Celia, Misoka, I

Celia,

Misoka,

I

Xue Yiwei

TRANSLATED BY STEPHEN NASHEF

RARE
MACHINES

Publisher and acquiring editor: Scott Fraser | Editor: Jess Shulman
Cover designer: Laura Boyle
Cover image: Max van den Oetelaar

Library and Archives Canada Cataloguing in Publication

Title: Celia, Misoka, I / Xue Yiwei ; translated by Stephen Nashef.
Other titles: Xilali, Mihe, Wo. English
Names: Xue, Yiwei, 1964- author. | Nashef, Stephen, translator.
Description: Translation of: Xilali, Mihe, Wo.
Identifiers: Canadiana (print) 20210259094 | Canadiana (ebook) 2021026005X | ISBN
    9781459748040 (softcover) | ISBN 9781459748057 (PDF) | ISBN 9781459748064 (EPUB)
Classification: LCC PS8646.U4 X5513 2022 | DDC 895.13/6—dc23

We acknowledge the support of the Canada Council for the Arts and the Ontario Arts Council for our publishing program. We also acknowledge the financial support of the Government of Ontario, through the Ontario Book Publishing Tax Credit and Ontario Creates, and the Government of Canada.

Rare Machines, an imprint of Dundurn Press
1382 Queen Street East
Toronto, Ontario, Canada M4L 1C9
dundurn.com, @dundurnpress 𝕏 f ⊙

To
this great globalized age
in your miracle
we bear witness to old joys and sorrows

∞ The Beginning of the Beginning

IT WAS THE most unusual winter of my time in Montreal, the most unusual winter of my time in this world. One thousand nine hundred and fifty-two days have passed since I left the city and, even now, I find the events that took place that winter around Mount Royal hard to believe. Sometimes they return, in my dreams at night or my daytime reveries, but are inevitably cut short by the same callous question: *Was it real? Was it real? Was it real?* I despise this question. It persists and recurs like a terminal illness, intent on severing the connection between me and that inconceivable winter, its inconceivable passion. Each time this question cuts short my reveries and dreams I feel the deep wound it inflicts.

For Montreal, it was a very ordinary winter. It was no longer than usual, and days when the temperature dropped below minus twenty you could count on both hands. But in that most ordinary of winters life opened a window for me it had never opened before and would never open again. To this day I still find the scene I saw through that window hard to believe.

It seems that everything began with the death of my wife. In her final days, my feelings for her underwent a huge transformation. I was repelled by the massive changes in her physical condition, perhaps even disgusted. I was scared by the pain she was suffering, perhaps even terrified. Of course, I still did my best to look after her, but the "still" in that statement conceals a change that had taken place. A cool rationality now dictated my behaviour rather than the warm spontaneity of feeling I had once felt. I no longer saw her as the woman with whom I had lived for twenty-three years. She was but a skeleton to which clung the barest remnants of sentience. When I held her hand it was out of a cold sense of duty, and when she lost consciousness for the last time, I was no longer flustered by what I knew was happening. I woke up my daughter, who had just fallen asleep, and asked her if she could call the emergency services. "Do you think I should?" she asked, her voice frail with exhaustion. I knew what she meant. That there was no point. "We should at least call," I said, out of obligation only.

The paramedics arrived in fifteen minutes, and eight minutes after that my wife stopped breathing.

It was during an annual checkup that my wife discovered something was wrong. Further tests established that the cancer that was growing in her pancreas was in its middle stages.

Only seven months passed between the checkup that revealed something was wrong and the moment she stopped breathing. For the first four months, her condition was relatively stable. When the chemotherapy started, she did all she could to stay in good spirits and stick to her normal schedule, even continuing to help out every now and again at the convenience store. But with the arrival of the new year her condition began to deteriorate rapidly. The morning she collapsed in the bathroom was the first time we called the emergency services and she was hospitalized. From that day she began to lose weight rapidly, her mood began to fluctuate violently, and her body, tormented by pain, began to edge visibly toward death.

The day my wife was hospitalized I entrusted the convenience store to a friend who had always wanted to buy it and spent all of my time by her side. Before I knew it, six weeks had passed, and in the first week of February her doctor told me that there was not much point in moving on to the next stage of treatment. I decided to take her home. Although my wife must have known what this meant, she was happy with the decision and her mood in the first days at home was noticeably better than it had been in the hospital. Every lunchtime a nurse would come to check up on her and every other day a religious friend of ours would visit to pray for her. This friend would ask me to join her. Neither my wife nor I were Christian, but our friend was convinced that my praying could still lessen my wife's psychological and physical pain. When it came to prayer, I have to admit, I was not very sure of what I was doing or even for whom I was doing it — as I prayed for my wife, I was also praying for myself, praying that when God came for me, he would not come so slowly. I did not want to suffer like she had. Within three weeks of my wife returning home, I was signing her death certificate.

My wife's death was perhaps a release, both for her and for me. In comparison, the death that followed three months later brought a purer sense of despair, a passing no death certificate could account for — the death of the relationship between my daughter and me. In truth, the symptoms of our worsening relationship had become clear when she started middle school. That was the time when her reliance on and attachment to me began to diminish and our conversations and interactions became increasingly rare. A clear example of this was her attitude to birthdays. Before starting middle school, she would look forward each year to the birthday present I gave her, and every year on my birthday she would make me a card, something, for some reason, she never did for her mother. But when she started middle school she stopped caring about my presents and even stopped remembering my birthday. So our relationship was already in dangerous waters when, after graduating from high school, she did not choose the university I wanted her to go to, or even the major I thought she should take. Despite all of this, I was not prepared for our relationship's demise. After she graduated from university, I knew that she was not planning to continue in education like I hoped she would, that she wanted to find a job right away, and a job far away from Montreal at that, but I did not think that meant that our relationship was doomed! When the last of her applications to work in Toronto and Vancouver was rejected, I was secretly pleased to see the downcast expression on her face as she moped around the house. Then, when I came home in the evening five days later, she told me she had been accepted for the only position she had applied for in Montreal. Before I had a chance to congratulate her, she told me she had found somewhere to live near her workplace and was going to move out in a few days. I had not expected this at all. "Why do you have to live somewhere else?" I asked her. "I want to," she replied coldly. She moved out that weekend, and the move was more drastic than I could have possibly imagined: she had not only moved out from the house, but also from my life. In the following four months she did not phone me once, nor did she answer my calls or respond to my emails. She did not even tell me where she was living. In the end I couldn't take it anymore and I sent her an angry email in which I wrote, "As your father, I at least have the right to know if you are dead or alive." I thought the anger would prompt her to reply quickly, if only to let me know that she was okay, and I waited, on edge, for ten days. It was a suspense more agonizing than that which had gripped me during her mother's final days, and I began to lose my hold on reality. On the evening of the tenth day I bumped into one of her middle school classmates in the supermarket and asked her if she had heard from my daughter. To my surprise, she responded without hesitation in the affirmative, saying they had eaten dinner together the night before. At first I was overjoyed because I knew that my daughter was alive and well (at least up to the day before), but this was followed by a sense of humiliation. She cared more for a middle school classmate than she did her own father. It was clear that I no longer needed to wait for her reply. Whether she was living or not, I knew our relationship was dead, though I would never know the reason. Perhaps there was no reason at all beyond the simple fact that all young people tend to turn against their parents at some point in their lives.

A month later I sold the convenience store I had run for thirteen years, a transaction that seemed to me pregnant with meaning — it symbolized departure, conclusion, even escape.

In some ways, perhaps, it was the third passing I had experienced that year. I had actually begun to think about selling the store from the moment my wife's test results came back. It wasn't only a matter of concentrating my efforts on looking after my wife. The awful news contained in the results of those tests was a wake-up call: life is tough and it is short. The test results felt like a sign that we ought to spend more of our time enjoying what we can of our lives rather than endlessly working. I hadn't acted on these thoughts, however, because I was worried my wife would read it differently, that she would see such a decision as a death sentence. After my wife was hospitalized my daughter had also brought up the idea of selling the store. She too said that the test results were a reminder that we shouldn't be toiling away from morning to night and getting by on only the bare necessities. Deep inside I agreed, but at the time I argued strongly against it. I told her that if we were to sell the store her mother's condition would only get worse. The store meant everything to her, more than her own life.

Before the year was finished another symbolic passing took place. Two weeks before Christmas I sold the house we had lived in for almost ten years and moved to the "snowy side" of Mount Royal, into an apartment building that was forty-eight years old, the same age as me. I did not want to spend Christmas and my wife's birthday (which was the day after) alone in our old house. And one of the reasons I chose to live where I did was that it was very close to my wife's grave. I would be able to visit it every day on foot.

After moving into my new home I tried a couple of times to phone my daughter again but she didn't pick up, so I sent her an email telling her I had moved, and included my new address. I added that I hoped she would be able to come for her mother's birthday so that we could pay our respects at her grave together. She didn't respond, but on the birthday she arrived at my apartment at noon. It was the first time we had met since she had moved out and I wanted to show her around my new home, but I gave up on that idea when it became clear she was not even remotely interested. We sat in the living room for half an hour, which began with me trying to get her to take a back-up key for the apartment, something I thought was important but she thought utterly unnecessary. Then I asked how work was going and she said it was going pretty well. I asked what her living arrangements were like, and she said they were fine. I asked whether she had got used to having to cook for herself every day, and she said she had. Finally, I asked why she hadn't answered my calls or replied to my emails, and she said she was busy. I couldn't get much more than that out of her, and the whole conversation left me completely demoralized.

We went to visit her mother. When I bowed to the grave my daughter seemed to find it very funny. She walked silently to the gravestone and brushed away the snow that had accumulated on top. I asked if she had dreamed of her mother, and she turned around to look at me but didn't reply. Then I asked her if she remembered the beef sirloin stew her mother used to make, to which she neither replied nor turned her head. I said that I hadn't dreamt of her mother once since she died. Wasn't that a little strange? Again, she neither uttered a word nor moved a muscle in response. I was at a loss. After a pause, my daughter told me she had arranged to go shopping with a colleague. I looked at my watch. We had spent less than twenty minutes by her mother's grave. I wanted to convince her to stay a little longer. In the end I said nothing.

My daughter intended to part ways at the entrance to the graveyard. This time I refused to give in and accompanied her to the subway station, even if during that hard-earned walk we barely uttered a word. As she made to descend into the station I told her I hoped she would be able to come home once in a while. She replied that she really was very busy, that she worked overtime almost every day. The way she rejected my request without a second thought hit me hard. "I have never felt so lonely," I told her, almost pleadingly. "Sometimes I think about leaving here — leaving, maybe even, this world." I don't know if it was what I said or the way I said it that got to her but she stopped on the stairs and turned around, a troubled expression on her face. This flicker of concern, if that's what it was, quickly disappeared, however, and she said matter-of-factly, "You shouldn't sit cooped up inside all day. Don't get caught up thinking about the past." Then she turned and left. I thought of pleading with her once more but couldn't think of anything to say. I watched desperately as my daughter went off down the stairs, hoping that she might turn around just once to look back at me. She didn't.

An icy shiver went right through me and for a moment I felt the tears welling up in my eyes. *Why can't you even turn to look at me? Why won't you ask me how I'm doing? Why can't you answer any of my questions with more than a couple of words? Can this really be just an inevitable part of growing up?* These questions bubbled up in my mind and I remembered how I had complained to my Taiwanese neighbour about my daughter. I told her I had become King Lear, a father forsaken, that a new "crisis of identity" was descending upon me. My well-meaning neighbour replied that I should not dwell too much on this sense of crisis. My daughter's behaviour was completely normal, she told me. All of her children were the same. But I could not accept this new "normal" and that they were all "the same." I was lonely. I was desperate. I wanted to leave here — maybe even this world.

I waited until my daughter had completely disappeared from view before swallowing back my tears and making to leave. It is perhaps from this moment that the story of my most unusual of winters ought to begin, because it was as I turned around that I noticed a young Asian girl about the same age and almost exactly the same height as my daughter. She was standing by the intersection of two streets, apparently unable to decide which one to take. In that moment it occurred to me that her presence might be a form of compensation, a way of balancing out what I had lost. I walked over to her and asked where she wanted to go, to which she replied the Mount Royal belvedere, where she could look out over the entire city of Montreal. "Why don't you come with me," I said. "I'm going that way." She agreed to my suggestion without the slightest hesitation, which seemed to compensate even more for what had just taken place between my daughter and me.

As we walked we chatted a great deal. She told me she came from Busan in Korea, that her father worked in a bank and her mother was a teacher. Like my daughter she had graduated the previous summer, but she was concerned that her English needed improvement so had enrolled in a two-month English-language course at McGill University. She had arrived the previous day and was hoping to use the time before her course began to see the sights of Montreal. I was curious about why she had chosen to come to Montreal in the winter, and she said she had specifically chosen this time to come. Winter was her favourite time of the year, something that could be traced back to her father, or more specifically to Vivaldi. Her father was an accomplished amateur violinist and one of his favourite pieces to play was "Winter" from *The Four Seasons*. She said the piece was a part of the spiritual bond she shared with her father. As she told me this I began to feel an old guilt rise up inside me. Why did my daughter and I not have a "spiritual bond"? Whatever the reason, I did not know if it was my fault or my daughter's. I didn't have many hobbies apart from reading, and my daughter had always been more captivated by numbers than words. The only books she read were detective stories, which was probably the genre I cared about least.

At the entrance to my apartment I parted ways with the Korean student, who had helped for a brief period to make up for the lack of relationship between my daughter and me. I told her to keep going along the same road we had been walking and she would reach the peak of Mount Royal. She bowed slightly and said she was fortunate to have met me, otherwise she would have been sure to have walked all over before finding it. Her gratitude brought me a warm sense of satisfaction, and I watched as she crossed the road and began to recede into the distance. My mood was completely different from just moments earlier when I had stood watching my daughter disappear into the subway; I decided to keep watching as the Korean student walked down the road. Little did I know that the first unusual occurrence of that winter was to take place just as she was about to disappear from view. When she came to the florist at the corner of the road she suddenly spun around to face me and lifted both her hands in the air above her head, as if she knew I was still looking at her, or perhaps had intuited what I was waiting for as I stood alone at the subway and wanted to make up for what my daughter had denied me. Thrilled, I too lifted both my hands into the air and watched as the Korean student held her arms aloft and, still facing me, continued to walk backward. I waited until she had disappeared behind the florist before I put my hands down. I was gripped by a strange feeling: that the Korean student had turned around and lifted her arms not as a way of saying goodbye, but as a kind of invitation. It was this feeling that caused me to run down the road, past the florist's shop around the corner, and to the girl's side. "I thought maybe I could walk with you a little longer." I was slightly embarrassed about saying this at first, but her cheerful response quickly made me feel better.

It had been almost ten years since I had been up Mount Royal in the winter. In the first few years after our arrival in Montreal, my daughter always looked forward to winter trips up the mountain because she loved ice-skating there. There were two rinks. The artificial one built next to Beaver Lake was open almost all winter, and when it got really cold, the lake itself would freeze, making a second, giant rink. My daughter loved skating during the holidays, and it also brought me great pleasure, especially when we held hands on the lake. I felt as though we were sharing something sacred, as though she would always be by my side, as though she would always need me to protect her. It was a time when I was full of love for life. But it didn't take long for my daughter to start changing. First she didn't want to hold my hand as we skated, then she didn't want me to go with her, and finally she stopped wanting to go skating at all.

I took the Korean student all the way to the edge of Beaver Lake, or rather, she brought me there. If it were not for her unexpected appearance at the subway entrance earlier, I would certainly not have found myself standing by Beaver Lake in the middle of winter again. As she looked at the landscape around her, she sighed, an exhaled vowel of astonishment that sounded very Korean. I also sighed, silently, marvelling at the scene with which I had once been so familiar but had not seen for ten years, at how life seemed to be made up of a series of recurring illusions.

The lake was not yet open for skating. I took three photos of the girl by the lakeside, from three different angles, and then we walked to the artificial rink where she stood for a moment eyeing the men and women, young and old, who were skating there. I was still thinking about life and its illusions when she turned and asked me a question that brought back vivid memories: "Can you skate?" I replied that I could but that it had been almost ten years. What she said next was also completely unexpected, the second unusual thing of that winter.

"Let's do it!" she said.

I started. I didn't quite believe what I'd heard.

"Let's go skating," she said.

We walked into the pavilion to rent skates.

The Korean student was agile in her movements as she changed her shoes, and before long she was standing with her skates on, waiting for me. This was totally unlike the other times I had come with my daughter, when I inevitably had to wait for her for ages. "How come you haven't skated for ten years?" she asked.

Once again the question brought back memories. "Because my daughter has grown up," I said.

She seemed to understand what this meant and lowered her head slightly before looking at me again and asking, "How old is she?"

"About the same age as you," I said. "These days she won't even come home and see me."

The Korean student did not ask me why, nor any other questions for that matter. She waited for me to get into my skates and then walked with me to the rink. It didn't take much time for her to get her bearings on the ice and soon she seemed completely at home. She skated beautifully, switching between skating forward and backward without effort, even managing a few jumps and spins. Each time she skated past me, she made a point of waving and saying hello, and each greeting filled me with warmth. Unlike her, I took ages to adapt to being on the ice, partly because it had been so long, but also because I wasn't really able to concentrate. I kept stopping to look at the girl as she moved so naturally across the rink and to picture myself with my daughter at this spot all those years ago. I was also still thinking about life and its illusions. There was no way I could have known that I would be here after ten years skating again, and in such unusual circumstances. A strange impulse came over me, a sense that this was not the end but a kind of beginning. From that day on, I resolved, I would come to skate here every day when I got up, every morning until the end of winter. What an unusual ritual that would be! It would be my way of dispelling the loneliness and emptiness I had recently found so difficult to bear.

After we had put our shoes back on and left the pavilion, I told the Korean student the way to the belvedere. She replied that she was already a little tired and, anyway, it had already gotten too dark to take good photos. She wanted to come with me down the mountain. She could always come to the belvedere another time. "Besides, it gives me the chance to practise my English!" she said. I was happy that she seemed to want to spend more time with me.

On the way down, she spoke to me about how she used to skate on a frozen lake as a child, and how her father would often play his violin while he watched her. "It was a really beautiful experience," she said. I was quietly envious of her for having such a father, and also of him for having a daughter like her. When we reached where I was living I paused for a moment before offering to accompany her to the subway. She seemed very pleased at the idea, saying, "We can say goodbye at the place where we met!"

At the subway station, she thanked me for spending so much time with her and I responded that I ought to be thanking her for getting me to skate again. Then I wished her the best of luck with her life in Montreal. She turned around and walked into the subway. My state of mind as I watched her descend into the station had changed completely from that of three hours earlier when I had stood watching my daughter from exactly the same spot. I was now full of gratitude and joy. I waited for her to disappear at the bottom of the stairs when, all of a sudden, she turned and rushed back up toward me to say the words that still, to this day, fill me with not only gratitude and joy, but also surprise. "She'll come back to you," she said. "For sure."

That was the third unusual thing to happen that winter, and it made me even more determined to honour the commitment I had made to myself on Mount Royal. After I got back to my apartment I went straight to the utility room. When I was moving to my new home I had thrown away a lot of old things I didn't need anymore, but I'd decided to keep the two pairs of ice skates that belonged to my daughter and me. At the time I'd only wanted them as a keepsake. I never thought they would ever see the ice of Mount Royal again.

That night I couldn't sleep. My mind kept running through the scenes of that strange day and of skating on Beaver Lake ten years earlier. I was filled with not only anticipation for my new start in life, but also apprehension. I didn't know if I would be able to keep to my commitment to going up the mountain every morning. Ten years earlier I had gone only during the holidays, and when I did it was usually in the afternoon. Plus I always went with my daughter and we would be chatting the whole time, as we walked up or down the mountain, as we put on our skates, as we moved around the ice. Now I was a solitary man. Would I really be able to skate every morning alone on Mount Royal?

As the sky began to get lighter, I got up. After going to the toilet I finished the novel I was reading, which had been translated from Persian. Six months previously I had resolved to read a certain amount of English every day, which was one way for me to deal with my solitude. Now I had two ways that supplemented one another; the first passive and thoughtful, the second active and physical. At ten minutes to eight I left the apartment. Just like I used to, I hung my skates over my right shoulder and my daughter's skates over my left. The effects of my lack of sleep very quickly dissipated as I walked toward Beaver Lake. At the time, of course, there was no way for me to know that this winter was to be the most unusual winter of my time in Montreal, but on some level I was aware that something had changed between the world and me. I was no longer a husband, no longer a father, no longer the owner of a business, maybe no longer even really a man.

Perhaps this is where the story about my most unusual of winters should truly begin.

∞ Celia

THERE WAS ONLY one person in the pavilion when I walked in, something I'd never seen before. In the past, by the time my daughter and I had made it up the mountain, it would already be the busy period of the holiday season and the pavilion would be so full of people it was hard to find a locker for your shoes. My daughter was always intent on using her favourite lockers in the middle of the low row next to the window that overlooked Beaver Lake. It always took some time to convince her to settle for another one, and then it would take just as long for her to put on her skates. Of course it never seemed like time wasted.

No time spent with my daughter ever felt wasted. But now everything had changed. As far as she was concerned, it seemed now that even a phone call with me was time wasted.

The other person in the pavilion was a woman. She was sitting sideways on my daughter's favourite lockers, her legs pulled up to her chest, her arms wrapped around her shins, and her head resting gently on her knees as she looked out of the window toward the lake. Her posture reminded me of a famous black-and-white photo. She was clearly just in from skating and her recently used skates lay on their side in front of her. The moment I saw her I was struck by the strange notion that she seemed to be suffering from some kind of sickness. But it was more complicated than that; there seemed to be something powerfully contradictory about her. On the one hand she exuded vitality, a willingness to take on everything hurled her way, but at the same time there was a vulnerability to her, a sense she might crumble at the slightest disturbance. A phrase immediately occurred to me to describe her: "healthy sufferer."

I had not expected my new life to be met so quickly with such a strange contradiction. I felt somewhat uneasy as I walked past her, a feeling intensified by the fact that she took no notice of me.

I walked to the row of lockers my daughter used to like least and took a seat facing into the pavilion, so that the woman remained within my field of vision. From there I was able to see her more clearly, how her hair was tied and the way her hands were clasped around her legs. These details seemed to bring me closer to her but I still could not see her face. I had no idea if she was looking at something out the window, pondering some difficult question, or merely lost in thought. Whichever it was, I figured it must be occupying all of her attention for her not to notice another person walking straight past her.

The previous night, as I was lying awake in bed, I had decided that I would not only carry my own skates each day, but also my daughter's. I hoped doing so might create the illusion that she had not left my side. So that morning as I'd walked up the mountain, I had chatted with my daughter like old times. I'd asked her the question I always used to ask her when we'd first immigrated to Montreal: "Do you like it here?" to which she always replied, "I do." This response was a major reason for my ability to persevere in my new life as an immigrant. My daughter's positive spirit was a blessing to her and me both.

I looked over at the healthy sufferer who was still sitting in the same position, and then down at my daughter's skates. I knew I would have to talk her down: "Look," I said. "Someone's already sitting there." But of course my daughter wouldn't give up that easily. She wanted me to have a word with the healthy sufferer. "There's no point," I said. "She won't let us sit there." My daughter asked me how I could know for sure. "Just now I walked past her and she didn't even notice," I told her. But my daughter wouldn't admit defeat. She said she wanted to wait. "She'll be there forever," I said. My daughter asked me again how I could possibly know. "Because …" I paused as I glanced once again at the healthy sufferer, and in that moment I thought I caught a glimpse of her secret. "Because she's lonely," I said. That's when I realized my daughter was not beside me. She had not been there for ten years and it seemed unlikely that she ever would again. The secret I had caught a glimpse of was not the secret of the woman in the pavilion but my own. I was the one who was lonely. I had never felt so alone.

None of the employees had arrived yet and the shutters were closed over the shop selling and renting winter gear. This was also something I had never seen before. I reflected on the fact that had it not been for my wife's passing and my daughter's leaving, I would never have met that Korean student the day before, I would have never walked up Mount Royal so early in the day, and I would never have seen this scene of the ice rink and pavilion looking so different from how I had seen it before. A passage in the novel I had just finished reading came to my mind. In it an old blind man spoke to the female narrator, a member of the Pahlavi family, former rulers of Iran, about Paris and love. He said, "Paris as an objective thing is meaningless. There is only the Paris in which individual lives unfold. The Louvre, the Eiffel Tower, Notre Dame — it is only when a person lives and experiences these places that the cover of their externality is removed and their true meaning revealed. The Paris you arrive in is different from the Paris that other people arrive in. The Paris you enter with the person who loves you and the Paris you enter with the person who doesn't love you are not the same Paris. The Paris you enter with the person you love and the Paris you enter with the person you don't love are even more different. One of these Parises is better than the other of course, aesthetically speaking: love transforms language, transforms the world, transforms how we see the world, transforms our relationship with the world.... Marriage does not change a person, but love absolutely must. Why did Hemingway call Paris a 'moveable feast'? Because he experienced love there. Paris transformed his love, the love that would be channelled into the great force of his literary creativity, this one and only love." It occurred to me at that moment that I understood this passage and what this somewhat obscure novel was trying to say. Mount Royal was now a part of my life. I could feel the new meaning that death and loneliness had bestowed upon it.

I made a point of taking my time changing into my skates because I wanted to see if the healthy sufferer would move from where she was sitting, but when I was finished she was in exactly the same position. She was still there when I was walking out of the pavilion. What had so captured her attention? How was it she had not even noticed a person who intruded upon her space? What was it about her appearance that brought to mind both vitality and fear? I was curious. I wanted to see her face, I wanted to hear her voice, I wanted to know her story. I had never felt so curious about a complete stranger before.

Outside the pavilion I could not resist turning my head to look through the window at the unmoving woman as I walked down the path and stepped onto the ice, though I knew I still could not make her out clearly. Thanks to my previous day's skating, it did not take long to find my feet, but my thoughts were not with the rink. I was imagining what the healthy sufferer's face might look like, what her voice might sound like, what her story might be. I was also thinking about how she related to me. Would I see her here every morning? Was skating her way of dealing with loneliness too? If she knew how curious I was about her and her life, would she be uncomfortable? These thoughts were interrupted by music, which broke through the silence of the mountain from a speaker hung from the lamp tower at the south of the rink. During the busy period they usually played pop songs, but that morning it was classical music — Beethoven's Violin Concerto in D, in fact, one of my favourite pieces. I still remember the first time I heard this piece at my middle school geography teacher's apartment, an afternoon toward the end of August in 1979. I was nearly eighteen years old and was getting ready to leave home for the first time on my own. I had four hours until my train to

Beijing and I decided to say goodbye to the teacher who had always showed an interest in what I was doing, even after I was no longer his student. After we exchanged a few words my teacher put a cassette in his new Sony music player, telling me he wanted to see me off with something special. Beethoven's Violin Concerto in D is a piece full of longing for the past and eagerness for the future. The first few notes stopped me in my tracks — it was as if Beethoven had written the piece specially for me and my first long journey away from home on my own some 170 years later. It transformed my journey that day, and every journey in my life after that. Thirty years had passed since that first trip away from home, and yet the force of the piece had not been worn down in all that time. I glided over to the modern-looking lamp tower and stopped to look up at the snow-covered speaker. I could almost see the pure notes floating out and into the pristine wilderness, into the untouched quiet, and finally up into the immaculate sky. I felt a strange joy take hold of me. Ever since the journey I had taken that day all those years ago I had found myself travelling farther and farther away from home. As the distance had increased, so had a certain anguish, which had come to form a knot of grief inside me that I had so far been unable to untie. However, at that moment beneath the lamp tower on the ice rink, I realized that all of my long journeys away from home had also been taking me toward something. They'd been taking me toward the very joy that had just taken hold of me, this unparalleled purity and tranquility. I took a couple of deep breaths of the fresh air and, to the accompaniment of Beethoven's violin concerto, I began again to skate, throwing my arms exaggeratedly into the air. I went faster and faster, faster and faster. But that was not enough to express how liberated I felt by this newfound joy and excitement, so I turned around and started skating backward, something I had never been particularly good at. I continued to go faster, and faster, faster still.... Then I felt the blade of my right skate wobble slightly, and before I knew it I had completely lost my balance. I fell hard, the inertia sending my body across the ice. I came to a rest at the edge of the rink.

I was overjoyed at the transformation that had come over me so quickly. Unfazed by the fact I was on my back on the ice, I spread my legs, stretched out my arms and lay on the ice with my eyes closed, happily listening to the familiar melody. My enjoyment was cut short by a voice: "Are you all right?" It was an unfamiliar voice, a woman's voice. Disoriented, I opened my eyes and saw the healthy sufferer looking over me. I quickly got to my feet and lowered my head as I brushed the snow off my clothes and muttered something about losing my footing and everything being fine. On hearing this, the healthy sufferer turned around and started walking away. I immediately regretted my hasty reply. Why hadn't I said it was more serious? Why hadn't I asked her to help me back to the pavilion?

As I watched the woman walk away, so full of vitality, I thought back to the previous day at the subway station when I'd parted ways with my daughter. I knew there was no way that the figure currently receding into the blinding white snowscape would turn around. I might never satisfy my curiosity to know more about the healthy sufferer. I had missed my only chance to get closer to her.... But then I realized she wasn't carrying her skates. Where were they? Why wasn't she carrying them? I felt my sense of curiosity growing. She must have left her skates in the locker, which meant that she was not really leaving the mountain, or at least she was planning on coming back. Maybe like me she had decided to come every day. This was a comforting thought. Perhaps the chance I had just missed would not be my only one.

Sure enough, she did not take the road that led down the mountain but continued walking farther toward the woods. As I watched her, I noticed that we were no longer the only people in the desolate expanse. By the side of Beaver Lake was someone sitting in an electric wheelchair. The healthy sufferer had noticed too and, having walked past, she turned her head twice to look at the figure in the wheelchair before continuing on into the woods. I watched as she came to a stop by an old elm tree. She reached into a hollow in its trunk and pulled out a pair of skis and ski poles. I didn't know what to think. What kind of person is so familiar with Mount Royal she discovers a tree hollow to store skis in? Was such a discovery a sign of her health or a proof of her suffering? The healthy sufferer deftly put on the skis and slid off into the depths of the mountain. She had just been ice skating and still had the energy to go skiing. How healthy must someone be to do this? Or how sick? I was desperate to find out the answers to these questions. I wanted to know everything about her.

I skated another couple of laps of the rink but my heart wasn't really in it so I headed back to the pavilion. I entered through the door I had come out of earlier so I could pass the lockers on which the healthy sufferer had been sitting. One was locked. It must have been where her skates were, in the very same locker my daughter had so often used ten years before. I paused by the locker for a moment and looked out the window as I thought about the past, and once again I saw the person in the wheelchair. The whole lake was visible from where I stood, and the figure seemed strangely enigmatic against the glistening, crisp background of the mountain. There was something unreal about the scene. It resembled a work of art, a work of divine inspiration. I suddenly understood why the healthy sufferer had not noticed me. She must have been absorbed in appreciation of this divinely inspired work.

I went back to my locker, sat down, and changed into my shoes. I was still in a daze. I wanted to wait for the healthy sufferer to return. I wanted to know everything about her. An elderly couple walked into the pavilion hand in hand, each with a pair of skates hanging over their shoulders. They took a seat on the lockers opposite me and began to slowly change into their skates. I couldn't resist introducing myself and asking them how old they were, to which the man replied he was eighty-four and the woman two years younger. I expressed my admiration that they were still able to go ice skating in their eighties and the woman replied proudly that they had been skating together since a year before their marriage, which made it sixty-two years! The man then told me it was their wedding anniversary and this was their way of celebrating. I felt a peculiar sadness as I thought of all the people, like my wife, who were not able to live as long as these two had been married. There were not many people in the world who were able to enjoy such a long, happy marriage.

I had been waiting for the healthy sufferer for almost an hour when I noticed the person in the wheelchair was gone. I decided it was time to leave, and as I walked down the mountain I pictured the moment I had opened my eyes as I lay on the ice and had gotten my first clear view of the face of the healthy sufferer. The grave expression on her face had prevented me from seeing how old she was but I could tell she was well educated and had a rich inner life. But perhaps most intriguingly, during that moment she was standing over me, I saw in her face even more clearly her contradictory nature. I knew it was this contradiction that was the primary cause of my curiosity about her.

I spent the whole day thinking about the healthy sufferer, about her contradictory nature and why I was able to see it so clearly. How had I been so sure from the moment I saw her that she was suffering? What was she suffering from? Curiosity about her displaced my feeling of loneliness. That night as I lay in bed I no longer thought about my wife's passing or my daughter's leaving, but the elegant way the healthy sufferer sat on the lockers, the caring way she asked if I was okay, the mysterious hollow in the tree. I even saw us skating together. I saw that she was just as skilled on the ice as the Korean student had been. I saw that she wore headphones, listening to music, and each time she overtook me I felt a closeness with her as she glided away again.

The next day I made a point of leaving the apartment half an hour earlier in the hope that I might be able to realize our encounter as I had pictured it the night before. I still carried my daughter's skates over my shoulder, but as I walked up the mountain I was no longer thinking about her. Instead, I was wondering how I would start talking to the healthy sufferer. I knew I had to be careful not to let her know how curious I was about her. I decided I would start by thanking her for her concern when I fell, then I could compliment her on her skating, then ask if she too had decided to come every day to Mount Royal to skate, then what she liked doing aside from skating.... I planned out the ways I could get her to let me into her world. Of course, I wouldn't let on that I already knew the locker she liked to use. That might make her uncomfortable. And of course, I couldn't tell her I had been thinking about her ever since our encounter the previous day.

When I entered the pavilion I saw that my meticulous planning had been for nothing. The healthy sufferer was sitting in exactly the same place as the day before with her coat and skates beside her, which meant she had already finished skating. This time she was not looking sideways out the window but sitting straight, her whole body facing Beaver Lake. As I walked quietly past her and saw that her hair was still tied in a bun, I was gripped by a strange and unsettling impulse to reach out and touch it. I took note of the strands of white that flecked her chestnut hair and realized she was perhaps not as young as it seemed from the effortless way she moved.

Just like the day before, she paid no attention to the fact that someone had intruded upon the space that was previously just hers. I took a seat on the row of lockers my daughter liked least again, but this time I did not dare look directly at the healthy sufferer. I did not want her to turn around and have our eyes meet. I was nervous — nervous because I had been thinking about her for a whole day, nervous because of the strange impulse I had felt to touch her hair. I sat with my back to the room and looked out the window as I nervously changed into my skates. When I walked out of the pavilion I didn't look back. All I wanted was to leave as quickly as possible. Only when I was on the ice did I hazard a glance through the window, but the healthy sufferer wasn't there. I skated over to the side of the rink that overlooked Beaver Lake to find her walking past the person in the wheelchair, who was sitting at the same spot by the lakeside. As she walked past she slowed down and turned her head to the wheelchair, as if there were something she wanted to say, but she seemed to change her mind and resumed her original pace, heading toward the big elm tree.

On the third day I decided to set off half an hour earlier again, but just as I was heading out the door the telephone rang. It was a classmate from middle school who was applying to immigrate to Canada. It was not the first time he had called me to talk about it and I had already asked him what had made him decide to leave. He said simply that everyone with money in China was considering emigration. We had not been in contact for many years and I did not know that he had become someone "with money." I also knew nothing of the situation for people with money in China, and had no idea emigration was the new craze. During the previous phone call, however, my classmate had told me that his wife was having serious misgivings about immigration. He practically had to force her into agreeing to apply, but when they had submitted the application materials she only became more nervous, and by the time they received the official notification of their interview date she seemed on the brink of a breakdown. She broke into tears almost every day, had stopped eating properly, and was unable to sleep. That was when she told him in no uncertain terms that she would not be going to the interview. My classmate did not know what to do and had called me to ask if I would speak with his wife and tell her about my own experience and the benefits of immigrating. I had refused, stressing that as far as my experience was concerned there might not be much in the way of benefits to talk about. Here he was calling again, telling me that his wife was next to him and wanted to talk to me. I had never met his wife and doubted very much that she had any desire to speak with me. Besides, I had no idea what I would say to her. When my classmate passed the phone to his wife I started by politely saying hello and introducing myself, but just that was enough to cause her to start sobbing uncontrollably. My classmate snatched back the phone and told me not to hang up, that she would be fine in a moment. He must have put the phone to one side because after that I heard the muffled sound of him speaking to his wife, chastising her one minute and pleading with her the next, until she finally stopped crying. As I waited, the idea came to me of trying to persuade her by talking about the love between a husband and wife. When she picked up the phone again I asked her if she loved her husband.

"Of course I do," she replied.

"In that case, shouldn't you be with him?"

"But I won't go with him if he leaps into a bonfire."

"Canada isn't a bonfire. It's a glacier."

She didn't reply so I went on to tell her that there were people who said immigrating was the best thing in the world and people who said it was the worst. Neither of these extremes were correct. "Immigrating is just a matter of moving your life to another place. If you still care for your husband, it shouldn't matter where you are as long as you are together, don't you think?"

She still didn't reply, so I went on to say that they were not immigrating yet. They might not pass the interview. Their application might not be accepted. And even if it was accepted that they did not need to register and even if they did register they could change their minds at any point in the process. "Why not give the interview a try? After all, you do still care for your husband, don't you?"

She still didn't reply but at that moment my classmate snatched back the phone. "Not bad! You know what you're doing!" he said excitedly. It sounded like my words must have had some effect. I did not know how this made me feel.

Thanks to that phone call I missed the healthy sufferer that day on Mount Royal. Rather than arriving at the pavilion half an hour earlier like I had planned, when I finally walked in it was forty minutes later. There was no one there and no one on the ice. I grumbled to myself about my wealthy classmate as I sat down to change into my skates. The whole situation had put me in a bad mood. I wanted to know whether the healthy sufferer had already left or was yet to arrive. But then I told myself that it didn't matter. What mattered was that she would come again. I walked over to her locker and saw that it was locked. Feeling slightly better, I decided to check the hollow in the elm tree. If it was empty it meant she was still somewhere on the mountain. I put both pairs of skates into my locker and jogged out of the pavilion toward the old elm tree. Were it not for the person in the wheelchair I would have run without stopping, but just like the healthy sufferer earlier, I couldn't help slowing down and looking back at the figure sitting at the lakeside. A new curiosity had come over me, which was why I did not feel disappointed when I found the skis inside the hollow of the elm tree.

The next morning, before I had even walked into the pavilion, I saw the healthy sufferer by the window, sitting in the same place as before, clearly just back from skating. This time I was adamant not to let the opportunity pass me by, and I walked straight up to her to say hello. She turned her head and looked at me with the same grave expression she had had on her face during our previous, very brief, conversation. I said what I had planned to say two days earlier, and thanked her for her concern when I fell on the ice. She nodded her head politely, and then turned around again to look out of the window. I was not going to let her bring our second conversation to an end as quickly as she had the first. I would not miss my chance again, to get her to notice that I had noticed her. "You didn't show up yesterday," I said.

She turned sharply toward me and said, "It's *you* who didn't show up," a certain censure audible in her emphasis on the "you."

The intensity of her response caught me off guard but also gave me a certain pride. It provided an opening in the conversation. "Oh, I didn't realize I'd missed you," I said softly. It was the first time we would miss each other that winter, but not the last.

I couldn't resist looking again at her hair tied in a bun at the top of her head and felt myself tensing up. But I urged myself to continue the conversation. "Are you from Montreal?" I asked.

She seemed to have been waiting for the change of subject. "I was born here, grew up here, and still live here."

But she didn't follow up with a question about me. "I guess I'm from Montreal too," I told her. "I've been here for fifteen years now." When I saw she was not going to take the bait, I went on: "But I come from China."

To my surprise, this sentence seemed to elicit another intense reaction in her. I saw a flash of discomfort in her eyes and her expression darkened. "China," she repeated, in a tone that suggested both disdain and dread.

I had never before heard a westerner use such a tone when talking about my motherland. I became aware of a distance that existed and would always exist between us, which only amplified my curiosity to find out more. "Have you been?" I asked.

The healthy sufferer stared at me with an uneasy look in her eyes but she did not answer my question.

The silence almost made me shiver. It was a silence more intense than the curt replies that had preceded it. Why? Why could she not answer this simple yes-or-no question? Had she been or hadn't she? The healthy sufferer seemed to become aware of the tension surrounding her silence and stretched out her hand. "I'm Celia," she said solemnly. "Nice to meet you."

∞ Misoka

I HAD TO wait until our last meeting before she would tear a corner off the newspaper I was holding and write me her name and its romanized spelling. This was almost seventy days after I saw her for the first time, the same morning that I first saw Celia. It was as I watched Celia stride into the woods that my eyes were drawn to the other woman in the snowy expanse that day. She was sitting in an electric wheelchair by the side of Beaver Lake, looking into the sun over its frozen surface. Strictly speaking I had not really seen her. I had just seen someone in an electric wheelchair, a figure too distant even to tell if it was a man or a woman. It was only on the day I missed Celia that I approached the wheelchair. The course of events that day unfolded as though part of God's intricate plan, a plan that, throughout the winter, I would find myself constantly caught up in. Celia was not at her usual spot in the pavilion, nor was she skating on the rink, so I ran toward the woods to see if her skis were still in the hollow of the elm tree. That was when I approached the wheelchair, which was always at the same spot. I slowed my pace as I came up behind it, and I took note of the person who seemed so out of place in this unforgiving environment. I was surprised to discover that it was a woman, and a young East Asian woman at that. In my fifteen years as an immigrant, especially the years during which I ran the convenience store and found myself interacting with a wide array of customers, I had developed a peculiar ability to distinguish between different ethnicities and cultures based on people's appearance and body language. Maybe this is one of the advantages of being an immigrant. I am able without much effort to tell the difference between West Europeans and East Europeans, or between people whose first language is French and people whose first language is English. Distinguishing Korean, Japanese, and Chinese people I find even easier, though that might not have anything to do with my being an immigrant. A brief glance at the side of this woman's face was enough for me to know she was definitely not Korean, but I could not yet be sure if she was Chinese or Japanese. There was something about her that was different from Chinese, and something that was different from Japanese. She piqued my curiosity, and as I was coming back from the elm tree I could not resist trying to get a better look at her. That's when I saw what it was that preoccupied her as she sat by Beaver Lake: she was writing in a notebook. A young, East Asian woman in an electric wheelchair was *writing* in the snowy expanse of Mount Royal. I found myself wondering at what might possess someone to do such a thing, what quiet, resolute zeal? It was hard to believe.

This truly is one of the more unusual images of a writer that one can imagine. The more I thought about it the more curious I became. I wanted to know what had brought her here, in such a severe winter, where she seemed so out of place. I wanted to know what had inspired her to choose this place to write, and what it was she was writing. I wanted to know who she was. As I was leaving the pavilion I asked one of the members of staff about her. He told me that she had started coming at the start of winter and she always arrived at the same time each day. As long as it wasn't too cold or the wind wasn't too strong she was sure to be there, sitting in her wheelchair at the same spot by the side of Beaver Lake. She began her day by straightening her back and exercising her arms and upper body before settling down in her chair and starting to write. On colder days, or days where the wind was too strong, she would move to a spot near the pavilion that provided shelter from the wind to do her exercises, before entering the pavilion to write. The member of staff also told me that the same wheelchair taxi dropped her off every day at the car park near the pavilion.

My curiosity about the woman in the wheelchair made up for the disappointment I felt about having missed Celia. Throughout that unusual day and all the way until I went to bed that evening, I was consumed with thoughts about the two mysterious women I had encountered on Mount Royal. I knew nothing about either of them, and I hadn't even seen the face of the woman in the wheelchair properly, but I had already perceived an important difference between them. Celia was clearly very healthy, but also appeared to be suffering from something, while the woman in the wheelchair obviously had some sort of affliction but had a certain radiance about her. To borrow a fashionable term, Celia seemed to exude a "negative energy" and the woman in the wheelchair a "positive energy."

The next day, the day I finally spoke with Celia, only confirmed my initial impression. Why did Celia say the word "China" with such disdain and dread? And why wouldn't she tell me whether she had been there? It only made me see even more clearly the peculiar negativity inside her. As I was getting ready to head home I saw that the Asian woman was already sitting by the car park, waiting. Her head was lowered as she studied what she had presumably just written in her notebook, so I decided to pass in front of her to see if I could get a clearer view of her face. Sure enough she looked up as I got nearer, but for some reason I didn't have the courage to look at her directly. I even quickened my pace so as to pass her more quickly. But out of the corner of my eye I saw the robust beauty that emanated from her dark skin and prominent cheekbones. It occurred to me that she hadn't always needed a wheelchair, that she must have been an athlete at one time, or at least someone who loved being outdoors.

I began to hope for a bitterly cold day with strong winds. When the weather forced her to come into the pavilion to write, the opportunity to get closer to her would arise. I did not have to wait long. The winter's second snowstorm brought with it dawn temperatures of minus sixteen degrees Celsius, which, combined with the strong winds, would amount to an apparent temperature of minus twenty-two degress Celsius. I experienced for myself just how terrible the weather was — on the way up the mountain I was almost blown over twice — but the warm anticipation I felt made up for the ice-cold temperatures. I was sure that the East Asian woman was already sitting in the pavilion and that this was my chance to get closer to her, a chance I would not miss. I had so many questions to ask. When I got to the pavilion I would immediately approach her and ask her if she was Chinese or Japanese, ask her what she was writing, ask her why she had chosen that place beside Beaver Lake to write, ask her how she had found herself the defining feature of a divinely inspired work of art.

The thought of Celia interrupted my reverie. Since the day we shook hands we had met on the skating rink once and in the pavilion three times, but her inexplicable reaction to my saying I was from China had diminished my interest in her. I did not understand what her reaction could mean or what her disdain was directed toward. The day we found ourselves skating at the same time she approached me and asked me a strange question. Which cities in China had I lived in? It was clear from her tense expression and nervous tone of voice that this question and my response were very important to her. I told her I was born in a small town near Chongqing, had moved to Beijing for university, and had spent the rest of my time before immigrating to Montreal living in Guangzhou. To my surprise, she was visibly relieved by my answer. I had no idea how to explain her reaction. She wouldn't tell me if she had even been to China but was intent on finding out which Chinese cities bore the traces of my presence.

So, on my walk up the mountain, as I contemplated my opportunity to get closer to the mysterious woman in the wheelchair, I found myself thinking about Celia. Ever since I had first noticed her I had spent my morning walk imagining what might happen if we met on the rink or in the pavilion. This time I felt completely different. I hoped she would not be in the pavilion, or on the ice, or even on Mount Royal. Her presence could only hamper my chances of getting closer to the woman in the wheelchair, and might even rob me of the courage I needed to start up a conversation with her. My feet began to feel heavy and I contemplated the contradiction between the mysterious East Asian woman and the healthy sufferer, a contradiction I would have to navigate carefully.

I saw the wheelchair the moment I walked into the pavilion, in a corner next to the main entrance. The woman must have chosen this spot specifically, as it was the place where it was easiest to remain unnoticed. She was absorbed in her writing and did not see me come in, which helped to relieve some of the tension I was feeling. I did not want her to notice me right away because I wanted to find out first if Celia was there. Looking around, I saw that she was not in the pavilion, and turning toward the window, I saw the skating rink was empty. Was this out of luck or design? Throughout winter, I would meet many situations that would make me reflect on this question. I did not know and had no way of knowing the answer, but at that moment the situation gave me courage. I walked up to my usual locker, put down my two pairs of skates, and then, looking out the window again, I took a deep breath, perhaps the biggest I had ever taken, and walked toward the wheelchair. I was overcome with nerves, as if I were approaching a judge's bench to be sentenced. When I reached the mysterious East Asian woman I said hello and took a seat on the locker next to her, so we would be at the same height. There was an anxious look in her eyes as she turned to look at me and swiftly closed the notebook in her lap. I was anxious too, and felt the same red I saw in her cheeks rising in my own. I pointed to the notebook and told her I had seen her with it every day and was curious to know what she was writing. She shook her head and told me in French that she couldn't speak English, which was surprising. Almost all East Asians I had come across in Montreal were more comfortable with English than French. This was the first time I had met one who could only speak French. Furthermore, she spoke a very proper-sounding French, not the heavily accented Quebecois French that most local people spoke. She must not have grown up in Quebec, which only complicated my confusion about her identity. Alongside the question of whether she was Japanese or Chinese, I was now faced with the new riddle of where she had learned her French.

I quickly switched to my stuttering, Sichuanese-accented French and tried to repeat my question. "My French is no good," I added, smiling.

She passed no comment on my French and simply answered my question or, to be precise, failed to answer it, because she said she did not know what she was writing.

"Is it fiction or non-fiction?" I asked.

She looked at me anxiously again and paused for a while before saying quietly, "Fiction, naturally."

I wondered why it had taken her so long to answer such a straightforward question. "It looks like you've written a fair bit already," I said, looking at the notebook. "You've almost finished that book."

This seemed to relax her a little. She moved her fingers over the cover of the notebook and said, with a certain pride, "This is notebook number five."

"Number five?" I said. I pointed at the book. "Are they all that thick?"

"Yes," she said. "But this is the only one that has my writings on Mount Royal."

I was surprised to hear she had written so much. "There must be enough for a whole book already then? When will it be published?"

"I don't write to publish," she replied.

"Then what do you write for?"

Again, she paused for a moment before turning to look out of the window. "To see," she said. "To see someone."

"Who?"

"Someone I can only see in this way."

"I've never heard of someone writing for that reason before," I said. "I've never seen someone writing in the icy wilderness before either."

She continued to stroke the notebook in her lap.

"How are you able to sit outside for so long? Don't you find it cold?" I asked.

"No."

"Why is that?"

"I don't know," she said, still looking out the window. Then, as if pleasantly surprised, she turned back and smiled slightly before saying, "Perhaps because what I'm writing is even colder."

It was a curious answer, and a series of new questions began to bubble up in my mind. Could she speak any other language? Why was she in a wheelchair? Was her fiction a full novel, and was this her first? What kind of novel was it? However, it was becoming clear that she did not want to talk for much longer. She opened her notebook as if to indicate to me that she wanted to get back to her writing.

I reluctantly got to my feet and made to leave, but my curiosity got the better of me. "I like your French accent," I said.

"Thank you."

"Do you write in French too?" I asked.

"Of course," she said. "It's my mother tongue."

"Your mother tongue?" I said, surprised. "I assumed you were Chinese or Japanese."

This question about her identity seemed to make her anxious again. "I'm sorry," she said coldly as she turned away to look out the window again. "I value my privacy."

I was immediately overcome with guilt and embarrassment, and I felt the red rising in my cheeks again. I cursed myself for not being able to hold my curiosity in check, for asking too many questions. At the same time, a part of me felt that I didn't deserve to be embarrassed for what was simply a well-meaning curiosity. "Sorry," I responded in a similarly cold tone, and walked away.

I had not expected our conversation to turn as inhospitable as the weather outside. I strode back to my locker and began changing into my skates with my back to the pavilion. I did not want to look at the woman I'd just talked with. I was unable to look at her. I felt both guilty for inadvertently touching on something she did not want to talk about, and embarrassed by the way she had so unreservedly refused to answer my question. But lurking behind these two emotions was another: fear. I was afraid that I had offended her so much that she would leave the pavilion, leave Mount Royal, leave my life and maybe even my thoughts. My curiosity had brought us together and I did not want my stupidity to make her disappear. Once my skates were on I headed to the door that opened onto the ice rink. I was desperate to know if the woman was still there but I didn't have the nerve to turn around and check. But as I was opening the door, I caught a glimpse of her reflection in the glass. She hadn't left. She was still there, writing. I felt a weight lift from my shoulders.

Although a weight had been lifted, it was not enough for me to focus my attention on the rink. I was numb to the sensation of the gliding blades and barely heard the music coming from the speakers. All I thought about was our conversation. "Perhaps because what I'm writing is even colder." Such a peculiar yet candid response! But what story could be colder than Mount Royal in winter? I had no idea. If she had not mentioned her mother tongue, I would never have encroached on her "privacy." But what kind of person considers whether they are Japanese or Chinese private? I had no idea. In all my years as an immigrant in Canada, I had asked many people who looked East Asian whether they were Chinese. I had encountered many self-assured answers along the lines of "No, I'm from Hong Kong," or, "No, I'm Taiwanese." In general, responses like these caused me to quickly lose interest in the person I was speaking to, but the mysterious East Asian woman's peculiar reaction had only made me even more curious about her. It dawned on me that there was something similar about her reaction and Celia's when I brought up China, as if they both had a strange relationship with the country in which I was born. These two women had very different energies, but they both reacted peculiarly to my mention of my native country. How could a Chinese man like me, who had been away from China for so long, not be curious?

It was quite some time before I realized that Beethoven's Violin Concerto in D was playing again, and that it had already entered the third, and my favourite, movement. The buoyant melodies drew me away from my speculations and back to the here and now of the ice rink. I became acutely aware of the wind, cold, and sunlight on my skin, as well as the way the ice skittered and slid beneath the blades of my skates. Like my first morning skating, I let myself be carried by the music, and I lifted my arms into the air. "Don't be scared off by a single refusal!" I told myself as I began to skate faster. "Be like Beethoven. Have the courage to grab fate by the throat!" The fear that had descended upon me in the pavilion started to crumble under the spirit of the moment, as did my embarrassment and guilt. I began to imagine our next conversation. I'd learned my lesson. I would be sure to stay clear of what she considered private. "Don't get caught up in the details!" I said to myself. Someone able to inspire such curiosity was worth getting closer to, irrespective of whether she was Japanese or Chinese. We were bound to have shared interests to talk about. Our previous conversation would act as a foundation for the next.

I went back into the pavilion in good spirits. The mysterious East Asian woman had left, but this wasn't surprising. I wanted to leave too. I wanted to go home as soon as possible. On my last lap of the rink I had been suddenly gripped by a desire to know the reason she used a wheelchair. I wanted to go home and look online for information about paraplegia, which I assumed she had. When my wife was ill I used to look up information on the internet about pancreatic cancer all the time. Aside from taking up a lot of time, it also distracted me from the pain of the situation and reminded me that many families were caught up in similar struggles, struggles that were doomed to fail.

The wind was getting stronger and stronger and I walked as fast as I could down the mountain. The snowstorm was approaching, and snowflakes had begun to circle around me. Outside the flower shop, I saw the florist give a bouquet of flowers to a middle-aged couple who were standing by a hearse, and I slowed down slightly as I heard the florist say in French, "Such an adorable child." I couldn't help turning my head to look back at the couple. Had they lost a child?! Feeling a pang of sadness in my chest, I clutched my daughter's skates as if I were about to experience the same fate. I quickened my pace, almost to a jog, until I arrived at my apartment. Without even taking off my jacket, I went straight to the desk and turned on the computer.

I was fully aware of the high quantity, and often poor quality, of information on the internet. I knew I would have to pore through a great deal of trite sentimentalism and obscure academia before finding what I was looking for. First I checked Chinese websites, then English, before finally searching in French. Seeing as French was the East Asian woman's mother tongue, it felt right to look at French sources. They would help me the next time I had the chance to speak with her. Through my research, I learned there are four main causes of paraplegia: external trauma, spinal tuberculosis, spinal tumours (usually blood vessel growths or large cell tumours), or metastatic cancers. I also found out that paraplegia can only be cured, if at all, by a long period of exercise and physiotherapy. There was no quick medical cure (such as surgery or drugs) currently available. Having concluded my research, I was not sure if it had done anything to satisfy my curiosity.

This trilingual research had taken the whole day, and by the time I was finished I didn't even have the energy to take a shower before collapsing into bed. Yet once again I was unable to sleep. My head ached as I cycled through the possible causes for the mysterious East Asian woman's need for a wheelchair. I hoped it was not the result of cancer or a spinal tumour, and

I did not want it to have anything to do with spinal tuberculosis. The only cause I felt I could bear was external trauma,
which led me to think about the possible scenarios: A car crash?
Domestic violence? A sporting injury? By the end of all this, my
brain felt completely fried, left with a dull throbbing. I laughed
to myself mirthlessly. I hadn't even wrapped my head around
paraplegia and I had nearly driven myself into a stupor.

I don't know when I got to sleep in the end but I know I
didn't sleep well. It was a restless night, plagued by an uninter-
rupted stream of dreams. In one of them I was an old man
hunched over a cane as I shuffled unsteadily through the snow
by Beaver Lake. I was surprised to see that I had lived to such
an old age, and even more surprised when I saw the mysterious
East Asian woman sitting in the same place in her wheelchair
after all these years. I walked over to her but, although she had
obviously noticed me, she did not lift her head from her notebook. "What made you want to approach me?" she asked. "I
didn't expect you to be here today," I replied. "Not now. I mean
back then," she said. I suddenly began coughing uncontrollably
and it took some time before I regained my composure and
pointed to the pen in her hand. "Because of that," I said. She
lifted her hand and the pen into the air. "No one approaches
a woman because of a pen," she said. "I've never seen someone
write in the cold before," I replied. She lifted her head and
stared at me, and I was astonished to see her face was just as
young as it had been before. "Especially someone in a wheelchair, especially a woman in a wheelchair, especially an East
Asian woman in a wheelchair," I continued, my voice cracking
with emotion. I looked away. Why was she exactly the same?
Why had I changed so much? Time had affected us in completely different ways. I was ashamed. I was distraught.

Then there was the dream, or nightmare, that woke me up in the end. A silver BMW was racing along a road by the sea, and in it were three generations of women. The mother was driving, with her daughter in the front passenger seat and the grandmother in the back. Then the mother and grandmother began arguing. I could not hear clearly what language they were using but it was obvious that the younger woman did not understand because she did not react at all to what they were saying. A sharp curve appeared ahead, a truck hurtling around it, the BMW heading straight for the truck.... As I lay there staring at the dark ceiling, I was sorry that I had awoken when I did. If I had dreamt a little longer I would have found out what happened after the crash. I wanted to know what happened after the crash.

It was already a little late in the morning, and I still felt a dull throb in the top-right side of my skull. The thought of this, and also the realization that the previous day's snowstorm would have made the road up the mountain difficult to walk on, made me think that perhaps it was better to skip that day's ice skating. But I also knew that these were really just excuses to avoid seeing the mysterious East Asian woman again. Where were the high spirits that had accompanied me down the mountain the day before? What had happened to the courage Beethoven had given me? Where had my excitement for our next meeting gone? I spent the morning sneering at my own cowardice. I did not have the strength to battle my rising sense of self-contempt, which had reached such a level by the time I was making lunch that I turned off the stove, picked up the two pairs of skates, and walked out the door. Sure enough, the road up the mountain was not as perilous as I had imagined and my headache had cleared. But Mount Royal at noon did not fill me with the same excitement as Mount Royal early in the day. It had lost all its purity and mystery. There were lots of people in the pavilion and on the rink, and not one of them aroused my curiosity. After a short ten minutes' skate I walked back into the pavilion, changed into my shoes, and went home.

As I finished my lunch, I thought back to the nightmare that had woken me that morning. I had no idea where such a strange dream had come from. Did it have anything to do with the East Asian woman? Of course, I *had* been hoping that her need for a wheelchair was a result of an accident, and not the symptom of a more serious disease. I went back to the computer and started looking for more information. I read five "inspirational" articles in a row. One about the American president Franklin D. Roosevelt was the most encouraging, and also the most enlightening. I suspected that the mysterious East Asian woman was most likely very familiar with the accomplishments of famous wheelchair users. I wondered if her strong will was in any way influenced by these people.

The inspirational articles improved my mood for the rest of the day, as well as my sleep later that night, and the next day as I walked up the mountain I felt at ease with the world. I was no longer perturbed about meeting the East Asian woman again, and no longer even worried about meeting her and Celia at the same time in the pavilion. When I reached the top, however, the pavilion was empty. There was not a soul to be seen, either on the ice rink or by Beaver Lake. I went to my locker, sat facing the window, and changed into my skates. As I was tying my laces, I started to make out a strange sound, getting gradually louder. It was the sound of an electric wheelchair, and it continued to come closer until it was right behind me.

"You're not upset by what I said the other day, are you?"

I turned around and looked at the woman. I did not know how to respond.

"I have nothing against you being curious," she said.

With that, she dispelled all of the shame I had been feeling on and off for the past few days. A comforting warmth rose up inside me.

"Curiosity is a pure thing," she said. "Just like Mount Royal in winter."

I looked at her full of gratitude, but still didn't know what to say.

"You are quite unusual, for a Chinese person."

This surprised me. "How did you know I was Chinese?"

She laughed. "How could I not?"

I didn't dare probe further into what she meant by that. She must have perceived my confusion but she seemed to have no interest in clarifying the situation, and instead changed the subject. "I have a lot of questions I want to ask you at some point," she said.

"Private questions?" I asked.

She laughed knowingly and then turned her wheelchair and began to roll away. But then she stopped, turned her head, and looked at me with a serious expression. "Have you ever been to the Old Summer Palace?"

My stomach lurched. Where had this question come from, this question, which by all rights I could say had encroached upon *my* privacy? I hesitated, but I did not want this conversation to end in the same manner as the previous one. "How could I not?" I replied, imitating her tone.

She didn't ask any more questions, but continued on her way out of the pavilion, along the path, and to her usual spot by the lake.

I had to wait until our last meeting before she would tear a corner off the newspaper I was holding and write me her name in kanji and its romanized spelling: Misoka. This was almost seventy days after I saw her for the first time. Then she pointed to the two kanji characters and asked me how they were pronounced in my mother tongue. "Mi Hua," I said in precise Mandarin. She repeated what I said perfectly, and then pointed to the first character. "That's the same 'Mi' as the one in Miyun Reservoir in Beijing." Those were the last words I heard from her that winter in Montreal, the last words I would hear from her ever again.

∞ I

JUST LIKE THAT, they entered my life, Celia and Misoka, two mysterious women with completely different energies, appearing before me like some irresolvable contradiction. And yet they both slotted so well into the pure winter of Mount Royal. They had made the mountain their own, or perhaps *our* own. But what intrigued me most about them was the peculiar relationship they both seemed to have with China. It truly was the most unusual winter of my time in Montreal. In the years that have passed since, I have asked myself the same question many times. Was it a matter of luck or design?

Two disasters had befallen me in the six months before that most unusual of winters; the first my wife's passing and the second my daughter's leaving. Together they had brought me to the brink of collapse. By autumn I had been overcome with a sense of terrible loneliness. Inside, I felt as grey as everything around me looked. I was numb to the vivid colour of the season. I felt like an inanimate pebble tossed in the ocean of time, dragged back and forth in its tides. The world no longer wanted anything of me and I no longer wanted anything from the world. By winter, this loneliness had morphed into a dull, throbbing pain inside me, a pain that hounded me through my sleepless nights and torpid days. It tired me, robbed me of hope, and transformed my relationship to time, particularly the future. I no longer looked forward to future events, nor did I feel anxious about what might occur. I just wanted to leave here, maybe even this world. The future no longer meant anything to me. My existence no longer meant anything to me. Then Celia and Misoka entered my life.

When this most unusual of winters arrived, I had already lived in Montreal for fifteen years, but "live" does not seem the right word. At no point in that decade and a half had the life I lived been my own. Like many Chinese parents, my wife and I had immigrated to Canada with a view to providing our daughter with a better social and natural environment to grow up in. It was the problem of education in China that made my wife first start really considering emigrating. During spring festival one year in the early 1990s, she came home late from meeting with some former classmates and I saw that something was on her mind. From the moment she came in, her every movement appeared guarded, uncertain, and her eyes were glazed over, as though fixed on something not in the room.

When she came to bed, she lay flat on her back with her hands clasped on her chest. I tried to move closer and place my face close to hers but she jerked her face away. I tried to put my hand down the front of her pants but she grabbed my hand and brusquely tossed it back. "I want it," I said softly in her ear. "I don't want anything right now," she replied, and then paused for a moment before saying, "All I want is to emigrate." It was the first time my wife had ever brought up such an idea and I sat up with a start, staring at her. "Where did that come from?" I asked. She lay there with her eyes still closed. After a period of silence, I repeated the question. "Because schooling in China is beyond repair," she said. She didn't open her eyes. There was evidently some strange fury inside her.

I had grown up in a family of teachers. From a young age I had amassed a great deal of experience of education in China, and along the way a considerable number of critical opinions. I had a lot of ideas about how to reform the education system, even some quite radical ideas, and I had written many articles about education and teaching. I understood and shared the concern my wife and many other parents had about schooling in China, but I did not think the situation was as dire as my wife was saying. Her timing wasn't great either — there was my wife talking about moving far away while what I wanted was to be close to her, right there in our bedroom. So from the very beginning we were at odds. In my wife's eyes, my refusal that night was a sign of my being "irresponsible," and it became an important event in our relationship. Even though my stance with regard to emigration was to undergo a dramatic transformation, and even though once we had emigrated I never said a word against our decision while my wife would complain all the time about our new life, I was to be forever tarred with the "irresponsible" brush. When my daughter stopped skating, it was because I was irresponsible; when she didn't continue with her violin lessons, it was because I was irresponsible; when she applied for university and ignored our advice, choosing the major she wanted to study instead, it was because I was irresponsible.

It was not simply that I would prefer not to emigrate. I was terrified of the idea, and for two main reasons. The first was that my major in university had been journalism, and in China it was understood that being a journalist meant being a "mouthpiece of the party." My position would be compromised if I became an international citizen. When I brought this up with my wife, she simply said I was being an irresponsible father. At one point she even said, "A good father would wash dishes if that was what was best for his daughter!" But most of the time she would say, "I never wanted you to work," or "I never expected you to be the breadwinner in this family." She really meant it. She was an ambitious and intelligent person, and she would only be willing to take the risk of moving to another country if she were sure she would be able to get a job when we got there. The second reason for my being terrified of emigration was the fact that my English was so poor, but my wife did not think this was a problem. She would be the primary applicant when we applied, so my English level would not be a factor in whether we were accepted or not. "Besides," she added, "you could do a lot worse than starting to learn now."

After submitting our application, my wife made me sign up for an English-language course. I've never thought much of evening classes, but the English-language course came with an unexpected benefit, thanks to my reading teacher. He was a skinny old man with a stony expression who spoke very slowly, but he was passionate about reading. He told us that if we wanted to truly master a language we had to understand the culture behind it, and the best way to understand the culture was to read its literature. As someone who had always felt strongly about literature, and especially its connection to language, I found his approach suited me perfectly. He recommended the book *Animal Farm*, and told us to try our best to read one page a day. That way we would finish it by the end of the three-and-a-half-month course, during which time our language ability would have advanced by leaps and bounds. He re-emphasized the importance of understanding a place's culture by telling us that a person living in China who didn't know Lu Xun could only be the object of ridicule and contempt. Similarly, wherever we were going, if we did not know that country's Lu Xun we would be unable to win the locals' respect. Before taking his class, I had never thought of reading literature in English, let alone being able to finish a whole novel, but sure enough, by the end, *Animal Farm* had become the first book I had read entirely in English. I was not sure if I had completely understood it, but it left a huge impression on me, more so than any Chinese novel or novel translated into Chinese had done. Being able to read literature in English was an unexpected benefit of that class. Not only did it help to lessen my fears about emigrating, but it was to become a useful tool for dealing with loneliness as an immigrant.

We got the news that our application was accepted when my daughter was seven years old. We chose Montreal because a distant relative of my wife's had already been living there for some years. In many ways, it was a silly reason for choosing where to live, because my wife had only met this relative, her uncle Lin, once in her life and it was more than twenty years before, when she was still in middle school. It was only when she decided we would live in Montreal that I even knew he existed. Everyone we spoke to had recommended we move to Vancouver or Toronto because they were completely English-speaking cities with large Chinese populations where we would not feel so isolated. But my wife ignored this advice and chose Montreal. She must have begun to regret her decision the moment we arrived, because the first thing Uncle Lin said when he picked us up from the airport brought a chill colder than Canada's infamous weather. "You were getting by fine in China. Why on earth did you come here?" he said to us, in the tone of a teacher chastising a disobedient child. My wife's face went red. She had not expected to receive such an inhospitable welcome the moment we arrived at our new home. When she replied, she seemed to have lost all of her previous conviction. "For our child," she said, but this softly spoken, almost automatic reply only provoked a contemptuous laugh from the man. "It's your child I'm worried about," he said. "The education here is a joke. When they study English they don't learn grammar, and when history class isn't about Quebec, it's about Canada. History? Compared to China's five thousand years it's not even worthy of the name." I glanced at my wife, who had an awkward expression on her face. "And as for mathematics, the students here are at least three years behind the kids in China," he went on. "You're gonna regret ever coming here."

We stayed with Uncle Lin for the following week. During the day, he insisted on accompanying us as we registered with various authorities and acquainted ourselves with our new environment. Then, in the evening, he insisted that we sit with him in front of the television as he watched Chinese dating shows. We said we were happy to do these mundane tasks on our own (in fact we would prefer it). We said we never really watched television even in China and didn't really like these programs. And we said that we had serious jet lag and needed more time to rest. However, despite all this Uncle Lin seemed oblivious to what we were trying to tell him. He continued to insist on following us everywhere in the daytime and pushing us to watch the Chinese TV show in the evening. On top of that he was always complaining — about Montreal's weather, its food, its health care, its transport system, even its racial diversity. He said that everywhere you went there were Arabs and Blacks and it made him feel unsafe. We spent our first week in the city on the receiving end of a torrent of complaints, which made us, a family that was already a little apprehensive about what was in store for us, even more apprehensive. I suspected that my wife was indeed beginning to regret her decision; not her decision to immigrate, but her decision to come to Montreal and specifically to wherever this relative was. It didn't take long for her to abandon her original plan of finding an apartment near where he lived, and instead we found a place on the other side of the city, about as far away from Uncle Lin as we could get. After that she politely declined whenever he suggested meeting up and we never once invited him to our home for dinner. We only met once or twice a year for the next five years, and after that we pretty much stopped seeing each other altogether. When my wife passed away I didn't even tell him.

My wife had started looking for work the moment our immigration application had been accepted, and before we had even landed in Montreal she had submitted over twenty job applications. After we moved into our own apartment she devoted herself even more fully to hunting for a job. She had always been a high achiever, but she also had a tendency to worry about things. Arriving in a strange new place had made her anxious, and Uncle Lin's endless complaining had done little to relieve her tension. It upset me to see her working so hard at all hours of the day, looking up jobs and sending out applications, and it was difficult to stand by as she went through the emotional ups and downs of checking responses from prospective employers. One day I finally told her that she should not get so worked up and that she should take some time off, but rather than gratitude all I got from her was the cold declaration that unlike me she was unable to be so "irresponsible." That was the last time I had the courage to bring it up.

My wife also applied for a government grant to help us learn French. We did not feel strongly about learning the language but we thought the money might be useful while we tried to get on our feet. However, the meagre grant did not make our lives any easier because it meant we had to become full-time students. Not only were there classes every day, but there was a lot to learn and a huge amount of homework. On top of that we had another full-time student to look after at home, and my wife was still frantically looking for a job. We were run off our feet and utterly exhausted. A saving grace was our daughter, who was taking to her new environment like a duck to water. She came back from school each day positively buoyant and was soon proficient in French. Her positive attitude was a great comfort to us.

Before the first semester of French classes was over, my wife found a job as a lab technician in a children's hospital. She had a Ph.D. in biology and I knew only too well what she thought of working as a lab technician. Not long after we got married, she had received a phone call from her Ph.D. supervisor, who told her that one of her classmates had been offered a job as a lab technician in a famous laboratory in the United States. It was the classmate my wife thought mostly highly of when they were studying for their Ph.D.s together, and if her supervisor was calling up to tell her that this classmate had received a Nobel Prize my wife would not have been surprised. When she heard the news, the incredulity that initially appeared on her face was quickly replaced by a look of disdain. "I can't believe she'd accept," she replied. "What a waste." I'm sure my wife could not have forgotten the disappointment she had felt in her classmate that day, but she was ecstatic when she heard she'd gotten the laboratory job in Montreal. I don't think I had ever seen her so happy. She took us to a restaurant in Chinatown, the first restaurant we had been to in Canada, and throughout the meal, she lavished both my daughter and me with her attention and care. We must have looked like a very close, loving family, but I did not feel the warmth of the occasion. On the contrary, I felt an inexplicable and powerful coldness. I smiled and laughed and said positive things, complimenting my wife more than once on the dishes she had chosen, happily remarking more than once on how much my daughter was eating, but inside I felt a peculiar cold, colder than the coldest of Montreal winters.

Once I finished the five-semester French language course, I found that my life, again, was to change completely. I spent most of my time at home, where my main responsibility was looking after my wife and my daughter. During the day when I was in the apartment on my own, I would sometimes feel lonely, so I decided to reread *Animal Farm*. From the very beginning I discovered there was much more to the text than I had gotten from it the first time, to the extent that I almost felt as if I were reading a different book. I knew it wasn't simply a question of my language capability having improved or my surroundings having changed. It was testament to the mysterious power of rereading. I remembered the independent book shop down the road from our apartment where there was a quote from a French author on the wall: "One understands a man not by the books he reads, but the books he rereads." Rereading allows us not only to better know a text, but to better know others, and ourselves.

The period during which my wife and daughter were at work and school quickly became the most carefree part of my day. It was the only time when I could control my own schedule and be free from the influence of other people's moods. The moment my daughter came off the school bus my life was no longer my own. My wife had devised a strict after-school timetable for our daughter, not only dictating exactly what she should be doing but also exactly what I should be doing. However, making sure my daughter completed all the tasks on my wife's meticulously drawn flow chart was not too demanding, and I did not resent it in the slightest. In fact, I looked forward to my daughter coming back every day. It was heartwarming to see how happy she was and how she was adapting and growing in her new environment. With my wife, on the other hand, it was a different story. Every day when she came back from the laboratory she was exhausted, which of course I understood was sometimes a necessary part of starting a new job, but on top of that she was often in a terrible mood. I began to dread the moment she stepped in the front door. I did not know if it was because she was tired of working in a job that was below her abilities or whether she was having problems with her colleagues, but I was too frightened to ask — and she was too proud, even if I had asked she would not have told me the truth.

One day she came home looking particularly glum and I told her to have something to eat before checking our daughter's homework. She said she wasn't hungry and that she didn't want to eat. But I put a bowl of gourd and pork rib soup in front of her anyway. She took a couple of perfunctory sips before going to my daughter's room to take a cursory look at her homework and half-heartedly read her a bedtime story in English. After that, she walked into our bedroom and slammed the door behind her. When I saw what a bad mood she was in I nervously cleaned up the kitchen. Walking quietly to our bedroom, I saw from the crack under the door that she hadn't turned on the light. This only made me more nervous. I softly opened the door to see in the moonlight my wife already lying in bed and facing away from me. I thought she might be asleep so I took great care to make as little noise as possible as I got ready for bed. After having a quick wash and rummaging around for my underwear in the dark, I quietly lay down on the bed. To my surprise, my wife's crisp voice cut through the night.

"What do you intend to do?"

I didn't understand. "What do you mean?"

"You can't waste your time every day at home like this," she said.

"Didn't you say —"

"I want you to get a job."

"How am I expected to find a job?" I asked. "Didn't you say you never expected me to work?"

"Naturally you can't be a journalist anymore," she said. "But you could study something else, try a new career."

"What could I study at my age?"

"You know, a colleague of mine, her husband had a Ph.D. in literature back in China, specializing in pre-Qin writing. Now he's a computer engineer."

I knew the colleague she was talking about. My wife didn't get on well with her at all. They'd gotten into an argument on my wife's second day at the lab. "Didn't you say she was a philistine?"

"But her husband is an admirable man, a responsible man."

I felt myself getting annoyed but I decided not to respond. I didn't like where this conversation was going.

I felt my wife roll over and look at me. "Why not go and take a course in computers," she said. "You're so smart, you'd get the hang of it in no time."

"You know I have no interest in computers," I said.

"So what are you interested in?"

"I don't know," I said. "I don't know."

"That's your problem," she replied. "You're not interested in anything."

I didn't respond. I did not want to argue with her.

My wife was silent for some time, and I thought the conversation was over, but then she said, "In any case, you can't keep sitting at home reading that book about animals all day."

I wasn't surprised she would say something like that. She had always been against my reading fiction and whenever she saw me reading a novel she would be sure to tell me to stop wasting my time with "useless books." I had gotten used to her attitude about literature and was not at all surprised that this doctor of biology did not know that *Animal Farm* was not actually about animals. However, it did surprise me that she suddenly wanted me to find a job. I did not know what had spurred this on but I suspected it had something to do with her recent mood. I rolled over and looked at the woman who seemed intent on demeaning me that evening and asked, "So why do you want me to find a job all of a sudden?"

She paused for a moment before saying, "Because I don't want to work anymore."

This was the first time I had heard my hardworking, high-achieving wife say such a thing, and the words struck me like a bolt of lightning. The image of us in the Chinese restaurant the day she got the job flashed in my mind. I remembered the peculiar cold I had felt that day, and I felt it take hold of my body once again as I lay in bed beside her. It took some time for me to summon up the courage to ask why.

My wife's response came immediately and decisively. "I never should have settled for that job."

A shudder shot through me. I didn't know what I should do to comfort her, or even to comfort myself. Carefully, I placed my right hand on her hip and felt her body tremble slightly under my touch. Then she did something she had never done before. She lifted her left hand from beneath the covers and placed her index finger on my chin. There was a warmth to that action that I had never felt from her before and tears began to well up in my eyes. I held her hand and lifted it to my mouth. That's when my wife made her peculiar proposal.

Even today I cannot quite believe that it was her who came up with the idea. She had never thought very highly of my brother, who owned two listed companies, and she had always looked down on struggling store owners whose work required more physical strength than intellectual prowess. However, that night in bed she suggested I borrow money from my brother so we could open a convenience store.

It was a long time before I discovered that it was her worsening relations with her colleagues and boss that had caused my wife to lose confidence in her ability to work for somebody else. To this day, I don't know the details. All she said was that her boss was racist and her colleagues jealous, but she did not tell me how that racism and jealousy was manifested. My wife quit the job for which she ought never to have settled a week after we bought the store, and the life we were to live without much variation for the following thirteen years began. Were it not for the results of her medical checkup that fateful day, I'm sure we would still be living it now.

The store opened every day at seven in the morning and closed at eleven at night, and for the first five years we were in business 365 days a year. After that it became 363 days a year as we closed for Christmas and New Year's Day. I was in charge of stock and it was primarily my wife who dealt with customers, though during busy periods we had a couple of friends who could lend a hand. With the opening of the store our lives entered a stable and monotonous cycle. Tomorrow would be just like today, just as today was no different from yesterday. We were rushed off our feet every day doing exactly the same things. I'm sure that life is tiring and repetitive no matter where you live, maybe that's just what life is about, but if we were still in China where I was the editor of an influential newspaper and she was working as part of a famous research group, it would have been tiring and repetitive in a different way. At least we would've been able to sit down in the evenings and reflect on just how boring everything was. In Montreal we didn't even have time for that. Every April when we had to submit our tax returns we noticed with an unpleasant start just how fast time was passing us by.

This was my life as an immigrant. If I had shared my experience with my classmate's wife on the phone, no matter whether she thought Canada was a bonfire or a glacier, she would no doubt have been stunned. Life is cruel to the immigrant, whether you have money or not. If my classmate and his wife decided to leave China, they would have to face the unavoidable hardships of emigration, like solitude, humiliation, and monotony, like repetitiveness, directionlessness, and helplessness. These were problems that could not be solved by money, difficulties that no frame of mind could counteract.

∞ Misoka

THE ENIGMA OF the paradoxical lives of Celia and Misoka, one a healthy sufferer, the other a combination of innocence and mystery, had piqued in me a curiosity that had long been stifled by the monotony of day-to-day life. I found myself questioning why people live the way they do, which not only reawakened in me a certain anticipation and anxiety for the future, but a sense of fulfillment in the present I had not felt for some time. In fact, it had even transformed the way I understood and made sense of the past. It was as though the rose of time had come into bloom and for the first time my life began to resemble

a whole, like the lives that are crafted in fine works of literature. The temperature was dropping as Montreal descended
deeper into winter, but the new questions that consumed me
prevented me from feeling the cold. I did not know if others
would see the contradictory nature of the lives of Celia and
Misoka, or if they even saw it themselves, but I had seen it.
After many mediocre years of immigrant life, after such a long
time during which nothing seemed to incite my curiosity, why
had I suddenly found myself able to see what I had seen? Even
today I do not know the answer to this question. I had seen
their contradictions, but beyond that I had seen the entirety
of their lives, the entirety of who they were. I had somehow
seen it! And yet, it was not only that. I had also seen myself, a
self I had never seen before, revealed through the intersecting
paths traced by three insignificant grains of sand one winter
upon the slopes of Mount Royal, like the three movements of
a sonata. This sonata had formed the most unusual memory of
my life, the most unusual memory to be found hidden in the
tranquil, snowy folds of the mountain. Today, after so many
years, each of its notes still sounds in my mind with the chime
of revelation.

The memory of that winter often brings me back to the
confused period of my adolescence and my relationship with
my uncle. I grew up in an ordinary small town. My parents
were mathematics teachers in the local middle school, and I
spent my childhood years among the dilapidated buildings of
the school campus. My uncle, on the other hand, was a poet,
well known throughout the province, who not only spent much
of his time in Chongqing, the huge city I always found so dis-
orienting, but also travelled across the country, visiting its sites
and meeting with its people. He was the picture of cultured

cosmopolitanism. I stayed with him and my aunt for a period of time every year for six years. The first three years they came to collect me by bus, the two years after that by train. The sixth and final time my uncle arrived driving a motorbike with sidecar. He was not accompanied by my aunt. He was with a woman I had never seen before. She was the last woman, before Celia and Misoka, about whom I was gripped with an intense curiosity.

When I heard the sound of the motor I stood up and ran out of the house, hoping, like every year, to charge into the arms of my uncle. But when I reached the front door I came to a sudden stop. He was with a strange woman wearing a purple dress with white petals printed on it. She was facing away from me and reaching for her luggage from the sidecar. My pulse began to quicken and my face grew red. I stopped and stood leaning against the door frame, unwilling to walk any closer.

It was the summer of 1974, and our small town did not see many women in purple dresses, let alone purple dresses with white petals printed on them. I was both excited and nervous at the thought that this strange woman was to be a guest at our house, a feeling that only grew stronger when she turned around. She was nothing like any woman I knew or had even seen before. She was elegant, beautiful.... I heard my uncle telling me to stop dawdling and help with the luggage, so I began to stumble toward them, as if walking into a painting or a dream.

After lunch my mother offered the woman the bed I shared with my brother so she could rest, and made us take our afternoon nap on the dining table. Before long she had dozed off, but I was unable to sleep. This was partly because of my brother, who was restless and kept knocking his feet against mine. But the main reason I lay there awake was that I could not stop thinking about the fact that this strange woman's sleeping body was so close to mine. I could even hear her breathing, the pure, almost luminous quality of her breath echoing around the room. Soon this sound was accompanied by the voices of my uncle and mother talking in the next room. I heard my uncle say that she was a "talented but unfortunate" woman. Her talent was clear to see in the prose piece she had recently had published in a Shanghai newspaper. Her misfortune, on the other hand, had begun the moment she was born. Her father was a commander in the nationalist Guomindang army, a hero in the war of resistance against the Japanese. He had died in the city of Xuzhou, three months before she was born, in the Huaihai Battle between the Communists and the Nationalists. After the Communists took power and before the land reforms took place, her mother and two brothers fled to Hong Kong, leaving her to spend the rest of her childhood with a distant relative. This relative's husband was a railway worker who couldn't write his own name. During the day he was the model of a level-headed and diligent worker, but when he returned home he transformed into a merciless and violent alcoholic. When he was drunk the whole household became victims of his cruelty. With the arrival of adulthood she was able to leave that oppressive household, but the life awaiting her was no more fortunate. She married the son of a factory owner who had never cared for her, instead harbouring a secret lifelong love for a neighbour from his hometown. Their marriage was plagued by conflict from the start, both verbal and physical. When their son died of typhoid at the age of three, their marriage followed shortly after.

I had never heard a story like it in my life, but despite this it seemed to me that I must have understood it, because as I listened I felt very clearly just how "unfortunate" this woman was. It did not make sense to me how such an elegant woman could be treated so badly, or how a woman who had been treated so badly could continue to be so elegant. I felt as if my mother too had mistreated her, because the moment she stepped into our home my mother had seemed hostile, as though they were bitter opponents in a long-running feud. When my uncle had finished his story, my mother showed no sign of empathy. "Women like that are the most dangerous," she said coldly. "Women like what?" my uncle asked. "Talented and unfortunate," my mother said.

The woman didn't seem dangerous to me at all. On the way to Chongqing I sat in the sidecar and she sat behind my uncle. She tried to hold down her dress but from time to time the wind would catch it and the hem would flap against my shoulder. It was the happiest journey of my childhood. Every detail seemed perfect. I did not understand my mother at all. How could this woman be dangerous? What kind of danger did she pose? As I looked at her sitting behind my uncle with her arms around his shoulders and a captivating smile on her face that I had not seen before on any other woman, I felt completely content. She had stopped being an unfortunate woman, I thought, because in the happiness I was feeling I could feel some of her happiness. In what way could a woman like that be dangerous?

My respect for writing has a lot to do with that sixth summer I spent with my uncle in Chongqing. During my time there I was affected by things I had never paid much attention to before. My uncle's house had a constant stream of visitors: writers, editors, and fans of literature, travelling from all over the province, and in some cases from all over the country, people of various shapes and sizes, speaking with all manner of accents, who came to discuss literature and recent events. When they talked, the world and the lives unfolding within it seemed enormous, and I felt my mind expanding under the deluge of new ideas. Their discussions filled me with both excitement and shame. I was ashamed to be from such a small town and such an average family. We hardly had any visitors, and the visitors we did have all looked the same, spoke in the same accent, said the same things about the same unchanging, everyday topics. When they spoke, the world and its lives seemed tiny and dull.

The main cause for my newfound respect for writing did not, however, lie in the animated discussions that took place in my uncle's library, but in a piece of writing published in a newspaper, a text I could hold in my hand and run my fingers over. My uncle often showed me the pieces he had had published, but for some reason I had never felt particularly strongly about anything he had written. One day, however, he removed a newspaper cutting from between the pages of a collection of Lu Xun's prose he was reading and handed it to me, telling me I should give it a read. It was from a Shanghai newspaper, and the text was the piece of prose written by the talented and unfortunate woman. It was the first time I had read her name, the first time I had seen her writing, and before I had even started reading, a strange, pleasant feeling took hold of me, much like what I had felt when the hem of her skirt lightly flapped against my skin on the road to Chongqing. I felt a certain respect for the name before my eyes, for the characters printed on the page, and a new respect for writing itself. Over the next few days I read and reread the piece, again and again, until what I initially didn't understand began to become clearer, then obscure again, then clearer once more, the pleasant feeling staying with me throughout. In fact, it remains with me to this day.

The talented and unfortunate woman was my uncle's most exceptional guest. She visited roughly every other day, and each time she entered the room I was thrilled. The peculiar sensation that her presence instilled in me only became more intense when I had read her writing. Sometimes, as I looked at her, she seemed incredibly real: the author of the piece that had been published in the Shanghai newspaper, the person standing in front of me. At other times, however, she seemed somehow unreal, because I could read her piece over and over, could trace my finger across each line, across her name, but she herself remained an impenetrable mystery. In what way was she dangerous? What danger did she pose? When she visited, she invariably took a seat in a chair in the corner of the library with a notebook in her hand. She rarely spoke with the other guests. Only when my uncle was there would she occasionally ask him a few questions about writing, to which his responses inevitably appeared to leave a deep impression on her. I will never forget the way she looked at my uncle, the unmistakable esteem in which she held him and which she clearly felt to her very core. I had never seen another woman look at someone in the way she looked at my uncle, and it made me think she was no longer an unhappy woman. I was able to feel her happiness through the happiness of my uncle. How could she be dangerous? What danger could she possibly pose?

That summer my mother arrived to take me home from Chongqing two days earlier than originally planned. I was initially upset at her premature arrival, but quickly realized that something was clearly troubling her. On the long coach journey home she didn't say a word. In an attempt to cheer her up I told her that the trip had been the most fun I had had at my uncle's home. My attempt at conversation did not seem to have the desired effect on her mood because she remained silent, so I went on to tell her how I had read the piece of prose that had been published by the woman in the Shanghai newspaper, the piece my uncle had said proved how talented she was. I told her I didn't completely understand it but that I still liked it very much. My mother replied that I had already told her so in my latest letter. It was clear from her tone of voice that she was still not in good spirits, so I went on to tell her that I had fallen in love with writing and that it made me happy when I wrote her letters or wrote in my diary every day. At this she looked at me with an uneasy expression and said, "Don't let yourself be led astray." She was looking even less pleased than she had been when we set off so, feeling defeated, I did not respond. After a period of silence, however, I could not help but ask her in what way that woman was dangerous. My mother looked at me and said, "Your uncle will be captivated by her. And it will destroy your aunt." I was more scared by the tone of my mother's voice than what she was actually saying. I didn't dare utter another word. Then my mother told me that I would not be spending my summer holidays with my uncle anymore. Surprised and stung by this new piece of information, I asked why. "Because you are no longer a child," was her matter-of-fact reply.

That evening I heard the hushed discussion between my mother and father, which explained the reason my mother had decided to cut my trip to Chongqing short, and why they would not be allowing me to spend my summer holidays there anymore. The problem lay in the latest letter they had received from me. "They were starting to have a bad influence on him," my mother said.

"It can't be that bad," my father replied.

"Take a look the letter and tell me that," she replied, before sighing deeply. "Women are bad news."

"Aren't you a woman?" my father said.

"That's how I know they're bad news."

It was not the scene of an East Asian woman sitting in a wheelchair by Beaver Lake in the icy cold of Montreal's winter that captured me all those years later, but the fact that she was writing, that she was utterly absorbed by her writing, so much so that she did not even seem to notice the cold around her. Writing had been my passion in my youth, a passion that had been sparked by the talented, unfortunate woman. The autumn following the summer that had apparently had such a bad influence on me, I secretly submitted a piece of writing to the same Shanghai newspaper that had published her work. A week after I received the rejection letter, I submitted again. A week after the second rejection I submitted a third piece. This time I did not even receive a rejection letter, and I did not submit my writing again. Although three consecutive failures had extinguished my passion for writing, my respect for both writing and writers never left me. It was the main reason why, decades later, I was so curious about the woman who was sitting on Mount Royal in the icy cold winter, writing.

Soon the talented, unfortunate woman was to find that she too was unable to continue to write. When I entered high school, she suffered the fate my mother had predicted for my aunt: a mental breakdown. My mother told me this piece of news without a hint of sympathy. "I knew this would happen," she said coldly. "In the old days they'd have called this karma." After this my uncle also stopped producing new literary works. No doubt my mother considered this karma too.

I never told Misoka the source of my respect for writing, but I had often thought to myself that she shared many characteristics with that talented and unfortunate woman. There was an innocence about both of them, as well as a certain quality I found it difficult to put my finger on, and they were both passionate about writing. Of course, if Misoka never ended up publishing any of her works I would not be able to say whether or not she was as talented. Furthermore, Misoka's secrecy about her past meant I was unlikely to find out exactly how unfortunate she was. But I had a feeling that there was one misfortune they shared. It was a feeling I had had the first time Misoka and I spoke, an inexplicable yet intense feeling, that perhaps she had never met her own father. Unlike Celia, Misoka tried to find the most inconspicuous spot to sit in the pavilion, which reminded me of the talented and unfortunate woman when she came to visit my uncle's house. I will never forget the image of her sitting in the same chair in the corner of the library. She shared a profound shyness with Misoka, a reluctance to be noticed.

The black coat and trousers Misoka liked to wear made the bright-red scarf wrapped around her neck particularly striking. The first time I saw her sitting by the side of the lake, what first caught my eye was her red scarf. Even during our first conversation I found my eyes repeatedly flicking toward it. I had the strange sense that I had seen it somewhere before. It seemed more than just a scarf. It was almost as if it were alive and listening in on what we were saying.

In fact it was the red scarf that sparked my third conversation with Misoka. She was placing it on her lap next to a French newspaper when she noticed that I was staring at the kanji characters embroidered on it. It was the first time I had noticed them and I was trying to read what they said when, in a sudden, swift movement, Misoka picked up the scarf and wrapped it around her neck, taking care to position it in such a way that the characters were obscured. She laughed awkwardly, which made me laugh awkwardly, but to my relief this time she didn't chastise me for prying into her personal affairs.

Instead she picked up the French newspaper and pointed to a photo of a political demonstration, asking me what was written on the banner the protestors were holding. The photo accompanied an article describing the recent tensions flaring up over a territorial dispute between China and Japan. According to the article, anti-Japanese demonstrations had been taking place over the last few days in some southern cities in China. The protestors were holding a banner on which was written, in blood-red, "Protect Our Homes. Defend Our Country."

A dejected look fell over her face when I told her.

"A lot of Chinese are still very hostile to Japan," I said. "I suspect a lot of Japanese are still very hostile to China too."

She looked at me and said, "Hostility only leads to tragedy," and pointed to the litter bin. "Better to throw all that hostility in the trash."

After I had thrown the newspaper away I returned to sit on the locker beside Misoka. She wanted to ask me some questions about Beijing. "I know nothing of Beijing today," I told her. "The Beijing I know no longer exists."

"Even the Old Summer Palace?"

I remembered how she had asked me if I had been to the Old Summer Palace the second time we talked. "Even the Old Summer Palace," I replied. "I saw it on TV and it's completely different from how I remember it."

"How do you remember it?" Misoka asked.

Her insistent desire to know more about the Old Summer Palace was still a mystery to me, but I closed my eyes and found myself back at the place that was so closely tied to my feelings of homesickness. "Back then it was not a tourist site, there were no walls around it," I said. "It was just a ruin, a true ruin."

"That's the Old Summer Palace I want to see," Misoka said.

I opened my eyes and looked at the mysterious East Asian woman whom I wanted so much to understand better. I had no idea why she was so interested in the Old Summer Palace, or what it was about that "true ruin" she wanted to see so much. Is it possible that she somehow knew that it had been my place of refuge during my university years? Is it possible that she too had developed a curiosity about me, that she wanted to pry into my past?

"Can you still see it?" she asked.

"As if I were there right now."

"You must know it very well."

"I used to go there often."

"How often?"

"I don't think anyone went there as often as I did," I replied. "It was a refuge for me when I was at university."

Misoka gripped tightly onto the ends of her scarf and looked at me with wide eyes. "This is so strange. How have I managed to meet someone who knows the Old Summer Palace so well?" she asked. "Can it really just be a coincidence?"

Her question touched profoundly on my memories. Was it a coincidence? Was it out of luck or design? It was a question that had been plaguing me for thirty years. I did not know the answer, I had no way of knowing the answer, but for the moment I did not want to be caught up in the implications of this question again. "What do you want to know?" I asked, making a point to hide from her how agitated I felt.

"Is it a bleak place?" she asked softly.

"Desolate."

"Desolate," she repeated quietly.

"The desolate setting suited my solitary character."

"There must have been fields surrounding the ruins."

"And lots of marshland."

"I can picture it, the marshland."

"And fruit trees."

"What kind of fruit trees?"

"I'm not sure. Probably peach, plum, or maybe apple."

"I also see lots of shrubbery."

"You're right. The little paths were lined on both sides with tall-growing shrubs. Cycling through it was like going through a maze."

"How wide are the roads?"

I made a gesture with my hands, to indicate to her that the roads were about one metre wide.

"That's how I imagined it."

"You've imagined it?"

"Yes. I have pictured those ruins many times."

I was about to ask her why but stopped, afraid she might think I was intruding on her privacy again.

Misoka seemed to be aware of my apprehension. She sighed and said, "I wish I knew what happened there."

"October eighteenth to the twenty-first, 1860. French and British troops burned it down —"

"No, not that."

"Then what? 1900? The Eight-Power Allied Forces?"

"That's all history textbook stuff."

What else could she mean? I looked at her and thought of the letter that Victor Hugo wrote, decrying the destruction of the Old Summer Palace. I asked her if she'd read it, presumably the most well-known French language text on the subject. "One day, two bandits entered the Summer Palace. One plundered, the other burned," I recited the famous lines.

"Of course I've read it," Misoka said. "That's also in the textbooks."

"What else is there then?" I asked.

Misoka was looking at me. "Like what happened in 1974."

"1974?" That was the year I had met the talented, unfortunate woman, the year I became obsessed with writing. "I've never heard of anything happening at the Old Summer Palace in 1974," I replied.

Misoka lifted her head, leaned it against the back of the wheelchair, and closed her eyes. "It was the winter of 1974," she said softly, as though speaking to herself.

"The winter of 1974?" I asked. "Why the winter?"

"Winter is my favourite season," she said, adding after a short pause, "because it is sowing season."

In what world was winter sowing season? Her answer did not seem to fit with reality, and it made me feel uneasy. I wanted to ask her what she meant but again I was worried about overstepping the mark. "Nothing happened in the winter of 1974," I told her.

"Something happened," she replied. "I'm certain of it."

I was utterly puzzled by what she was saying. I heard a disapproving voice inside me. *How could you know? What could you know that I don't?* Those ruins were the place I knew best in Beijing, and Misoka could only "picture" them by closing her eyes and imagining. I could not accept that she knew more about the Old Summer Palace than I did. What happened in the winter of 1974? I found myself constantly perplexed by Misoka, just like I did with Celia. In the enigma of these two women's lives I saw an unusual paradox. Something drew me toward them, but the closer I got the more confused I became.

It was becoming clear that my third conversation with Misoka would not be able to continue for much longer, and besides, I was worried that Celia might appear. I had always dreaded the moment when the three of us would meet face to face. At the very best it would be an awkward encounter. I stood up but before saying goodbye, I removed a book from my rucksack. It was a popular novel written by a Chinese woman living in London and I had bought it two days previously from a second-hand bookstore. I asked Misoka if she had read it, and she said she'd heard of it but hadn't read it yet. I gave her the book and told her I had read the English-language version and that I had bought this French version especially for her. "It's about three generations of Chinese women," I said. "It might interest you."

She took the book and scrutinized its cover for a few moments before looking at me and saying earnestly, "Actually, I'm more interested in understanding Chinese men."

This was not what I was expecting! I felt the blood rush to my cheeks. I did not know what to say. What was she trying to say? I tried to maintain my composure, making an effort to appear calm. "What do you want to understand about them?"

"Like why a Chinese man would fall in love with a Japanese woman."

What did she mean by that? I was even more at a loss. Was she talking about something she had experienced or something she had imagined? I did not have the courage to pursue the topic further so I put on my rucksack. However, before I could walk away Misoka said something that only made things even more awkward. She pointed to the place where Celia usually sat and asked bluntly, "Who is she?"

So she had noticed Celia too! Or perhaps I should say she had noticed the relationship between Celia and me. I stood there uncomfortably as I thought of how to respond in a way that would not upset her. "A friend," I said. "Just like you."

Misoka was clearly upset by the second half of my reply. "Just like me?" she said sardonically.

Our conversation had entered very sensitive territory. I decided it was best to say as little as possible. Anything I did say would have to be worded very carefully. I did not want to be misunderstood, or to cause offence.

For a moment Misoka didn't seem to know how to continue either, but after a period of silence she asked me, "Do you think she's pretty?"

It was another trap. If I told her I thought Celia was pretty, she would certainly be upset, but if I told her I didn't, she would think I was lying, which might upset her even more. I didn't respond.

"She has lovely skin. Naturally lovely skin," Misoka said. "Not like me at all."

Again, Misoka would not be pleased if I agreed, and if I told her I preferred her dark skin she might not believe me. She would be upset either way. Again, I didn't respond.

Misoka looked again toward the spot where Celia usually sat. "I saw you talking the other day," she said. "You were sitting very close."

She was obviously trying to let me know that she knew about our relationship, to make me feel embarrassed. I tried to keep my cool. "She was explaining Shakespeare's sonnets to me."

This clearly wasn't what she was expecting. "Shakespeare?" she asked.

"Yes," I said. "She's a Shakespeare expert." As soon as I finished I realized I'd said the wrong thing again.

A frown appeared on Misoka's brow. "So she's not like me at all," she replied. "She's an expert and I don't know a thing."

I was annoyed with myself for speaking so carelessly. Then I remembered Celia telling me that she "only read Shakespeare." Perhaps I could make up for my mistake. "Actually I think it's perhaps a problem with her," I replied. "She says she only reads Shakespeare."

This seemed to confirm Misoka's suspicions. She looked up at me and asked, "Do you think everything's all right with her, in terms of her health?"

I didn't dare reveal my true feelings about Celia, so I said, "After skating she goes skiing. She must be in pretty good shape."

"But it looks to me like she's suffering from something," Misoka replied. "That was my impression when I first saw her."

I was completely shocked. Her impression was exactly the same as my own! I did not have the courage to tell her that I felt the same way, so I just looked at her incredulously.

"She must have been hurt," Misoka said, "psychologically."

"Everyone has been hurt psychologically," I replied.

"But with her it's serious," Misoka said. "I can tell."

Celia's strange response to my mention of China came back to me. Could it have something to do with a psychological hurt she had suffered?

"In fact I would say the psychological blow she received was lethal," Misoka continued.

There was surely no way for Misoka to suspect that any psychological blow Celia had suffered might have something to do with China, but I didn't want to continue talking with her to find out. It was the first conversation Misoka and I had had about Celia, the first encounter between the three of us, the insignificant grains of sand whose paths had for the first time that day intersected and begun to influence one another. I began to have an ominous feeling that the complex interrelations that were to develop between the three of us were bound to bring more sorrow to the snow-covered slopes of Mount Royal, to that most unusual of winters.

∞ I

MY SPECIAL RELATIONSHIP with the Old Summer Palace arose because of the solitude and homesickness that haunted me during my six years as a student in Beijing, the first time I had made a life for myself somewhere new. I was frequently overcome by a longing for home, a sense of alienation, a feeling that my life was without moorings. During these times the Old Summer Palace was my refuge. Its draw to me and my need for it became evident the first time I saw it. I suspect that a ruin exists for every lonely person, a place with which one can enter a kind of dialogue, and I was lucky enough to find mine at the time I needed it most.

Before Misoka, I had never told anyone of my special relationship with the Old Summer Palace. It was too personal. I went there often in my university years, I believe more
often than anyone else, and it seemed to me that I came to
know its every path, its every rock, its every secret ... but I did
not know what happened there in the winter of 1974. I loved
the Old Summer Palace during winter most of all, because
in winter every detail seemed especially vivid, especially real.
Everything, perhaps, appeared especially *ruined*. I made an effort with every visit to walk farther, to see the remnants of a
section I had not seen before, but in the end I would invariably
return to what once was the Big Fountains site in the Western
Palaces to take a seat on my favourite rock. The rock, which
was shaped in a smooth arc and into which was carved a floral
design, must have originally been part of a domed roof. It had
lost its former splendour, of course, but maintained, it seemed
to me, a certain dignity to which even time had to pay heed. I
often found myself simply sitting there, staring at the desola-
tion around me without a thought in my head. At other times
strange ideas would occur to me, such as the notion that the
Old Summer Palace had always been destined to be sacked and
burned by foreign powers, that it was this act that had allowed
it to become the true Old Summer Palace. But such thoughts
quickly made me uncomfortable. So much of what was "true"
in history was built on a foundation of destruction — this was
its tragedy. It reminded me of the talented and unfortunate
woman who had to be destroyed so many times before she truly
appeared before me. Why had things turned out the way they
had? Why did they have to turn out this way? The cruelty behind the destructive forces she had faced had revealed itself in
her mysterious silences, and later in what happened to her while

I was at high school. I remember the night I heard the news of her mental breakdown, when I lay in bed secretly weeping under the covers. It wasn't just what happened to her that filled me with grief, but the way my mother had spoken about it. My mother's words had had their own destructive character, perhaps even more cruelly destructive than the incident itself. It was with this thought that I became aware of the horror of language. That being said, I knew that nothing my mother said would be able to change the significance of the talented, unfortunate woman in my life. She was the first woman to move me, to intrigue me, to make my heart ache; the first woman to capture me with her scent. She was a worker in a plant that made confectionery not far from my uncle's home, and on the days when a southwesterly wind swept through Chongqing you could smell the distinctive aroma that floated over from the state-run factory. I liked to stand at the window, greedily inhaling the sugar-scented air, and my uncle often joined me. "That smell always gets me in the mood for writing," he once said, and I knew that like me he was thinking of the woman. After her collapse my uncle never got back into the writing mood, despite the fact Chongqing's southwesterly winds continued to bring that familiar scent from the factory.

I studied for a two-year master's degree after finishing my undergraduate course, and I continued to make trips to the Old Summer Palace to sit on the rock by the ruins of the Big Fountains in the former Western Palaces and reflect on the depth of my solitude, the weight of my nostalgia for life at home. These were the most carefree moments of my time in Beijing and I still look back fondly on the time I spent sitting among the ruins. The most vivid of these memories were the two occasions my silent contemplation was interrupted, the first of which took place one day at dusk, in the autumn of 1983. I was thinking of the journey I had taken to Chongqing on my uncle's motorbike. Having travelled most of the way, we had stopped at a simple country restaurant to have a bite to eat. Throughout the meal, the woman who ran the restaurant sat in a chair by the entrance and stared at us enviously. "What a happy family," she said, on four separate occasions, and the talented, unfortunate woman, on first hearing this, pulled a face at me. It was the first time I understood what people meant by the warmth of family.

It was when I was indulging in the memory of this warmth that I felt someone tap my shoulder. Startled into the present, I turned around to find a plainly dressed girl with delicate features. "Do you mind taking a photo?" she asked. She handed me her camera as I got to my feet and motioned to me to stay where I was before skipping deftly across the fragments of rock to the remnants of a large arch. I took three photos: one with her left hand on the arch, one with her leaning sideways on it, and one with her reclining against it. Then she ran back and said, "Sorry. I didn't mean to interrupt your thoughts."

Somewhat embarrassed, I laughed and handed the camera back to her. "I was just thinking of a little thing that happened a long time ago," I told her. I knew, of course, that it was not a little thing, because I had never experienced anything like it before or since.

The girl put the camera in its leather case, which she then put in her rucksack. Then she looked up at me and said, "You must come here a lot."

"How did you know?"

The corner of her mouth twitched slightly (this image is still the clearest part of this memory) and she said, "Just now when I approached you, you looked like you belonged here, among the ruins."

It was an interesting observation. I looked at her, then all around me, and realized that I did indeed seem to fit in with this world.

The girl looked at her watch. I assumed she would say she had to leave, but to my surprise she sat down on the rock I had just been sitting on. She patted the rock with her right hand, indicating that I could take a seat beside her. "This is the first time I've been here," she said.

I sat down beside her. "Is there something special about today?"

She smiled, but didn't reply.

"It looks like the ruins are having an effect on you," I said.

"I was imagining what it would be like the whole way here," she replied.

"Is it like you imagined?"

"Pretty much the same," she replied. "I even imagined you."

"Me?" I said, somewhat skeptically.

"Well, maybe not you. A blurry figure."

I turned to look at her and thought about her interesting turn of phrase.

She did not turn to look at me but lifted her eyes to the darkening sky. "I imagined that I would meet someone I was meant to meet," she said, putting emphasis on the words "meant to."

I continued to stare at this girl who seemed to have descended from nowhere, whose features were difficult to discern in the grey light of dusk, whose voice even seemed somewhat muffled by the surroundings, but who also gave me an impression of a certain purity. It was not her appearance that gave me this impression, but something about her whole existence that made itself known in the way she spoke, the way she moved. The world, it seemed to me, had been good to her. She had never fallen victim to its destructive forces, and it was clear to me that she never would. She would forever remain as she was when she first entered the world, she would forever be herself, her life intact. I was sure that her background was somehow different from that of everyone I knew, and sitting next to her I could not help but think of the talented and unfortunate woman. The contrast between the lives of these two women was enormous. For the woman I had first seen on my uncle's motorbike, the opportunity to reveal her brilliance only appeared after a period of destruction.

The girl and I chatted for a while. She told me that she was a third-year student at the Central Academy of Fine Arts, and the artist who had had the greatest influence on her was Marc Chagall, whose work was "immaculate." She said that her opinions were always different from other people's, so her family had labelled her a nonconformist. Her classmates all dreamed of a future in the huge cities of Paris or New York, whereas she longed for a life in the countryside, some idyll far away where she could plant her own food, read books, and paint. She also told me how, more than art and the image, she was passionate about words and reading. She particularly liked to read works that were difficult to understand, like Borges's stories and Shakespeare's sonnets.

The sky was already completely black by the time we got ready to leave. I had spent the night at the Old Summer Palace twice before, and had often arrived or left after sunset. I had never been remotely afraid on these occasions, but that evening, as I felt the dark enveloping the ruins, I began to feel a rising fear. I knew it was a result of the girl's peculiar beauty, the way she seemed untouched by the world, and the sense of responsibility it instilled in me. Her purity had to be protected, and I was afraid that it would be harmed in some way by the darkness. She, on the other hand, remained calm and carried on chatting as normal. It was only when I mentioned for the third time that it was getting late that she finally stood up. She had left her bike on the other side so I walked mine alongside her around the circumference of the ruins before we cycled away along the winding paths, with me taking the lead. It was clear from her tone of voice that she was not afraid of the dark. "I also imagined that the person I met would show me the way riding a bicycle," she said loudly from behind me, and the confidence in her voice calmed my nerves. "I know all these paths very well," I told her.

The following two days passed very slowly. I kept thinking back to our conversation, and staring at the address she wrote in my notebook when we parted ways. On the afternoon of the third day, having finished writing an essay for my History of Chinese Journalism course, I got on my bike and raced to the Old Summer Palace. This time I did not venture out to discover a new section of the ruins, but immediately sat down on my rock by the Big Fountains. I crouched down, rested my face against the rock's cool surface, and wrapped my arms around it, feeling its contours with my fingers. It was no longer the same rock I knew so well. It was the rock the girl and I had sat on together, and now it contained the memories and words we had shared. I took a seat, removed a sheet of paper from my rucksack, and began to write my first letter to the girl I had met three days previously in these ruins. In it I wrote that I had been thinking about the question she had asked me before we went our separate ways, and that over the last few days my opinion had changed. I no longer believed that our meeting was an accident. It was meant to be.

Her response came very quickly. She said she also believed our meeting was meant to be, not simply because she had imagined so many of the details of our encounter in advance, but also because our conversation had flowed so naturally. She could tell that I was not only able but willing to engage with her unorthodox views and suggested that we continue our discussion through these letters. She hoped that in each letter we would talk about a book each was reading or had read. Then she began to talk about the collection of Pirandello plays she had just finished reading.

We met occasionally, but for the most part our relationship was based on our letters. In the two months that followed we would each receive a letter from the other about every two days. At first our correspondence put a lot of pressure on me, because both the breadth of her knowledge and the depth of her insight were much greater than mine. Her letters were full of profound observations and elegant writing that shook and challenged my preconceptions. Meanwhile, my letters contained only superficial opinions and commonplace expressions. A sense of shame and inferiority overcame me each time I placed my reply in the mailbox. She never made fun of my letters — in fact she often engaged earnestly with what I had written — but this did nothing to make me feel less inferior. The gulf between us was too great. Anyone who read our letters side by side would have clearly seen the obvious freedom of her spirit in comparison to my own, which was evidently restricted, perhaps even enslaved, by ordinary ideas and entrenched opinions. This was perhaps the general difference in the way we wrote, but she

surpassed me in the specifics as well, in every topic we discussed. She had read every book I mentioned, whereas I had read
none of the books she talked about. An even more specific example is the letter in which she discussed the "Dark Lady" from
Shakespeare's sonnets. She told me she had spent a great deal
of time trying to understand who this mysterious lover must
have been to the poet, and in the end had drawn a portrait of
her. When I saw the portrait she enclosed I could not help but
laugh. "Why does it look like a self-portrait?" was my obtuse
response. She answered my question in her reply with a single,
puzzling sentence: "I believe that the *Mona Lisa* was da Vinci's
self-portrait."

The sense of inferiority I felt about her also had another
source: the mystery of her family background. On the first day
we met, I had intuited that her world was very different from
my own, but she herself never touched on this question. The
more we wrote to one another and the deeper our conversations
became, the clearer it became to me that this question was
important to the relationship we were forming, and the more
it bothered me that she always found a way to evade the topic.
Little did I know that the answer to the question would lie in
Death of a Salesman. One day we arranged to meet at her campus at noon and then set off in the direction of the National
Art Gallery. As we passed the Capital Theatre she asked me if I
had heard of a play called *Death of a Salesman*. To her surprise,
I replied that I had seen it that spring when it premiered in
the theatre, and that I had managed to get a great seat in the
middle of the twelfth row because someone had returned his
ticket. I had even spotted Arthur Miller himself sitting a few
rows in front of me. She stopped walking and stared at me,
before saying something I could not immediately understand.

"So that day in the Old Summer Palace wasn't the first time we met," she said. I looked at her, confused. "I was there too," she explained, "and I was sitting in the row directly behind Arthur Miller." I was stunned. Was it another accident? Or was it meant to be? I must have seen the back of her head that day in the Capital Theatre, just like she had seen me for the first time from behind as I sat on my rock in the Old Summer Palace. It was almost unbelievable, and we both sighed at the peculiar coincidence. We went on to discuss the play and how it touched on questions of family and the father-son relationship. I told her that my family was very similar to the family in *Death of a Salesman* and that I did not like parents who were too over-bearing or families that were too competitive. She replied that her family could not be more different than the family in *Death of a Salesman* but that she still didn't like them. She preferred lively, spirited families who were not subject to societal influences. It was surprising to hear her speak so frankly about her family, and even more surprising when she went on to say she was sorry for not telling me about her family earlier. She then told me the name of her grandfather and grandmother. Even though she had prepared me for what she was about to say, and even though she spoke as if there were nothing remarkable in her words, they struck me like a bolt of lightning. The names of her grandparents were names that everyone in China knew.

Three days later I wrote her the last letter I would send her. It was the only letter in our regular correspondence in which I did not mention any books. I simply told her that I was grateful for everything she had given me, that she had changed the way I looked at the world, and that from now on reading would be a faithful companion for the rest of my life. I did not tell her how I felt about myself around her, but I did mention

Death of a Salesman, how it had made me realize the tragedy of a life plagued by a sense of inferiority. Finally I returned to her question of whether or not our meeting was meant to be, and wrote that an encounter that was meant to be did not preclude a separation that was meant to be. In fact, perhaps it necessarily preceded it. I closed by saying that this was the last time I would write to her.

She apparently did not read it that way, however, because the reply I received two days later was no different from the letters she had written before. She wrote mostly about Nabokov's *Pnin*, and then in the last two lines she invited me to visit her that Wednesday at dusk in the ruins where we had first met: she had something very important to discuss with me. I didn't go, nor did I send a reply, and a week later I got another letter. In it she wrote about her opinion of the final two chapters of Camus's *The Outsider*, and at first it seemed just like all of her other letters. The only strange thing was that she did not mention the fact I had not come to meet her. I didn't reply to this letter either, and a week later she sent me a collection of Shakespeare's sonnets. The package contained none of her writing and I knew that this was the last correspondence I would receive from her. The book marked the end of our literary relationship.

The second time I was interrupted in the Old Summer Palace was when I spent the night there again, in the summer of 1985. It was about 10:30 p.m., and I was lying in my usual spot on the patch of bare ground by the ruins of the Big Fountains. Staring at the sky, I thought about my grandmother teaching me to make *jiuzao*, a kind of fermented glutinous rice, and the image of her leaning over and peering at the pot to see if the rice had finished steaming appeared in front of me. A wave of loneliness and homesickness rushed over me again and the stars above me began to wobble and blur. Then I heard voices. At first I thought I must have imagined it but as I listened more closely I heard that they were coming from the other side of the ferns. A man and a woman seemed to be having an argument.

"What are you waiting for?" the man said. "You'll end up catching a cold."

"What will we do if I get —"

"You won't."

"I'm scared."

"Don't be."

"If I do you're done for."

"You won't."

Then the woman let out a short cry. "Not so fast!" she said.

"You're being so annoying," the man replied.

"Are you not worried?"

"You need to relax."

"If I do you're done for."

I lay there nervously listening to everything they said. Of course I knew what they were doing, but I did not understand why the woman kept saying, "If I do you're done for." Why did she not say, "I'm done for" or "we're done for"? What exactly was the relationship between them? To this day I still do not know the answer to these questions, but at the time they made me feel even more alone and long even more for home. I could not understand why a man and a woman could embark on the most intimate of acts in such an antagonistic manner. I remembered the last letter I had received from the girl I had met two years earlier in the Old Summer Palace. She had written about *The Outsider*, how in this increasingly fake world we were all outsiders. It occurred to me that my loneliness arose from my estrangement from what was true, and my longing was really a longing for the truth, that most sacred of homes. With this thought I stood up. I had just heard the man and woman leave. A terrible fear swept over me and I decided to leave too, rather than lying there awake the whole night, tormented by my sense of total detachment. I got on my bike and raced away as if fleeing some vast fraud, seeking some sacred truth. I had no idea that it would be my last time leaving the Old Summer Palace.

No doubt I was a reclusive sort of person from the moment I was born, but it was almost certainly made worse by my parents' favouritism. My brother is five years younger than me and even before he was born I never felt much love from my parents. Once he had arrived it quickly became obvious that my parents preferred him to me. According to them, he did "everything right" whereas I did "nothing right." They even came to say things like this to my face, as well as to guests who came to visit. The first time I became aware of their opinion of me was during a parent-teacher meeting in my third year of primary school, when my teacher told them that I had difficulty concentrating in class. This comment apparently piqued their interest because my father immediately began heaping praise on my teacher's perceptiveness and asked whether she could help them discover any other problems with my character. My mother, on the other hand, started drawing comparisons with my younger brother who had just started kindergarten and asked how it was possible for two sons from one family to be "poles apart." I simply sat there, overcome by shame, staring at the floor. After that, my parents frequently made such observations about my brother and me and I began to get used to it. Perhaps you could even say that my parents were correct in their judgment, because sure enough I had not inherited their mathematical abilities whereas my brother is pretty much a mathematical genius. After many years, their favouritism proved to be accurate. In high school, when it came to choosing between studying science or humanities, my grades gave me no choice but to study humanities, an inferior subject by Chinese standards. Such a fate, for the son of two mathematics teachers, was difficult for them to countenance. Even after I had left the town they never let it go.

Before leaving China I spent ten years working for a respected newspaper in Guangzhou. I saw an advertisement for the job two months before graduating from my master's degree. My classmates were all looking for work in Beijing and tried to persuade me not to leave. They had no way of knowing the psychological roots of my reluctance to stay, the intense sense of inferiority I felt that made me want to leave the capital as quickly as possible. I got an acceptance letter shortly after I applied and had packed up my things two days before my final thesis defence interview. I left Beijing the day after the defence and went home to spend two weeks with my parents before travelling to Guangzhou to start work. For a long time, however, I did not have a specific job title, and I started being "trained" first in the advertising department before being transferred to the editor-in-chief's office to continue my "training." Only toward the end of spring the following year did I officially become an editor in the Society section of the newspaper.

Guangzhou was the second place I would make a life for myself away from home. To begin with I found it difficult to adjust to the climate, the language, and the food. On the train from Chongqing to Guangzhou, a retired teacher in the opposite bunk told me that the only way to survive in Guangzhou is to do what he did when he first arrived: marry a local. He called this "planting your roots in local soil." But it was only after starting work in the Society section that I even found any "local soil" that was available. It happened when I went to interview the director of a biology research centre for a story I was writing. About halfway into the interview the director, who spoke Mandarin with a very strong accent, realized that we were both from Sichuan province. He immediately asked me how I was doing in Guangzhou and when he found out I was single he almost jumped out of his seat with excitement. He told me that a member of their team was an honest but brilliant female doctor with whom he thought I would make a great match. She was a local, born and bred in Guangzhou, and when it came to her economic situation, "Let's just say you have nothing to worry about there." Her family was also reasonably well off. Her father worked as a shipbuilding engineer and her mother as a tax auditor. "But she's a little older than you," the director said. "That doesn't bother you, does it?" The director apparently took my silence to be a tacit acceptance of his proposition because he picked up the phone on his desk and dialed a number. While he waited for someone to pick up, he asked me how much longer I needed for the interview. I said, "Around forty minutes," and forty minutes later the woman with whom I would spend the next twenty-three years of my life appeared.

She was not particularly good-looking or particularly warm, and she did little to capture my attention. The muted atmosphere between us that day was how it all began, and since she never truly captured my attention throughout our relationship, I suppose it was also how it ended. At the prompting of her director she swapped business cards with me and, again only once the director had suggested it, escorted me out of the research centre.

In the following three weeks I called her three times, but our brief conversations never really interested me. I assumed that would be the end of things, but a week later she called me for the first time. Unlike in our previous conversations, this time she asked me about my life, whether I had adapted to Guangzhou's humidity, whether I liked Cantonese food. From this turn in our conversation, a new opening seemed to appear in our relationship, and the next day I called to ask her if she was free that weekend to come with me to Yuexiu Park. To my surprise, she enthusiastically agreed. It was our first date, but because I wasn't entertaining any hopes for our relationship I wasn't even slightly nervous. As we strolled around the park, we discussed the resistance the economic reforms were meeting, how prices were skyrocketing, and the effects of the new industries on the environment. Then, seemingly out of nowhere, she asked me if I had ever had a girlfriend. I responded without hesitation that I hadn't. She seemed pleased by this answer and replied that she had not had a boyfriend either. She had begun to think that maybe something was wrong with her because she had never been much interested in the opposite sex. After graduating from university, all of her female classmates seemed desperate to find boyfriends but she had felt no such urge. She felt the same way now, she told me. If it was not for her parents' constant nagging she'd be inclined to continue as she was.

Over the next four months, her "not being much interested" gradually sapped any passion I might have had for our relationship. She did not let me hold her hand as we walked or let me give her a kiss on the cheek when we said goodbye. But one day everything changed. She was sitting on the edge of the bed in her dormitory, I on the chair in front of her. For some reason I asked her whether she had been hurt psychologically as a child. She didn't seem to object in the least to my peculiar question, but as she spoke her eyes began to fill up with tears. I handed her a tissue and she wiped her eyes before smiling at me, looking embarrassed. It was probably the most intimate gesture she had ever made toward me, and without knowing what I was doing I took her face with both hands and kissed her on the mouth. A look of utter shock appeared on her face but she didn't get angry. Later, on the night we first had sex, she told me that that was the moment she had first decided to marry me.

But it was a full three months later, after our newspaper had finished a series of articles triggered by a local news story, before I accidentally proposed. The news story came from an anonymous letter we received, which claimed that cheating was taking place on a huge scale in the middle school exams throughout the city. Our department head immediately assembled a team of journalists to investigate. He suggested we begin with this story and go on to write a series of articles about education reform in general, and he chose me to lead the project. It was the most significant assignment I had been given since I started working there almost two years before, and it awakened my sense of social duty and conscience. During that period I worked every day until midnight, terrified that I might overlook some small piece of information or potential source. When they came out, the series of articles garnered a great deal of attention and we received innumerable letters and phone calls from readers. It was an exciting time and we all got caught up in the thrill of our work and its impact.

However, the furor eventually also caught the attention of certain government departments. After the fourth batch of articles was released, we got an order to cease the publication of all related reports, as they were said to be undermining social stability. Our department head was suspended from work pending an investigation, and I was transferred to the Entertainment section of the newspaper to report on celebrity gossip. Needless to say, I was not happy with the transfer and went to the bureau chief to ask if I could stay in my current position, explaining that I had no interest in the entertainment industry. After a long speech about the newspaper's "development strategies" and "long-term trajectories," the chief added flatly, "With time you can acquire an interest in anything."

I didn't start working in my new position straight away but instead decided to take some time somewhere quiet to think about my future. I settled on a tourist spot that had recently caught my attention, Zhangjiajie National Park, in the west of Hunan province. Throughout the train journey I was preoccupied by the lovers who were sharing my compartment. They spent almost the whole trip together in the lower bunk opposite, first sitting side by side and then with the girl lying down and the boy sitting next to her. They never stopped talking, as if there were no limit to what they had to say to one another, and I found myself moved by how close they were. My mood alternated between a genuine happiness for them and a profound melancholy for my own situation. The lovers and I got off the train at the same spot and ended up on the same bus to the park. The girl spent the journey with her head on the boy's shoulder. As I looked at them it occurred to me that the doctor of biology who was my girlfriend would never understand this biological behaviour.

When the bus arrived, the couple and I went to different hotels and I assumed that we would not see each other again, but the next day I saw them asleep in each other's arms in the grass by a small stream. They exhibited a freedom I found it hard to fully comprehend, and I thought of the girl I was "meant to meet" in the ruins of the Old Summer Palace. In my mind she was the very embodiment of freedom. If I had come to this pure and untouched place with her, maybe we too would have fallen asleep together in the grass. I looked up at the azure sky and thought of the couple. When they had first lain down they must have let out a heartfelt sigh at the sky's beauty. Only a free soul could truly understand the splendour of the sky. I admired them, I envied them, and at that moment I understood that I had achieved what I'd wanted to achieve when I left the city. I now knew how I wanted to live my life. I was desperate to go back, desperate to get on the train to Guangzhou, and when I arrived, I would go straight from the train station to the doctor of biology's office.

On the way back I kept thinking about how I wanted to start anew, to bid farewell once and for all to a life that had given me so little happiness, to the relationships that had prevented me from enjoying my freedom. I would finally speak to the doctor of biology with whom I had spent the previous six months and tell her no. But that was not how it played out when I found myself standing in front of her. Instead, I proposed. I still don't know what caused this sudden reversal in my intentions, but two weeks later we had finished the paperwork, and a month after that was our wedding.

Not long after getting married, my wife asked me a question. Would I look after her if she ended up paralyzed? I did not like the question, I thought it was tasteless, and it seemed to show that she was not living in the present but the future, or, more specifically, in her anxiety about the future.

"That won't happen," I said.

"But what if it does?" she said.

"It just won't," I insisted.

My refusal to answer upset my wife and she told me that it proved I did not really love her. It is true that she had never stirred feelings of love in me, but if she did end up in bed paralyzed I would of course look after her. I would be attentive to her every need. She ought to have been as sure about this as I was. But my attentiveness would have been fake, a result of a cold sense of responsibility, not the mysterious quality called passion or that even more mysterious quality called love. Misoka had instilled in me just such a passion. The moment I saw her I became gripped by a kind of obsession with her. The evening after she wanted to talk about Chinese men, I dreamt about the passionate life she and I might share. I lifted her from her wheelchair, took her to the bed, and slowly took off her clothes, one item after the other. I used a warm, wet cloth to clean her body and sometimes my fingertips would brush against her skin. I was full of gratitude for her, all of her, even the parts of her body that could not feel. This was the kind of obsession that could conquer time, could conquer all feelings of alienation. In my vision, Misoka followed my hand with her eyes, followed the path it took over her skin, and then suddenly burst into tears. She told me to get off, to get off her immediately. She said she was too dark, too ugly. Her mother had always said so. I fell to my knees on the bed and placed my face against hers. "You are my Snow White," I told her. I had first heard of Snow White on my first summer trip to my uncle's home when I was eight years old and I was captivated by his lively telling of the story. Forty years later, in the snowscape of Mount Royal in Montreal, I had finally seen *my* Snow White. She was sitting on her own in the blistering cold of morning in a wheelchair by the side of Beaver Lake. And she was writing, writing, writing …

∞ Celia

AS I GOT to know Celia better, what came to intrigue me about her was less what she did or how she looked and more what she said. Like my wife she often had violent and unexpected reactions to some of my opinions, though unlike my wife I never felt that this was an attempt to demonstrate superiority or authority. It seemed instead to come from a position of wisdom, or perhaps that strange kind of despair that wisdom can instill in a person. For example, at one point I referred to "civilization" in an approving manner and she interrupted me, saying, "There's no good to be found in civilization."

At first I wanted to ask what brought about such a cynical view but when I thought about the certainty with which she had asserted it, I decided it would somehow be frivolous to ask for her reasons. There was perhaps a certain wisdom to her opinion of civilization (I seem to remember Taoism saying something similar) but it was also definitely tied up with despair. Misoka thought that Celia had suffered a "psychological blow." Could the wound it inflicted have something to do with the wisdom or despair, whichever it was, I detected behind her words?

On another occasion, when we were both skating, she saw that I had stopped and was standing beneath the speaker listening to the Violin Concerto in D major. She skated over and told me that her favourite Beethoven pieces were his string quartets. When I asked her why, she said, "Because they sound like a conversation between one man and three women." I was a little unsettled by this remark because it was almost as if she were making fun of my situation. After my wife's passing and my daughter's leaving, I had no women in my life, but now Misoka and Celia had appeared, and what's more their presence constantly brought back memories of a third woman from my past.

Then there was the time we were reading one of Shakespeare's sonnets. We came to the word "loneliness," and she lifted her head to the sky and cried out, "Fuck!" Normally I would have thought this completely at odds with her otherwise dignified manner, but at that moment it seemed to reveal something about her character more truthfully and accurately than anything she had said before. "Fucking loneliness," she said. "It's a cancer, a cancer none of us can escape." I had not seen this side of her before. Whether she was the picture of health I saw skiing into the woods or the woman suffering from some mysterious affliction, I always thought of her as someone who was at home with her solitude.

"Are you afraid of being alone?" I asked cautiously. "You always seemed like you weren't."

"Of course I'm afraid," she responded curtly. "Perhaps more afraid than anyone."

I thought back to the terror of my own solitude before I had met Misoka and Celia. I could not imagine a more intense fear.

"Loneliness is the mother of all error," she said. "I think all the mistakes we make are the result of loneliness."

She said it in a way that sounded convincing, almost philosophical, but it did not fit with my experience. I had broken off the literary relationship I had formed among the ruins of the Old Summer Palace, which was a mistake but not one that arose from loneliness. Similarly, I made a mistake on my return to Guangzhou from Zhangjiajie National Park when I went to the doctor of biology for whom I felt nothing and said the exact opposite of what I had spent the long journey planning to say. But again, this mistake was not caused by loneliness, or at least not entirely.

"A poet once said, 'God's loneliness moves in His smallest creatures,'" she went on. "Perhaps this is the reason I cannot accept God. He gave man loneliness — he created the conditions for man's sin — so that man would need salvation."

It was another unconventional, even blasphemous, statement to which I did not know how to respond. I thought back to the time when my wife was near death and we had prayed for her. What would Celia think of us seeking divine help in a time of desperation? How would she face her own death? It was clear that she had not only left God far behind but to a certain extent the whole world. As I pondered the question of whether this was a result of wisdom or despair, it dawned on me that even now that I knew her better, she still puzzled and fascinated me as much as ever.

It was true that there was something special about our relationship now that I had managed to get closer to her. I was surprised to find out that Misoka had noticed, but also grateful that she had let the fact of her discovery slip. I no longer had to be as cautious or nervous as I was before. I could now face head-on the inexplicable miracle that had occurred: while I was on the brink of collapse, two unfathomable women had appeared and brought something in me back to life.

It was Shakespeare who provided the opportunity to build a more intimate relationship with Celia. I will never forget how this came about. I had opened the door of the pavilion and heard the sound of Celia playing the recorder. I stood some distance behind her and waited for her to finish before walking over to compliment her on her playing. "I was just improvising," she replied shyly.

I was impressed. It had sounded to me like a completed piece.

She lifted the recorder and waved it slightly in the air. "This is the only instrument I can play," she said. "My mother taught me a bit of piano, but I've forgotten everything."

I told her I could play too, so she rubbed the mouthpiece off with the sleeve of her jumper and handed it to me. I played the only piece I knew all the way through.

"A sad song," she said. "I used to be able to play it on the piano."

I was excited to hear that she had recognized the piece. I told her that at the turn of the century a Japanese musician had taken this American song and added his own lyrics, turning it into a popular Japanese tune. This inspired a Chinese student, who was studying in Japan at the time, to change the lyrics again the year of the outbreak of the First World War. The result was a song that Chinese children have been singing for the past century. As I finished telling her the story of the melody's international journey, I noticed the same uneasy look in Celia's eyes I had seen when I first asked her if she had ever been to China. I realized that I had said too much and awkwardly handed the recorder back to her. "I've never seen a recorder like that before," I said. "It must be very old. It has a beautiful sound." I hoped that by changing the subject I might make her feel more comfortable. Sure enough she seemed to relax.

"It's a family relic," she said as she ran her index finger over the length of the recorder. Then she looked up and asked, "You haven't played for a while, I'm guessing?"

"Too long," I said, uncomfortable memories floating up in my mind. "Time passes quickly."

Celia looked at me sympathetically. "You're thinking of your daughter," she said.

"How did you know?" I asked.

"She's a recorder teacher, is she not?"

"And how do you know that?" I said a little too loudly, unable to disguise how unsettled I was.

With her recorder, Celia pointed to the ice skates that were hanging over my shoulder. "Because you bring her ice skates with you every day."

"How did you know they were hers?"

Celia didn't answer my question. "She's grown up now."

"You know that too?"

"I also know that she doesn't need you anymore."

"How?"

Celia smiled and said, "Because I have the world's greatest teacher."

"The world's *greatest* teacher ..."

"Yes," she replied. "He knows all of humanity's secrets."

I couldn't imagine what kind of teacher she could be talking about. "Who is he?"

With that Celia told me about her academic career. She had received a Ph.D. in English Literature from the University of Toronto, and her thesis had been about madness in the theatre of Shakespeare. She had read his work countless times and could pretty much recite his four great tragedies by heart. She would be surprised to hear of someone who had read Shakespeare more than she had. Not only did she reread him constantly, but she pretty much "only read Shakespeare." And so, she had answered my question.

I had never met someone who was so excessively committed to a single author and I wondered if it was a symptom of whatever it was she was suffering from. However, I also realized it was an opportunity, one that was linked to the fated encounter I had had decades before in the Old Summer Palace. "You must be very familiar with his sonnets," I said.

"Of course," Celia replied.

"Excellent," I said. "I would like you to be *my* teacher."

She smiled and asked, "Why the sonnets?"

"Because —" I paused for a moment before deciding to reframe my answer. "Because when I was younger I tried to read them, but I didn't really understand."

"Were you reading the original?"

"No, translations."

"Poetry cannot be translated."

I did not want at that moment to get into a discussion about translation. "Would you be my teacher?" I asked.

Celia paused for a moment, looking at me. "The sonnets are his least valuable work," she said. "If you really want to read Shakespeare you should read his plays."

"We can at least start with his sonnets," I said. "This is an opportunity for me."

This seemed to unnerve her. "Opportunity? What opportunity?"

I hesitated. I had to be careful not to say too much. "I have some questions about them. I was hoping you'd be able to help me answer them."

"What questions?"

"For example, I remember that half the poems were written to a Dark Lady."

"Not half," Celia interrupted. "About a sixth. Sonnets one hundred twenty-seven to one hundred fifty-four."

The precision of her correction derailed me slightly, but I continued. "I have a lot of questions about the Dark Lady."

"Like what?"

"Like what she looked like," I said, without really thinking.

Celia looked surprised. "That hadn't even occurred to me!" she said, as if to herself.

"Because you're an expert," I replied. "It's the sort of question only a layman would ask."

Celia was still looking at me but I could tell her attention had travelled to another place, another time. "The one hundred thirtieth sonnet is where he spends the most time describing her appearance," she said. "We know from that sonnet that her 'breasts are dun' and that her hair is like 'black wires.' But there are only four lines that describe her face. The first line says her eyes 'are nothing like the sun,' the second says that 'coral is far more red than her lips,' and the fifth and sixth lines tell us that her cheeks have none of the colours of 'roses damasked, red and white.'"

I felt Celia's soft voice wash over me as she articulated her thoughts woven through with fragments of Shakespeare's poetry. I was impressed by the strength of her memory, as well as the extent of her patience with someone who was far from a literature specialist. "Why did he make a point to emphasize her darkness?"

Celia sighed. "I've often thought about that. I wondered if this Dark Lady may not have been as dark as he implies," she said. "I believe he might have been exaggerating it, as a way of emphasizing her otherness, and in this sonnet her unattractiveness, in order to ease the suffering inherent in love."

I wasn't sure if I fully understood her point, but it was clear that it was a powerful one. "You really are a great teacher," I said. "I'm sure to learn a lot from you."

Celia let out a laugh. "All right then," she said. "Let's start with the sonnets."

The next morning, with Celia's help, I entered the world of Shakespeare. The moment I arrived in the pavilion she handed me a book of his sonnets. She had told me that she owned many different versions and that she would choose one that best suited my needs. "We'll begin with sonnet number ninety-nine," she said sternly. "I'll give you ten minutes, in which time you should be able to read it at least three times. I want to see what questions you have."

I had not expected the first lesson to begin with a test, and I began to get nervous. I walked to my usual locker, put down the two pairs of skates, and flicked to the page with sonnet 99.

It took a minute to read it through the first time, but I didn't understand any of it. I took a few deep breaths and told myself to calm down before reading it again. This time I felt I understood. He was cursing a series of flowers, those "sweet thieves," who had stolen his lover's beauty. But what questions should I have? The way Celia had put it, it seemed she already had in mind what I should ask. Again, my nerves began to get the better of me. I did not want to disappoint my teacher in her first class. I read the poem a third time, this time more slowly, and felt I got an even better grasp on what it was trying to say, but I still did not know what question I should be asking. I suspected that Celia did not want a question about what the whole poem meant, or about the meaning of specific words.... I walked back to where Celia was sitting and meekly told her that I couldn't think of a question.

She motioned for me to sit down next to her. "How many lines does it have?" she asked, smiling.

I counted. Then I counted again. "What?" I said, staring at Celia. "There are fifteen lines!"

"That's what I was hoping you would ask," she said.

I looked down at my feet like a guilty schoolboy.

"With poetry you have to be very perceptive," she said. "Every detail is important."

I realized that this was what she wanted to teach me in our first class. I lifted my head and looked at her, grateful to have such a remarkable teacher.

"A sonnet with fifteen lines points to a lot of possibilities," she went on. "Perhaps it's unfinished, which points to a whole series of other questions, like how an unfinished piece found its way into this collection. Maybe there was a certain carelessness involved in its compilation. The vast majority of Shakespeare's works were not vetted by him before they were published, the sonnets included."

"So which line is the extraneous one?" I asked.

Celia smiled and said she had asked herself this question before. "There's no obvious superfluous line," she said. "If you wanted to turn it into a proper sonnet with fourteen lines, you would have to rewrite it from scratch."

"Maybe Shakespeare didn't notice there was an extra line when he wrote it," I suggested.

Celia seemed happy with my suggestion. "That's definitely possible," she said. "Especially if we take into account the development of the sonnet form." She went on to explain to me the history of the sonnet. The first sonnets were written by the Italian humanist Petrarch to his lover Laura. These poems were exquisite in form, graceful in content, and the vowels of the Italian language only made them flow more beautifully off the tongue. Laura was the epitome of beauty. Fair-skinned, golden-haired, and with bright red lips, she was the very ideal of love. Sonnets thus began as a hymn to love and to beauty. However, by the time they had reached Shakespeare, the form of the sonnet had coarsened and its content had become vulgar. A different idea of love and beauty had formed. The Dark Lady does not have red lips, her skin is not fair, her hair is not golden, and most importantly her love is not the sole property of one man; her desire is not chaste. Both inside and out, she is the very antithesis of Laura. Shakespeare broadened the scope of the sonnet. It touched not only on love and desire between those of the opposite sex, but also on lust and affection between those of the same sex. Not only did it praise the beauty of love but it also explored its artifice, its superficiality, and even its odiousness. One could say that Shakespeare shattered once and for all the Italian humanist's innocent dream of beauty. Compared with Petrarch's, Shakespeare's sonnets revealed more "modernity," to use a fashionable term, which, of course, was a literary achievement. "But sometimes it comes across as too callous," Celia concluded. "Take sonnet number one hundred twenty-nine. The rage is almost savage." She sighed deeply.

This was how our special relationship began. I would ask her questions about the sonnets whenever I had the chance, almost every time I saw her and often by email if I could not wait until our next meeting. She was far more patient with me than I could have imagined, never failing to engage thoughtfully with even the most inane of my questions. It was the second literary relationship of my life but this time it centred around one book alone, a book that nonetheless tied the two relationships together. The curious symmetry could not but make me return to the same unanswerable question. Was all this meant to be, or was it merely a matter of chance?

The temperature continued to drop and the time came when Beaver Lake was open to skaters. At this point I developed a routine whereby I split my fifty minutes on Mount Royal into three parts. I spent the first ten minutes warming up on the smaller ice rink, followed by thirty minutes skating wildly on Beaver Lake, after which I would return to the rink for ten minutes for a slower, more leisurely skate. The only variation to this order of things was if Misoka was beside the lake, writing. I did not want to disturb her, even though a bond had formed between us. It was always important to understand and respect the distance between people, which was something I kept having to remind myself. It seemed that because of the distance between me and these two women, my curiosity about them didn't diminish as time passed, and the more I knew them, the more they fascinated me. Each meeting only intensified my desire to meet them again, something I had never felt about the woman with whom I had shared my life for twenty-three years.

The first time we three "insignificant grains of sand" appeared together in the pavilion was four days after Misoka first mentioned Celia to me. There was not much wind that day and it was not particularly cold, so Misoka ought to have been at her usual spot by the lake, but when I walked into the pavilion, she was there, waving at me. She told me she had a question she couldn't wait to ask me, a question it turned out that would bring back sad memories. She asked if I had ever visited the Old Summer Palace "in the rain." I replied that I hadn't, which was true. But if I had gone on that Wednesday many years ago to see the girl waiting for me there, my answer would have been different. That evening there was a huge storm in Beijing, and as I sat in the library looking out the window I was overcome by regret and guilt. But I convinced myself I had to ignore those feelings if I was ever to escape the cycle of self-loathing I was intent on leaving behind. Misoka was obviously disappointed in my answer. She said she wanted to know if there was anywhere in the ruins one could go to shelter from the rain.

That was when Celia entered the pavilion, which was strange because it was the time she usually went skiing. Stranger still, she did not walk to her locker but instead came over to where Misoka and I were talking. I felt the blood rush to my cheeks and my heart begin to race. I nervously stepped back. I didn't want to seem too close to Celia in front of Misoka. "Did you see the email I sent last night?" Celia asked, as if Misoka were not there. I glanced awkwardly at Misoka, who had already buried her head in her notebook, and realized with some relief that the opportunity to introduce them to one another had passed. Embarrassed, I told Celia that I hadn't turned on my computer in two days so I had not seen her email. "I suggested we skate together. We can discuss the question you have about sonnet ninety-seven while we skate," she told me, apparently oblivious to how self-conscious I was feeling. She was talking about the sonnet we had started to read a few days earlier, a poem about winter, and I had told her I didn't understand what Shakespeare meant by the phrase "hope of orphans." It was only when she told me that I ought to read "hope of orphans" as "orphaned hopes" that I realized that "orphan" was being used as a metaphor to describe the line's main object, "hope." My question had been answered, but Celia now asked me a question of her own, one that had nothing to do with the poem we were reading.

"Have you ever known an orphan?"

It caught me by surprise and I thought for a moment before replying, "I have often felt as if I were an orphan."

"I have that feeling a lot too."

I looked at Celia and became aware that this statement seemed to be addressed to the person whose presence she hadn't acknowledged. I immediately felt sorry for Misoka. "I've already been skating today," I said coldly to Celia. Out of the corner of my eye I saw Misoka's head lift slightly. She knew I was lying, and she must have known I was lying for her.

I could tell from Celia's expression that she too could tell that this wasn't the truth and that I had lied to her because of the way she was acting in front of Misoka. But she didn't let on and continued just as before. "That's a shame," she said. "Well we can discuss it after the film tomorrow."

"The film tomorrow?" This was the first time I had heard of any film.

"That was in the email too," Celia said. "Didn't I tell you there was a Woody Allen retrospective coming up? I've already booked tickets."

I vaguely remembered her mentioning the retrospective a few days earlier, and that Woody Allen's humorous look at the relationship between the sexes would help me understand Shakespeare's sonnets, but I thought she had only been mentioning it in passing. "I'll have to see if I'm free tomorrow," I said in the same cold tone, before awkwardly saying goodbye to Celia and awkwardly not saying goodbye to Misoka. I left the pavilion that day without removing the two pairs of skates from my shoulders.

I could not make sense of Celia's decision to invite me to the film and the fact that she had even booked tickets. Before this she had turned down all of my invitations. Since we had started discussing Shakespeare's sonnets I had invited her twice to go to a concert and both times she had said she wasn't free. When I'd asked her out for a meal she told me she had "no interest in food." Her response on the three occasions I suggested grabbing a coffee was "Another time maybe." I had started to think it was not only my invitations she would turn down but invitations in general, that perhaps what she took issue with was being invited. When I got home I turned on the computer and read her email twice. I began to get excited at the prospect of meeting for the first time outside of Mount Royal. I quickly replied to confirm that I would meet her the next day at two in the afternoon by the movie theatre on Park Avenue.

It was one of those theatres that only play classic films. Celia and I arrived at almost the same time, and after we had collected our tickets we looked through the posters advertising the retrospective. It soon became clear as Celia talked to me about Woody Allen that she knew all of his films, and I was quick to express my admiration. "I'm guessing you don't know Woody Allen that well?" she asked me.

"I don't know him at all," I said lightheartedly. "The only thing I know about him is the scandal."

Celia did not see the funny side and I saw the troubled look I knew so well appear on her face. I immediately regretted what I had said, a feeling that only grew more intense when Celia remained stony-faced throughout the film, which frequently had the audience in stitches. I kept kicking myself for not being more careful with my choice of words.

Were it not for the uneasy cloud that had descended upon that special afternoon, I would have been able to appreciate it much more. I had never been invited by a woman to the movies, let alone a woman whom I found so interesting. It was a *unique* experience for me, in the truest sense of the word. Celia had once told me that the rarest asset in this consumerist age was uniqueness, something I had not really understood at the time. It was only that afternoon, as I experienced it for myself, that I began to recognize the value of the unique. I barely paid any attention to the movie. Instead I was listening to Celia's breathing, observing her reactions, savouring her scent. Perhaps it was simply an effect of the dark in the movie theatre, but that afternoon her body seemed more distinct to me — more vividly *there* — than the times we had sat so close looking over Shakespeare's sonnets on Mount Royal. No woman had ever made me feel that way. The feeling was, to use Celia's word, completely unique.

Celia and I both lived on the other side of Mount Royal from the theatre, and she suggested that instead of taking a bus we walk across the mountain. "We have never been together on Mount Royal at dusk," she said.

I was obviously thrilled at the opportunity to extend our afternoon together. We approached the mountain from the road by the McGill University gymnasium and walked for a long time in silence before Celia felt like talking. When she did she told me that today was the second time she had seen the film. The first time had been when it first came out thirty years ago and she saw it with her husband. When she finished, she corrected herself: "Ex-husband."

Why was she telling me this? Why had she invited me to see a film she had seen thirty years earlier with her ex-husband? It seemed to me that this meant she did not care about me at all. But after we'd walked a little farther, my opinion began to change. Perhaps the fact that this enigmatic woman had invited me to see a film she had seen thirty years ago with her ex-husband indicated a genuine care for me. Maybe it was a symbolic act, a sign that our relationship was going to develop further. She must have told me about it, I thought to myself, because she wanted to share more about her life with me.

But I was wrong. She had nothing more to say to me on the subject. Instead she asked me if I liked movies. I told her I used to, but that in these fifteen years since immigrating to Canada life had been so busy that I'd had no time to watch films. Celia said film was something she could not live without and that Woody Allen was among her favourite directors. She had seen all of his films.

I saw an opening and could not hold back from asking something that had been on my mind all afternoon. "So how come you didn't laugh once? Isn't it supposed to be funny?"

Celia stared at me and said nothing, and I immediately regretted saying something that could be interpreted as poking fun at one of her idols. It was clear Celia did not want to discuss it. I didn't know what to say to fill the gap in the conversation, so we walked in silence until we reached Beaver Lake. This was the place where we would have to split up and walk our separate ways home so I stopped and thanked her for the invitation. I told her that I had truly enjoyed our walk together and the Woody Allen film. She said she had enjoyed it as well and added that it was amazing to her that after all these years the film could still give her so much to think about.

That should have been where our conversation ended, but after taking two steps away from me Celia turned around and apologized for interrupting my discussion with Misoka the day before. I told her it wasn't a big deal, it was just a casual conversation. Celia continued to stand there looking at me, and it was obvious that there was another question on her mind. I waited for her to ask it.

"Is she Chinese?" Celia asked.

"I don't know," I replied.

This was clearly not the answer she was hoping for. "Is she Japanese?"

"I don't know."

"What do you mean you don't know?" she asked. "I always see you together."

Just like Misoka had noticed my relationship with Celia, Celia had noticed my relationship with Misoka. The topic had caught me by surprise, but this time I wasn't nervous. That being said, neither was I particularly keen to explain everything to Celia. So I remained silent.

"She seems to be very interested in you," Celia said.

I could hear the emotion in Celia's voice. "She's not interested in me, she's interested in Beijing," I said, "specifically the Old Summer Palace."

Celia nodded. "It must have something to do with her writing," she said.

"I don't know," I replied.

"You don't even know what she's writing?"

"No, I don't. I don't think she wants anyone to know."

Celia went on to tell me that she had noticed Misoka from the very beginning of winter, and I thought back to the first time I saw Celia sitting, statuesque, on the lockers, engrossed in something outside the window. "Do you know what I first thought when I saw her?" Celia asked.

Once again I said that I did not know.

"That she was an orphan."

Celia truly was an exceptional teacher. With that last observation she brought us back to the topic of our previous lesson on sonnet number 97.

∞ I

I'LL NEVER FORGET the bureau chief's words the day I asked him to reconsider my transfer to the Entertainment section of the newspaper: "With time you can acquire an interest in anything." The image of his hand turning the pages of the newspaper, his head not even lifting as he spoke, remains vividly in my mind to this day. I did not believe him. I wouldn't have even if he had tried to pretend he believed it himself, which he hadn't. I never managed to acquire an interest in the Entertainment section of the paper, just as my wife never managed to acquire an interest in our conjugal life. Perhaps, to borrow my mother's expression, it was karma. I should never have listened to the retired teacher on the train to Guangzhou who convinced me that marriage should be a life strategy (or a means of dealing with loneliness). I had already come to this conclusion with the arrival of our wedding day, which was a thoroughly Cantonese affair. The whole process, from cheerfully meeting guests to the rituals I had to carry out with my wife, strange tricks and games I could not understand, surrounded by a language that was still remote to me, all made me feel thoroughly alienated. I felt like a guest, an outsider who would never truly feel at home. The wedding did not make me feel as if I had "planted my roots in local soil"; it only emphasized the fact that this soil would never be local for me, that perhaps I would never truly be able to plant my roots here. The wedding only brought me regret. What I had said to the woman who would be my wife after I had returned from Zhangjiajie National Park was a mistake, the biggest mistake of my life.

My parents did not attend the wedding. Their reasons were all related to their physical condition: their backs were sore so they could not take the train and their hearts were weak so they didn't dare fly. But I knew the problem was psychological rather than physical. There was no way for them to accept the wife of a son who did "nothing right," let alone a woman from Guangdong, where they spoke a different language, where they ate anything that moved but could not eat chili! If it was my brother getting married I was certain they would've been there in a flash, on the back of an ox cart if necessary, and they would have had no ailments to complain of. Although I never shared my parents' views with my wife, she must have known what they thought of her, and when they failed to turn up at our wedding a shadow was cast over our marriage that could not be dispelled.

It was only when we started living together as husband and wife that I started to become aware of how incompatible our lifestyles were. What disappointed me most was how she disapproved of my "wasting time" reading literary works and journals. On the other hand, the differences in our eating habits mostly amused me, particularly the fact that she could eat durian all day and thought it smelled delicious, while a mere hint of its nauseating stink forced me to leave the room. She was also passionate about her work, whereas I had been unable to muster any enthusiasm for my job ever since I'd been transferred to the Entertainment section of the newspaper. She even treated the household like her workplace where she had to be in control of every detail, right down to what brand of soy sauce and cooking alcohol we bought. A colleague of mine visited our home once and gave me the nickname "apparatchik." The implication of course was not lost on me, and it was no surprise when later my act of dissent against the "wise decision" to emigrate was met with such a dictatorial response.

The most difficult difference between us concerned our conjugal affairs. Not only did she have no interest, she repelled any of my attempts to help her "acquire" one and seemed, if anything, intent on diffusing my own desires. Whenever I attempted to elicit a physical reaction in her, she would act as if she had not noticed and start talking about global affairs or some trifling encounter at work. It was as if the object of my intimations could not have been more remote from her. On those occasions when I could hold back no longer, she would only reluctantly acquiesce, saying things like, "I have work tomorrow," or "I'm tired." I had learned to pay no attention to these barriers she put up between us, and I developed the ability to satisfy my yearnings in the solitary acts I carried out in her body. Often she would urge me: "Get it over with," or "Isn't that enough?" I had learned to ignore these exhortations. And as I approached the end she would whisper to me, "Be quiet," or "We don't want the neighbours to hear." But I had learned to ignore these suggestions too, just as I had learned to accept that she was unable or unwilling to "acquire an interest" in these things. Over time, I lost interest as well.

Were it not for the results of my wife's medical tests many years later, that twenty-three-year-long mistake would no doubt have continued to this day. I would not have met the Korean student the following winter and followed her up Mount Royal, my life would not have become entwined with those of the two unfathomable women I met there, and that winter would not have become the most unusual winter of my time in Montreal, the winter that changed the way I looked at the world. I would come to see the death of my wife as something that was meant to be, an inevitable narrative link in the unfolding story of my life. I even saw the mistake of our twenty-three-year-long marriage as essential in some way. It made me want to thank her on behalf of that winter in Montreal, to express thanks for our erroneous marriage. I even wanted to thank my parents. My reclusive character was in no small part a result of the way they treated me as a child, which was without doubt a major reason I made that fateful mistake the day I returned from Zhangjiajie National Park to Guangzhou.

Of course, such thanks would also have to be extended to the two most exceptional customers I had in the convenience store, the two people who had, prior to that most unusual of winters, had the greatest impact on my life as an immigrant.

Eric was a handsome Black man who lived on a small street about two hundred metres away from the store. The first two times he came he simply bought a few items and left with barely a word, but the third time he started a conversation with me when he saw I was reading an English novel. He told me he was born in Saint Lucia in the Caribbean, and that after getting a Ph.D. in sociology at Columbia University he had moved here to take a job as a lecturer at McGill University. When I told him I liked literature he asked if I had ever heard of the great poet from his native Saint Lucia. Somewhat embarrassed, I admitted that before he had mentioned it to me, I had not even heard of Saint Lucia, let alone any of its writers.

"Derek Walcott," Eric said proudly. "One of the greatest English-language poets of the twentieth century." He went on to say that Derek Walcott was the only Black writer to be generally considered one of the "greats" in that domain.

I confessed that it was the first time I had heard that one of the greatest twentieth-century English-language poets was Black.

"Are you Chinese?" Eric asked me.

When I told him I was, Eric said he was not in the least surprised that I had not heard of Derek Walcott. Three years earlier Eric had met a famous Chinese writer in New York who knew many white American writers, even some less well-known figures, but who had never even heard of Toni Morrison let alone earlier Black writers like James Baldwin or Ralph Ellison. He shook his head and said to me that he had noticed a lot of racism among the Chinese population.

"What do you think is the reason?" he asked me.

It was not the first time I had heard people complain of Chinese people's racism, and I shrugged before replying.

"Perhaps because we are people of colour too." He didn't seem to understand exactly what I meant, so I added, "I mean maybe it's an expression of our own sense of inferiority."

It was the first time Eric had heard such an explanation and he said he found it interesting. He went on to tell me of some of his personal experiences of racism from my people. Every semester, he said, there were Chinese students who signed up to his lecture course and then switched out when they found out the teacher was Black. There was also the time he mentioned to a student that he would be interested in teaching in China. The student responded without hesitation that it was unlikely he would find a place. When Eric asked why he was told that Chinese people would be concerned that a Black teacher's English would not be authentic enough. Finally, when he had made a joke with another student about getting a Chinese girlfriend, the student had replied that there was no way that could happen. The student said, "What Chinese parents would accept their daughter marrying a Black man?" He'd gone on to add, "Maybe if you were in the NBA there would be a chance. The Chinese are more likely to compromise if there's a lot of money involved."

Eric was knowledgeable but not at all pretentious. I liked talking with him and he also seemed to enjoy our chats. Our conversations were spontaneous and relaxed but we both got a lot from them. Every time he came in I would teach him a few Chinese phrases and characters, which he would jot down in a little notebook he used especially for our impromptu Chinese lessons. I, on the other hand, learned a lot about the English-language world from Eric. I was most grateful for his guiding me through almost the entire history of the American civil rights movement. It started one rainy evening when he came to the store to give me a photocopy of Martin Luther King's "Letter from Birmingham Jail," which he had referred to more than once during our previous conversation. Reading it, I was gripped not only by Martin Luther King's words but also by a desire to know more about the civil rights movement that formed the context to his writing. Eric must have known the impact "Letter from Birmingham Jail" would have on me, because on his next visit he brought with him two books, one on the history of the civil rights movement and another on American society in the 1960s. From that day on our conversations frequently revolved around these topics and it was through these discussions that Eric helped me better understand American society and come to terms with my own immigrant life in the city of Montreal. Once I had finished these two sociological books, Eric suggested I read some literature by Black writers. He recommended that I start with Ralph Ellison's *Invisible Man*, adding that in western society Chinese people were "invisible," too. He told me that Ralph Ellison's novel was sure to give me lots to think about with regard to my identity. Many people started off "invisible," he said, and life was the process of rendering oneself "visible"; in fact it was perhaps the most important step when it came to dealing with a sense of inferiority. The ideas he shared with me helped me gain a new perspective on my own position as a Chinese immigrant in Canada.

Just as I was getting to the end of *Invisible Man*, Eric moved to Toronto to start a new job. For the next six months we remained in contact by phone. Eric was still studying Chinese, I was still reading Black literature, and our conversations were just as they had been in the convenience store. But over time the frequency of our phone calls began to decrease and Eric seemed to be losing interest in our conversations. I thought that perhaps something had happened, but the two times I asked him about it he said that everything was fine. That Christmas Eve I phoned him three times but he didn't pick up. Each time I left a message asking him to call me back, he never did. That was how our relationship ended.

It was in the period leading up to Christmas of the same year that another interesting customer entered the convenience store, a Chinese man quite unlike most Chinese people I knew. He had a refined manner, was elegantly dressed, and gave the impression of someone who had seen the world but also stood somewhat apart from it. He was always wearing sunglasses and I never found out whether it was to protect his eyes or his identity. The first time he came in, he bought three phone cards worth five dollars each and then left. The second time, five days later, he bought another three five-dollar phone cards, something my wife and I thought very strange. It was rare for Chinese customers to buy more than one phone card at a time, let alone three. With one phone card you could make eight hours' worth of international calls, enough to last a couple of weeks for most people, but he had used three phone cards in five days. One of my wife's favourite pastimes was guessing our customers' backstories, particularly if they were Chinese. She was always very pleased with herself when she was more or less right, which she often was, but this time she had no idea. After the man with the sunglasses visited a second time my wife followed him out to see which street he lived on. When she came back she said he probably didn't live near the store because he had gotten on a bus. I didn't pay her any attention so she snatched the "useless" book from my hands. She wanted to discuss what this strange customer's story might be. Who was he? Why did he need three phone cards in five days? Who was he calling?

"You don't think he's a corrupt official on the run, do you?" she asked excitedly.

"Would that satisfy you?" I replied coldly.

"It's not a question of what would satisfy me."

"Then stop thinking about it."

Annoyed that I was spoiling her fun, she threw the book she had snatched from my hands onto the counter and stalked into the back room. She soon came back, however, with a pot of instant noodles and stood beside me. "Who could he be making so many calls to?" she asked.

I really could not be bothered with all this speculation. "Why don't you guess when he'll come back and how many phone cards he'll buy," I said. "That's a bit more your concern."

Five days later the man came back and, just like before, he bought three phone cards. Remembering what my wife had said the last time we had spoken about him — "Try to start a conversation with him next time!" — as I handed him the cards I asked him how I should address him. He lifted his head to look at me but I could not make out his eyes through his sunglasses to see what he thought of my question.

"My surname is Wang," he said in a leisurely drawl. "Everyone calls me Hermit Wang."

When my wife came to start her shift I told her what I had learned, but instead of congratulating me she laughed condescendingly. "Anyone can say their name's Wang. Anyone can call themselves Hermit Wang," she said. "You needn't have bothered."

I didn't argue with her. I knew that my first conversation with Hermit Wang had not been a waste of time. I was confident that the next time he came things would be different.

Sure enough, when Hermit Wang appeared five days later, he came straight to the counter without saying anything. It was proof that our previous conversation had not been for nothing. I didn't say a word either and simply handed him three phone cards, a gesture of recognition that our relationship had changed. Unlike during his previous visits he did not leave as soon as he had the phone cards. Instead, he strolled around the store, picking up and eyeing a pack of digestive biscuits. As he began to make his way back to the counter, I realized he was about to ask me something. I had no idea what he would say, which was a new experience — in general I knew the kinds of questions customers liked to ask, especially Chinese customers. It was always about costs, profits, or plans for the future. How much money did I make from the convenience store? How much was the rent? How much tax did I pay? What was the monthly turnover? What was the profit? Why not open a fresh meat counter? Why not a coffee corner? How did I deal with customer flow, logistics.... They all seemed to know a great deal about business. Even more baffling was the fact that many Chinese students were just as well-versed in these affairs as the adults. They asked exactly the same questions. Why did no one ask me about *Invisible Man*? Why did no one ask me if I liked winter sports? Why did no one ask me if I missed home? Business was the last thing on my mind when I was their age. That was in the eighties, the decade of hopes and ideals, when the world was more innocent, when China was still innocent. China and the world would never be able to return to that time.

Hermit Wang did not ask me any of these questions with which I was so familiar. "You look to have been here some time. I have a question I don't know if you've thought about before," he said. "Have you ever wondered what you are doing standing here? Is the fact you're standing here an accident, or were you supposed to end up here?"

My pulse quickened. It had been a long time since I had considered such philosophical matters. I lived a normal, repetitive life now. I tried not to pose myself too many "why" questions, especially questions as odd as the one Hermit Wang had just asked. I was standing here because I was the owner of this convenience store, because I sold products for money so I could raise my family. I had not considered the question of whether it had happened accidentally or necessarily. To me it had simply happened naturally. But I knew this was not the answer Hermit Wang was looking for, that his question was broader than that. What he meant by "here" was more than the convenience store.

"I've never thought to ask myself that question before," I said meekly.

"I suppose you haven't thought much about what kind of age you are living in either," Hermit Wang said.

"Not really," I said. "But I can tell when things change. I can tell that the age we are living in is very different from the 1980s, which is a shame I think."

Hermit Wang nodded. "It's good to be able to recognize that. It shows that you see the bigger picture." He paused before going on. "You can only understand the meaning of life if you can see the bigger picture, and without understanding the meaning of life you cannot live a meaningful life. Most people are blinded by the ups and downs, the losses and gains directly before them. They do not see the bigger picture. They do not see what life means." He paused again, as if waiting for a reaction from me, but all I could do was stand there looking slightly bemused. How else could I have reacted?

Hermit Wang went on. "If you could see how you would be living twenty years in the future, would it affect how you chose to live now? If twenty years ago you could have seen your life today, would you still be living in this city you have come to inhabit? Would you still be living with the same person you have come to live with today?" I could see he was getting excited but he was making an effort to remain composed. "There are only two ways for someone to see the bigger picture," he said, pausing for a moment to see if I was still listening. "The first is the way of the philosophers: let all these metaphysical questions fill your mind and draw you up to your spiritual apex. The second is the way of the dead: let all your most meaningless and absurd experiences wash over you and drag you down to the depths. Only from these two vantage points can one get a perspective on life. Only then can one see the bigger picture."

I was completely gripped by Hermit Wang's words. I had never heard anyone say anything like it but at the same time it felt like something I had always been desperate to hear. When he had finished speaking he simply turned and walked out, but his leisurely drawl seemed to reverberate around the narrow space of the empty store. I stood there and thought about what he had said. What was I doing standing here? The monotony of my existence had drained me of my enthusiasm for life and I no longer asked myself these questions. I thought of the ruins of the Old Summer Palace, a place that approached both the apex and the depths. While I was there I had occasionally caught a glimpse of the bigger picture; I could look to the past as well as the future. But now, as an immigrant in Montreal, I could only see the present, or, to use Hermit Wang's expression, the ups and downs, the losses and gains directly before me. How had this happened? Before Hermit Wang had appeared, there had been Eric, who had told me about the twists and turns of the Black civil rights movement and the tumultuous society of America in the sixties. In doing so he had shown me that there was another life outside my own everyday struggle, but it was a call that came from outside. Hermit Wang was Chinese and had used my native tongue to tell me what I had always been desperate to hear. His words were proof that he looked at the world in a completely different way, that he had lived a completely different life, and it was that very difference that filled his call with the power to shake the foundations of my beliefs. I felt a profound respect, even awe, for Hermit Wang, and I found myself looking forward to the next time we met. I thought back to my wife's tawdry speculations about his life and felt ashamed. Later when she excitedly asked me what had happened, I told her reproachfully to stop trying to guess Hermit Wang's backstory. "You'll never know what kind of person he is," I said. "But mark my words, there's no way he's a criminal on the run."

Funnily enough, the third time I spoke with Hermit Wang he proved me wrong. We had been discussing loneliness when he said something that shocked me.

"I should come clean. I'm a fugitive."

I bent down to pick up the book I had knocked to the floor in shock, telling myself to remain calm in the face of this new danger. I stood staring at him stupidly, wondering what crime he had committed and whether he was likely to do something again. But what he said next dispelled my fear and in fact filled me with an even greater respect for him.

"Everyone is a prisoner. They have been imprisoned by family, by school, by work, imprisoned by their own fear, anxiety, despair. They are imprisoned by superficial prosperity, meaningless fame, illusory power. Simply put, they are imprisoned by the vicissitudes of everyday life and most haven't even noticed. They don't know they are prisoners, even worse that they are prisoners on death row. They feel neither the need nor the inclination to escape. Do you remember Tan Sitong's theory of *luowang*, the nets of society in which we as citizens are all trapped? He had long seen through the reality he was in, and so he strove to destroy all the *luowang* that made up this world. It was with this determination that he wrote, 'I smile toward heaven from beneath the executioner's blade,' on the walls of his cell before he was publicly beheaded in Beijing by Empress Dowager Cixi's Qing government after the failure of the Hundred Days' Reform. And then there's Javert, the police inspector from *Les Misérables*, who always thought himself the model of truth and justice. When he realizes that he has in fact been prisoner to his preconceptions, he has no choice but to kill himself, to escape the judgment of his conscience." Hermit Wang took another look at me before going on. "There are few Javerts in the world, and even fewer Tan Sitongs. It was very late in my life before I understood I was indeed a prisoner, and even later before I escaped." He paused again. "Thankfully we live in a globalized age. Without it escape would be impossible. In the past, if you came to this realization, you would be locked up in a mental asylum."

I was surprised to hear him express gratitude for this globalized age because I suspected he was someone who did not think much of the present day at all. In fact, of all the fantastical theories he would later share, it was his critique of our so-called globalized age that left the deepest impression on me. He once said that the Marxism with which we were all familiar in China was far from inspiring; it put too much emphasis on materialism, on class struggle. He preferred theories that categorized the world in terms of the age of religious authority, the age of aristocratic authority, the age of democracy, and the age of chaos. The globalized age was an age of chaos, and it was marked by the collapse of authority, the destruction of the individual, and the disappearance of meaningful relationships. He asked me if I had heard of the expression "Everyone will have their fifteen minutes of fame." He told me this was characteristic of an age of chaos, an age in which people had lost the sense of distance and duration that was a result of embracing what it meant to be human, in which people had forgotten how to stop for a moment, to pay attention and take their time, to linger and be absorbed. Everything had become fast food: fast-food education, fast-food careers, even fast-food marriages and fast-food love.

Another time he spoke of the problem of "near and far." The development of science in this globalized age meant that we could hear voices from thousands of miles away or receive news from all over the world whenever we wanted. This technology seemed to have brought us closer to one another, he said, but in fact the explosion of cheap information, the accumulation of sights, sounds, and facts, had divided our attention and robbed us of our ability to truly empathize. Not only had people not been brought closer together, they had been driven further apart. Everyone had an opinion about everything these days but they no longer thought about anything. This was a result of the deluge of information. Information did not help you to see the bigger picture. In fact it prevented you from seeing it. He even said, "Information is not your friend but your rival." (This sentence has remained with me ever since.) He then spoke about the paradox of near and far as it affected the Chinese. Chinese people lacked clean air and safe food. They had to travel very far to satisfy this nearest of needs. It was the same problem with education, one of the most basic, nearest of needs, and Chinese parents had to spend a large amount of money to send their children far away to satisfy it.

It was the question of the public and the private that Hermit Wang liked to speak about most. He told me that he despised the fact that the private space afforded to individuals was withering away in the contemporary age, and that this was why he chose to live as a kind of hermit. Thanks to computers and phones no one had any privacy to speak of anymore. Everyone lived in a virtual public space into which they chose to pour their most private information. Everything was a matter of either performing one's life or prying into other people's. Everyone was both exhibitionist and voyeur. In this virtual world people seemed to be freer than before, but actually it had limited their freedom, robbed them of it. Privacy was a basic constituent of what it meant to be human. In an age of information abundance, the happiness of a life was inversely proportional to the amount of information there was about it.

My conversations with Hermit Wang continued for the better part of a year, and the day before he moved away he came to the store to say goodbye. Just as he had never told me where he lived, he never told me where he was going next. He simply said that it was unlikely we would ever meet again. He told me he was very grateful for our discussions and hoped I didn't mind him "prattling on." He rarely spoke with strangers and still did not know why he had decided to talk so much with me. I felt privileged to have earned his trust. I told him I had found everything he had said enlightening and that his words would stay with me forever. I insisted on walking him to the bus stop and when we got there he brought up what had first intrigued me about him.

"Do you not think it strange," he asked, "how many phone calls I make?"

I told him I had wondered about it at first but afterward had not really thought about it. Hermit Wang lifted his hand as if to take off his sunglasses but seemed to think better of it and returned his hand to his side.

"Indeed," he said. "It seems I have not truly managed to free myself from this age."

I waited until Hermit Wang had gotten on the bus before turning around and heading back into the store. There was something tragic about his last words and I still find myself thinking about them to this day. They were proof that the mundane still had a hold on him. I had never met someone so lucid, so apparently uninhibited. I could not imagine what it could be that would not let him go.

Eric and Hermit Wang had given me a great deal to think about but despite everything they had said, nothing would have changed were it not for that routine health checkup. It was only when the results were confirmed that I finally saw that the life I had been living for twenty-three years was coming to an end. After speaking with the doctor I told my daughter what he said before telling my wife. My wife's reaction was far calmer than I could have anticipated. She remained composed throughout the day and carried on with her tasks as if nothing had changed. It was only with dinner that evening that I noticed a change in her mood. On the one hand I wanted to comfort her, but on the other I was afraid of making things worse by adding fuel to the fire. I was on edge the entire evening and carried out my every movement with the utmost care. We managed to make it to bedtime without incident, and as I leaned over to switch off the light I prayed she would not say anything and we could get a good night's sleep. Unfortunately things did not turn out that way.

"How long did the doctor say I have to live?" she asked matter-of-factly as soon as I turned off the light.

"Don't start thinking about that," I said. "The main thing now is getting you treated."

She did not respond. I didn't know what to say.

"Do you remember, whenever we talked about death, you always said you would die first," she said.

"I don't want to die after you," I replied.

"Are you afraid of being alone?"

"No."

"Then what is it?"

"I'll think it's my fault."

"That's not up to you, I'm afraid."

I hesitated slightly before saying, "I know this marriage has not brought you much happiness."

"I thought that was what I should be saying to you," she replied.

A wave of anguish washed over me and another silence followed.

"Did you ever regret immigrating?" she asked suddenly.

I did not respond right away. "No," I said.

Another long silence.

"You?" I said, not really sure why I was asking.

My wife took some time before responding. "Didn't we do it for our daughter?" she said. "She'll thank us for it later."

This answer that wasn't really an answer brought me back to the day we went to the restaurant to celebrate her new job and the cold I had felt, that inexplicable and powerful cold.

She turned onto her side with her back to me and said, "Back then I was imagining our life here. I never thought about dying here."

"Don't get caught up in all that," I said. "The doctors are working out how to treat you. We need to concentrate on doing as they say."

The next morning when I woke up my wife said she wanted to go back to China one last time before starting the treatment, to say goodbye to her mother. I told her not to use words like "last time" and "goodbye," that thoughts like that could only have a negative impact on her treatment. She looked at me with a hurt expression and told me that of course she would not use those words in front of her mother, that she would not even tell her mother the reason for her unexpected visit. She went on to say she hoped I would be able to accompany her like three years previously, when we had gone back to attend her father's funeral. Of course I was more than willing to go with her. I thought my accompanying her might help with how she responded to the treatment. Before long we had booked our tickets and entrusted the convenience store to the friend my wife thought most reliable.

Just as with our previous visit, my wife did not contact any of her classmates or colleagues during her time in Guangzhou, nor did she want to go out to eat or see the city. She told me she wanted to spend all of her time with her mother and eat her mother's food. Something I had not expected was her desire to visit my parents with me. Three years previously, after the funeral, I had gone on my own to see my parents in Chongqing. This time we were more pressed for time and I had not even thought I would be able to visit them myself, let alone that we might go together. However, after ten days in Guangzhou, we travelled to Chongqing to spend two days with my parents. They were living in an apartment my brother had bought them two years earlier in the most expensive complex in Chongqing. My parents had long abandoned their hostile attitude to my wife and were very happy to see us. They were only upset to hear we could not stay longer. My father told me he didn't especially mind how much I saw of him, but thought I ought to come back more often to spend time with my mother, who was beginning to show signs of dementia. After lunch on the second day, when my wife was taking her afternoon nap, I went to the hospital to see my uncle, who was in the late stages of lung cancer. That day he was in good spirits and asked me several questions about life abroad. I in turn could not resist asking him about the talented and unfortunate woman. He was surprised to hear that I still remembered her. He hadn't seen her for many years, he told me, but she was probably still at the psychiatric hospital. He went on to share with me a strange coincidence. The apartment complex my parents were living in had been built on the site of the confectionery factory where she used to work.

Before we left Montreal, what had worried me most was my wife's psychological state. I did not want her to suffer any mental distress. She always complained about China whenever we went back: the filthy air, the traffic, the terrible service, and the obsession with wealth and status. This time, to my surprise, she was serene and forbearing throughout the trip. Part of this was of course due to the fact that she barely went outside, but I was also certain that, in addition to affecting her body, the terminal illness was having an impact on her psyche.

There were, however, two incidents that could only be described as distressing. The first took place on our last evening in Chongqing when my brother insisted on taking us out to Chongqing's fanciest restaurant. Nothing untoward happened during the meal and I was just beginning to relax when the bill arrived and my brother suddenly came down with a bout of verbal diarrhea. He began by making fun of our decision to emigrate, adding he didn't know whose "lousy idea" it was but that no matter which way you looked at it, it was a myopic and terrible decision. Then he embarked on a lecture about loving one's country: China was the future and hope of humanity; without China the entire world economy would collapse; the Americans were ignorant and arrogant, unaware of the fact that it was China that was keeping them afloat and at any moment could choose not to. He then said that the textbooks all told us that material abundance was the prerequisite of communism and that in China now everything was in abundance, even romantic partners ... and so he went on until he brought up the money he had lent us to buy the convenience store. At the time he had told us we could return it whenever we wanted, so we had never felt particularly pressured to pay it all back, but that day in the restaurant he decided to announce to everyone present that he was cancelling his "foreign debt."

"Don't worry about it," he said. "It doesn't even amount to a fraction of what I made on the stock market this week."

I didn't dare look at my wife to see how she was reacting but I could tell that she was struggling to keep her anger in check. I did not know what I could say that would lessen the humiliation she was feeling or stop my brother making things worse.

"Looks like the time has come for the Chinese to repay the countrymen of Dr. Norman Bethune," he said.

My wife finally could take it no longer. She replied in a calm, measured tone that we would return all of his money the minute we got back to Guangzhou.

The second distressing event took place as we were saying goodbye to her mother before heading to the airport. All of a sudden, the old woman grabbed hold of her daughter and burst into tears.

"What are you crying for?" my wife said impatiently.

The old woman only cried even louder. "I don't know if this is the last time we'll ever see each other," she said through her sobs.

The comment was like a knife in my stomach. "How can you say something like that?" I said reprovingly.

"Why shouldn't I?" the old woman replied. "At my age, every day could be my last."

"Don't say stuff like that," I said a little too loudly, worried about how my wife was taking her mother's comments.

"I'll say what I want," the old woman said as she took a tissue from my wife and wiped her eyes. "I said it at the time. Why on Earth do you want to emigrate? 'For the child! For the child!' you said. What does that even mean? Are there not children in China? They all seem to get by all right!"

I reminded my wife that we didn't have much time.

"You don't know how much your decision hurt your father and me," the old woman went on. "I am sure he wouldn't have left us so soon …"

My wife hugged her mother and told her quietly that we had to go.

"You don't know how lonely I am here," the old woman said. "You don't know."

My wife told her again that we couldn't stay any longer.

"Honestly, living like this is no better than death," the old woman said, adding after a pause, "I'm sure this is the last time I'll see you."

My wife spent the taxi journey to the airport with her head turned away from me, looking out of the window. I didn't dare say a word, but when the taxi got onto the motorway, my wife took my hand and said, "Last time we came back it was to bid farewell to the dead. This time it's no different."

"Don't say that," I said.

She was quiet for a moment before turning to me. "I don't want to come back here again," she told me.

I did not know if she had temporally forgotten her condition or if she was choosing to ignore it, but I felt tears well up in my eyes. I held tightly onto her hand.

"Don't say that," I said.

∞ Celia

I DIDN'T KNOW what to think the first time I saw Celia and Misoka talking to one another. It was a complicated feeling, no doubt similar to how Misoka felt when she saw Celia and me together or how Celia felt when she saw Misoka and me together, but at the same time there was a major difference. I saw two people with whom I had a connection, whereas of the two people Misoka and Celia had seen there was only one (me) with whom they felt personally connected. Of course I knew Misoka and Celia were bound to meet at some point, especially since both had expressed such an interest in one another. They had each intuited something about the other's life and it was evident that both of them were keen to explore it further. Nonetheless, I was concerned that a relationship forming between Celia and Misoka might affect the relationship I had with each of them.

I did not greet them when I walked into the pavilion and instead headed straight to my locker where I swiftly put on my skates with my back to them. By the time I was leaving the pavilion I saw that Celia had already returned to her locker. Their conversation had finished, but this did not improve my mood, which remained with me through my warm-up exercises and out on Beaver Lake where I found it difficult to muster any enthusiasm for skating. Before long Celia had come onto the ice too, and she stood at the side waiting for me, then motioned for me to stop.

"Jealousy might be a literary stimulant," she said, "but in life it's toxic."

It was lucky that I had not entirely come to a stop when she said this because it only made me feel worse. I increased my speed and started skating away. Celia had apparently anticipated that I might react this way because she immediately started after me and it wasn't long before she had caught up.

"This is not even the first time we've chatted," she said. "Didn't she tell you?"

I had talked with Misoka the previous two days and neither time had she brought up the fact she had spoken with Celia before. I felt as if I had been deceived in some way.

"We saw each other in the supermarket on Sunday," Celia said. "She saw me and said *bonjour*."

I was surprised to hear that it was Misoka who had begun the conversation, but I made an effort to appear as though it didn't bother me. "She's curious about you," I said.

"Me too," Celia replied. "I was curious about her the moment I saw her."

"I think it's different," I said, half jokingly. "She seems to see you as a rival. You seem to see her as a lover."

Celia was clearly not too pleased by this comment. "She's young enough to be my daughter!" she said.

It was the first time Celia had ever revealed anything about her age. I was surprised to discover I had the ability to break through the defences she had carefully constructed around herself, and it made me feel better. I no longer felt unnerved by the possibility of these two mysterious women becoming close. Perhaps it posed no danger to my relationship with each of them. It might even help me understand them both better. "What did you talk about?" I asked.

"All sorts of things," Celia said. "Even the story she's writing." Celia paused for a moment. "She's much more outgoing than I had expected."

I found it hard to picture Misoka being so open with a stranger. I stopped skating and looked disbelievingly at Celia as she came to a stop too. "What is she writing?" I asked.

"She described it as a 'classical love story,'" Celia said.

"I had no idea," I said. "I had no idea she'd be so outgoing with you."

"Now you know that subtle difference between the first five-sixths and the last sixth of Shakespeare's sonnets," Celia said. "It is possible for there to be a greater attraction between those of the same sex. This is a truth that science cannot account for."

I wasn't in the mood for Celia's aphorisms. "So did she tell you about her life?"

"She didn't tell me as such," Celia said. "But I've worked it out from our conversations."

"What have you worked out?" I said, excited to hear what Celia had to say.

She refused to answer. She said she had thought about it, but in the end decided it was not up to her to share this information with me. It would be better to wait for Misoka to tell me in her own time.

Celia's cryptic comments only returned me to my earlier mood. These two mysterious women now shared a secret. They trusted each other more than they trusted me. It was a situation that would only increase my desire to find out more about both of them but now the separation between us had become clearer. I would have to work harder to overcome it.

Looking back on it now, I realize that the beginning of Misoka and Celia's relationship was not only a turning point in my relationships with each of them, but in the entire story of that winter. The events of the following day were a sign of that change.

I was already skating on Beaver Lake the following day when the first streaks of light began to appear in the sky. I had deliberately arrived earlier than usual because I wanted to avoid seeing either Celia or Misoka. My plan was to be finished skating and already heading home by the time they arrived.

It was the first time I had witnessed the sunrise on Mount Royal, and it was a truly beautiful experience. More than once I could not resist stopping my skating to face eastward with my eyes closed. Occasionally my eyelids would let in a glimpse of the rising sun's subtle glow and for a moment it felt as if my entire life were being briefly illuminated by its soft rays. In the pure air and perfect quiet at dawn, I felt winter's rarely acknowledged warmth. From somewhere deep down a primordial gratitude awakened in me, a gratitude for the vagaries of life that had brought me to this world and this moment. I remembered Hermit Wang's question and realized it did not matter what I was doing standing here. It did not matter if it was an accident or meant to be. All that mattered was that I *was* here, that I had, for whatever reasons, come to be here.

Then I heard a voice, a woman's voice calling me from a distance. It was a strange experience hearing my name reverberating through the immaculate silence of Mount Royal. It was as if the whole world were listening, waiting, existing in anticipation of how I would respond. I turned toward the direction of the voice and saw Celia standing by the old elm tree, waving her ski at me. I had no idea what she was doing here so early, and I didn't know whether she was about to go or had just returned from skiing, but I was excited to see her. I forgot all about my previous intention to avoid her and Misoka and waved back at her enthusiastically.

Celia picked up her skis and placed them in the hollow in the tree before walking straight to where I was on Beaver Lake, which involved tramping unsteadily through thick snow.

"What are you doing here so early?" she asked.

"What about you?" I replied.

"Trying to avoid you!"

"Me too."

A rare smile appeared on Celia's face before she turned to point toward the elm tree. "That's my natural locker. It's where I store my skis all winter."

I did not let on that I knew her secret and expressed polite surprise before asking her how she had found it. "Surely you didn't learn that from your great literary teacher?" I said jokingly.

She did not take it as a joke. "It's not entirely unrelated," she said. "The relationship between humans and nature is a complicated one."

This observation did not strike me as particularly ground-breaking. "That's what the Taoists think too," I said.

"There are emotional bonds between trees too," she went on. "They too harbour secret love for one another, as well as jealousy."

She had brought up jealousy again and I was no longer sure if she was talking about trees or people, or if she was talking about people in general or one person in particular. I looked at my watch and realized that Misoka was due to arrive at any moment. I did not want her to see me with Celia so early on the mountain.

At that moment Celia lifted her head and said, "Did you hear that?"

I listened and could just about make out a rhythmic tapping sound.

"A woodpecker," Celia said.

"A woodpecker?" I said. "At this time of year? I thought it would be too cold for them." As I spoke the sound became more distinct. It seemed to be coming from the woods.

"The woodpecker never leaves. It is a solitary animal. It goes about its business on its own. Perhaps it is the most solitary life on Mount Royal."

"You can tell from the tapping," I said. "I've never heard such an empty sound before."

Celia paused to listen. "I imagine it knows every tree here," she said.

There was a warmth in Celia's voice that I had not heard before. Something about the woodpecker meant a lot to her. I looked at the area of the woods from where the tapping seemed to emerge. "I've never seen a woodpecker before," I said.

Celia looked at me and said something I will never forget. "I am a woodpecker."

Whatever had come between us the previous day seemed to disintegrate with this confession. Our special relationship was back, along with my yearning to get closer to her. I looked at Celia, the woodpecker standing before me, and saw more clearly than ever her solitude and her familiarity with these woods. It was undoubtedly this quality that had meant she was able to find her own "natural locker" in the hollow of an elm tree.

Then Celia changed the subject and asked me if I had ever been to the ski resort some 150 kilometres from the city. I told her I had not and she asked if I had ever thought about going. It had never really occurred to me but I told her that I would like to visit someday. She told me she had a small cabin there and that she used to go every season.

"But ever since the autumn of last year I've been too afraid to go there alone," she said.

"Why?" I asked, thinking woodpeckers were not supposed to fear solitude.

"I'm worried something might happen."

"Something might happen?" I asked. "Like what?"

Celia didn't answer my question but instead asked me one of her own, a question that caught me completely off guard. "Would you go with me?"

From the way she asked me I was not sure if she was inviting me or pleading with me to go with her, and four contradictory emotions began to bubble up inside me: excitement, embarrassment, apprehension, and guilt. I was excited and embarrassed because apart from my wife I had never travelled to a strange place with anyone of the opposite sex before, let alone someone of the opposite sex by whom I was so fascinated. The cause of my apprehension and guilt on the other hand was the other woman who had fascinated me that winter. How would Misoka react if she knew I had accepted Celia's invitation, if she knew what stage our relationship had reached?

At the centre of this emotional commotion was a voice that kept saying, "You can't go, don't go"; a voice I discerned as clearly as the earlier sound of the woodpecker. But something came over me just as it had the day I returned from Zhangjiajie National Park to Guangzhou. "When?" I asked.

"Right away," Celia said.

"Right away?"

"Don't think this is an off-the-cuff decision," she said. "I've been thinking of inviting you for some time, ever since we started reading the sonnets together."

I heard the voice inside me again. "I'll have to think about it," I said.

"What do you have to think about?"

I didn't know how to answer this question. I stared at Celia as I scraped at the surface of the ice with the blade of my skate.

She repeated the question.

I paused for a moment before saying, "How do we get there?" as if I had already accepted her invitation.

"The train's easiest," she said.

It was an intriguing prospect, but I still didn't want to go "right away." I told her I hadn't slept well the night before and that I was tired. I wanted to go home and get a little rest before deciding if I would go with her.

"In that case we'll take the last train," she said in a tone that implied that the matter was already settled. The feeling that I had been pressured into making a decision that was not my own made me uncomfortable. Unlike Hermit Wang, I was apparently unable to extricate myself from the world and its mechanisms.

"What do I bring?" I asked.

"Enough clothes for three nights," she said. "And don't forget the book of Shakespeare's sonnets."

"Three nights?" I had not thought we would stay for so long.

Celia could tell I was nervous. "I usually stay for three or four days," she said. "We can use the time to read the rest of the sonnets!" Before I had time to protest she said we should meet at the Starbucks in Central Station at 5:30 p.m.

As I watched Celia walk away, a cold sweat came over me. I had no idea what to make of her invitation and a series of questions came to me that I could not answer. What was she worried might happen if she went alone? Could my being there really stop it from happening? Was that the only reason I was invited? What else might she be asking of me? But I had no time to linger over these thoughts. I had to get off the mountain before Misoka arrived and saw the state I was in, so I rushed to the pavilion and changed out of my skates.

On the way home I was still on edge. My thoughts revolved around the inexplicable phenomenon that was Celia. It had been more than a month since I had first spoken with her, during which time I had come to understand more and more about who she was, but I still did not know the answers to everything that had first puzzled me about her. Who was she really? From the moment I had seen her I had intuited that she was suffering from something, but what was it? How was it related to what she was worried might happen at the ski resort?

Also, just how small was her small cabin? Where would I be expected to sleep? The more I thought the more my state of mind began to change. My sense of embarrassment and guilt had gone, and my apprehension had transformed into a huge terror that as good as crushed any remaining excitement I might have felt. More questions posed themselves that played off my fear. I began to wonder about my own safety. Was it possible that "something might happen" to me? Could something happen to both of us?

I thought of phoning my daughter to ask for her advice but then I remembered that she was no longer answering my calls. I realized this was probably for the best, because even if I'd been able to speak with her I had no idea how I would have explained my situation. Would I really have the courage to tell her that I was planning to spend three days in a cabin with a strange woman I had met by Beaver Lake? Would I really have the courage to tell her that the reason I was going was because this strange woman was afraid that something might happen if she went on her own? Would I really have the courage to tell her that now I was terrified that something might happen to me? No matter how I put it, I was sure my daughter would only make fun of me. But there was no getting around the fact that the terror I felt was real. What if something really did happen?

I decided I had to leave something behind for the only "relative" I had left in Montreal. When I got home I tidied up all my documents and put them in an envelope that I left on the desk. Then I turned on the computer and wrote my daughter an email. For a moment it occurred to me that I was writing my last will and testament. I told her that I had decided to spend three days at a famous ski resort, but that I wasn't sure about the state of my health. I asked her to come to the apartment if I had not contacted her after three days.

Around noon I cut up the smoked fish that was left in the fridge and fried it up with some eggs and rice. Not long after I finished my lunch I felt something wasn't sitting right in my stomach, so I decided to go for a walk. The moment I stepped outside I bumped into my talkative Taiwanese neighbour. She said I wasn't looking so good and asked what was the matter. I lied to her that I had been up all night watching the Korean soap opera she kept recommending to me. She told me I should know at my age how to take care of myself and not to get carried away. She went on to say that two people in our apartment building had died last week, one of them younger than I was. She sighed dramatically and said that but a hair's breadth separated life from death. It was clear that these apparently casual comments were directed at me and they only made me more concerned about my trip with Celia.

I walked two laps of the building, consumed by unsettling thoughts, before heading back to my apartment. After packing my things I turned on the computer again to see if my daughter had responded. She hadn't. I reminded myself that it had only been an hour. At the same time I was sure that she had probably read my message, which was a comforting thought. I then lay on the bed to calm myself down and get some rest. To my surprise, I fell asleep very quickly. I was even more surprised when I was woken up by my wife. It was the first time she had appeared in my dreams since she died. She was draped in a white shawl, approaching from somewhere far in the distance, accompanied by a simple tune on repeat that was getting gradually louder. The closer she got, the larger she appeared, and the more afraid I became. When she got to the side of the bed the melody came to a sudden stop. It was as though the whole scene had been rehearsed in advance. Through the translucent white shawl I could see her nipples and the black of her pubic hair; however, what truly caught my attention was her face: it was utterly lifeless but for the murderous gleam in her eyes. I had no idea what she intended and I didn't dare ask her. Just when I was thinking about how to escape, I noticed that her lips were opening and closing. She was trying to say something, but I could not hear her voice. I fixed my eyes on her lips and realized she was saying the same thing over and over again. That's when I heard it. She said it again. She kept saying it, louder and louder, just like the melody that had been playing earlier: "I won't let you go. I won't let you go. I won't let you go." The sound was almost deafening now and it continued to get louder and louder, louder and louder, and then it stopped.

I was lying awake in bed. I hardly ever dreamt when I slept in the afternoon, let alone feverish, peculiar dreams like that one. I felt the sheets and realized that I was dripping with sweat. I knew what my dream was trying to tell me. Just like the voice inside me earlier that day, it was warning me about the trip that I was planning to take. My apprehension and terror were gone. I looked calmly at the alarm clock on the bedside table and started thinking about just not turning up at the train station, but then I remembered how my wife always criticized me for being irresponsible. I got out of bed, had a shower, and left the apartment. I would meet Celia and tell her to her face that I was not going. I would even tell her about my dream and urge her not to go either.

I got to the Starbucks in the train station ten minutes early and found a seat by the entrance. I flicked through my book of Shakespeare's sonnets as I considered what I should say to Celia. My thoughts were interrupted by a woman telling a man to hurry up in Mandarin and I looked over at the big clock in the centre of the train station. It was already five minutes after the time Celia and I had arranged to meet. I watched the crowds of people walking this way and that and thought of what Hermit Wang had said about seeing the bigger picture. It seemed to me that for someone like Hermit Wang the scene of all these people striding so purposefully in every direction would be evidence of the absurdity of our world. After fifteen minutes I began to get nervous. I decided to wait another thirty minutes, plagued by unsettling thoughts. Why had she not come? Had something happened to her? What could have happened? After a restless half hour during which time the open book of sonnets sat unread on the table, I stood up to leave, but when I reached the entrance to the coffee shop I decided to wait another ten minutes. Fifteen minutes later I started walking to the bus stop, filled with an ill-defined sense of apprehension.

On the bus home I was exhausted, both physically and mentally. In the end I had not gone to the ski resort, which in some ways was a victory, but concerns about what had happened to Celia meant I was far from relieved. I realized that she often made me feel this way. In the twelve hours from our meeting that morning to her absence at the train station, her actions and words had first filled me with fear, which then led to confusion, and finally drained me of energy. Perhaps this was what made our relationship so special. Standing in the elevator of my building I thought about collapsing straight into bed the moment I got home, but then I remembered the email I had sent to my daughter. I decided I should write her back, explaining that I had cancelled my plans so she would not worry about me. I turned on the computer, overcome with fatigue but still nurturing a small hope that my daughter might have replied. I did discover an unread message. However, it was not from my daughter. It was from Celia. She had sent it that afternoon. If I had checked before leaving for the train station I would have seen it.

In the email Celia said that she had decided to cancel our trip but did not say why. She went on to say that she would be at Beaver Lake that evening at eleven, but did not explicitly invite me. I read the email again. By the look of the time she had sent it, Celia had decided to cancel our trip at the same time that my nightmare had convinced me not to go. Was this a coincidence? Or was there more to it?

The email, rather than calming me, became the third instance that day that Celia had sent my thoughts into an anxious spiral. Why had she suddenly decided to cancel? Why would she not tell me why? Why was she going to Beaver Lake so late at night? Why had she told me she was going but not asked me to come? I lay down on the bed without changing out of my clothes. I was utterly exhausted and was in urgent need of some rest, but all the questions I had about Celia had me in such a state that I couldn't sleep. From 9:40 p.m. I found myself continuously turning to look at the clock, just as I had done when I was waiting for Celia in the train station. At 10:20 p.m. I could bear it no longer and got out of bed. I turned on the computer and saw that I had no new emails from Celia, which meant that she had not changed her plans to be at Beaver Lake at eleven.

I had never been up Mount Royal so late before. The impression was similar to that of Mount Royal at dawn and I felt that familiar gratitude for its purity and quiet. I reached the pavilion and made my way toward the lake, shining in the crisp light of the moon that also illuminated a solitary figure standing in the snow.

"I did not think I'd show up," I said.

"I *knew* you would," Celia replied.

"Because of the great teacher again?" I said, serious.

"No," she said. "Because of this." She passed one of her earbuds to me.

When I heard what she was listening to, a cold shudder went up my spine. I pulled the earbud from my ear. "What is this?" I asked, unable to prevent my voice from trembling.

"Ravel's *Boléro*," Celia replied. "Do you like it?"

"I can't believe it. What a strange coincidence," I said, trying to control the emotion in my voice.

"What coincidence?"

I was reluctant to tell Celia about my nightmare that afternoon but at the same time I wanted to get to the bottom of this melody's uncanny reappearance. I did not know what to say.

"Have you heard it before?" Celia asked.

"Only in a dream," I said. "But how could a dream antici-pate reality?"

Celia had no way of knowing what I meant. She looked out across the lake. "Your mind must be playing tricks on you," she said.

I did not respond. She wouldn't understand the connection between what I had dreamt that afternoon and what I had just heard. I waited a moment before asking her what it was about Ravel's *Boléro* that had told her I would come to see her that evening.

"A melody playing over and over, at first too quiet to hear, but each time getting louder until it overwhelms your senses.... This is what made me see you approaching in the moonlight, from the distance, getting nearer, getting larger ..."

I stood there, shocked at the resemblance to my dream.

"This is Celibidache's 1971 version. He's my favourite conductor," Celia said. "A perfectionist, a spiritualist, an artist of sublime solitude." She looked at me. "Sublime solitude is the only true solitude. The truly sublime is the solitary sublime."

I still did not have the courage to put the earbud back in my ear, to hear the echo of my nightmare in the real world, and Celia did not insist on my listening. She put her earphones away and suggested we walk to the belvedere. I looked up at the indigo sky, the pearly white moon, and felt a contentment I had not felt for some time.

We began to walk. I thought Celia would tell me why she had cancelled our trip, but instead she asked me a question.

"Do you like the winters here?"

I thought for a moment before replying, "I like *this* winter."

Celia glanced at me with a look that suggested she had liked my answer. "A lot of people say everything about Montreal is great except for the winter," she said, "but it's what I love most about Montreal."

In the space of a couple of months I had come across three women who, for their own separate reasons, each loved winter. For the Korean student who first brought me back to Mount Royal, it was because of her father's playing of Vivaldi. For Misoka it was because winter was "sowing season."

"Why do you like Montreal's winter?" I asked.

"Because it brings us the sublime and the solitary," she said.

"Like the conductor you love."

"And the snow, which covers up all that is ugly, which covers up all the hurt," she said, "just like at the end of Joyce's 'The Dead.'"

I had not read "The Dead." What had captured my attention was Celia's use of the word "hurt." She had never mentioned it in this way before. I was sure she was not talking about hurt in general. She was talking about her own in particular.

My suspicion turned out to be correct. Celia went on to tell me that there were two events in her life that had formed her "darkest memories," memories that were at the very core of who she was, of the kind that "no amount of snow can conceal." She spoke of the memory of her father, once a happy child whose character and fate had been transformed by his career and marriage. From an early age he was obsessed with art and wanted to become a painter, but his father forced him to study law. As a result he was miserable as an undergraduate. He had no interest or confidence in what he was studying or how he was living his life. Then one day his legal history lecturer spoke about the story of Kandinsky who had studied law before embarking on his career as a painter. It was a defining moment for Celia's father, who decided to follow in the footsteps of the great artist. He began to commit to his studies, and before long he was getting the highest marks in his year. After receiving his doctorate, he began working in his cousin's firm and quickly became a famous property rights lawyer. Everyone who knew him, including his father, assumed that he had realized his greatest ambitions. No one suspected that this was all merely preparation for the really great moment in his life. He was awaiting the arrival of his thirtieth birthday when, like Kandinsky before him, he would abandon the world of legal affairs and embark on the eternal path of artistic creation.

His plans were to be thwarted by his marriage. Celia's mother was the daughter of a good friend of her grandfather. Both her grandfather and his friend ought to have known how unsuitable Celia's parents were for one another, but they insisted on arranging the marriage as a testament to their friendship. Celia's childhood would take place against the backdrop of two parents in conflict. They argued every day, be it about matters of great import (like whether Che Guevara was a modern-day saint or whether America should invade Panama) or trivial affairs (like whether the kitchen floor should be mopped once or twice a day or how well-done a steak ought to be). When Celia's father announced on his thirtieth birthday that he would be resigning from the law firm and enrolling at the Paris Academy of Fine Arts, her mother fainted before he had even finished his sentence.

So Celia's father had been unable to take his idol's most important step on the road to becoming an artist, and this was the reason he was unable to look at Kandinsky's paintings without crying. He lost all enthusiasm for life and spent as much time as possible away from home. He put all of his energy into his work, which made him more successful as a lawyer, but it was a success that only deepened the wound of his failure to achieve his greatest ambition. The only person he liked speaking to was Celia, and their conversations revolved around how to choose one's career and marriage partner. He told Celia that everyone he had met could be divided into two types: those who had found a way to do what they loved and those who hadn't. He said many of the latter type were unhappy and regretted their decisions, no matter how successful they were. Meanwhile those who had followed their dreams never seemed to have any complaints or regrets, irrespective of the difficulties they faced. On the subject of marriage, he told her that no one should change who they were because of their partner, so the success of a marriage lay in the compatibility of the couple's personalities and aims. He said the minimum requirement of such compatibility was that one spouse truly appreciate the other. The highest embodiment of it was when both spouses appreciated one another. When Celia listened to her father speak of these things she could see in his eyes an abyss deep in his soul.

Celia's parents divorced when she started university. Before long her father had closed his famous and successful law firm. He bought a cabin at the famous ski resort where he took up a reclusive life and Celia visited him there every season. He was finally painting every day, which was what he had always wanted, but from his paintings the daughter could tell that he was still unhappy. He had been unable to fill the abyss in his soul, and two days before Celia's wedding he ended his life with a bottle of sleeping pills. It was only twenty years later that Celia understood why her father had chosen that time to kill himself. He had wanted to prevent her from entering what he thought was an ominous marriage.

The cabin her father had bought must have been the same one she had invited me to that morning, the place where we were supposed to have been staying that night, but at the time I thought nothing more of it because I was engrossed in her story. I was wondering whether these memories had anything to do with why she still suffered to this day.

We walked back from the belvedere and stopped at the entrance to the pavilion. I thanked her for telling me about being here and also about the details of her past. I told her that this was the most remarkable night of my fifteen years as an immigrant in Montreal.

"You said you liked this winter," she said. "I think this is the most remarkable winter of my life."

"I saw you the first day I came up here," I told her.

"The moment you walked in a strange feeling came over me."

"I thought you hadn't even noticed me."

"I'm someone who tries to see the bigger picture in life," she said. "I even foresaw this evening." She slowly moved her face closer to mine.

I did not pull away. I closed my eyes and felt her cold lips press against my own. Her arms wrapped around me and her scent stirred in me desires that had lain dormant for many years. In the negative twenty degrees of that winter's night, a certain potency and pleasure coursed through my body and rekindled something inside me.

Our lips only parted when we could hold our breath no longer and then we looked at the dark sky, breathing deeply.

"Thank you," I said toward the sky.

Celia stretched out her hands to hold my head and kissed me on the forehead. "I foresaw this night from the start," she said, before turning around and walking to her bicycle, which was parked by the side of the pavilion.

I asked her if she would be safe cycling home so late. She told me she did it all the time, got on her bike, and cycled away. I watched the outline of her body slowly disappear into the night and thought back to the first day I saw her skiing into the woods. What had happened between that day and tonight was hard to believe. On my way home I almost ran down the mountain, my cheeks wet with tears.

It was only when I got home that I realized how cold I was. After a hot shower I still hadn't warmed up. I climbed into bed but the chill refused to dissipate. It accompanied me as I dreamt of walking with Celia into her cabin by the famous ski resort. It reminded me of the cottage in the snow from the film *Doctor Zhivago*, where the protagonist stays with Lara. Celia and I sat back to back by the stove, reading Shakespeare's sonnets. She wanted me to read the first lines of sonnets 40 and 144. First we read the opening of sonnet 40, a sonnet written to a male lover: "Take all my loves, my love, yea, take them all." Then we turned to sonnet 144, which was written to the Dark Lady: "Two loves I have of comfort and despair."

"Here we see the fanaticism and frustration of the bard," Celia said. "It's clear that neither of these two lovers of different genders is able to satisfy his unbridled passion for love."

I was not in the right state of mind to appreciate her explanations. I was frightened by the sound of the wind outside the window.

"Your mind is wandering," Celia said.

I turned to look at her but my attention was still directed outside the window. "Will something happen?" I asked.

"The biggest danger is not out there," Celia said. "The biggest danger is in here, in the soul."

I stared at her, my eyes wide with fear.

"I don't know if you know," Celia said. "I am not well."

I pretended surprise, as if this were the first I had heard of it.

"I am on medication," she said.

Again I did not want to let on that I had known all along.

"Recently my sleep has gotten worse," she said.

"There must be ways of dealing with it," I said. I did not want to mention trying Chinese medicine in case it touched upon the sensitive subject of her relationship with China.

"I often wake up with a start after sleeping an hour or two and then can't get back to sleep," she said. "Then I go to Mount Royal."

"There must be ways of dealing with it," I repeated, taking hold of her hand.

"I often think of my father," Celia said. "I am going to end up like him …"

I shivered and held her tightly in my arms. "Don't …" I said softly.

"From the day he passed away I knew how things would end for me," she said.

"It won't happen that way," I said. "It won't."

Celia held me tightly too. "You know," she said, "I have died three times already."

I had no idea that she had entered such a dark place. I rested my face against her soft hair and hoped that my care for her might help banish some of the darkness that had accumulated inside her. It was at that moment that I saw, through the snowy window, two murderous eyes staring at me. My God, *she* had followed us here! Terrified, I pushed Celia away. She turned her eyes toward the window.

"A wolf," she said calmly. "A lonely wolf."

∞ Misoka

OF COURSE, AFTER that day my relationship with Celia was bound to change. I now knew that she was not simply a "sufferer"; she was someone who had died and could die again at any moment. In my lowest and loneliest periods I had also at times felt the urge to leave this world, but for me it had never been more than a momentary impulse. For Celia it was a symptom that hounded her at all times. Her experience of death revealed to me the darker aspects of her life and a world that was more profound than I had previously thought. It was why she appeared more radiant in the moonlight than the light of day, why she was more enchanting in dreams than in reality. Of course, there were many questions from the previous day that I still could not answer. Why had she cancelled the plans we had made? Why wouldn't she tell me her reasons? Did it have anything to do with my own decision that afternoon not to go? How had the melody she loved so much made its way into my nightmare?

It was not only my relationship with Celia that had changed but also my relationship with Mount Royal. I had never been there so late, and I never thought that in the bitter cold of its night I could feel such a fiery potency and pleasure. From that day on I would certainly not see it in the same way. I would never forget that indigo sky and its pearly white moon or the passion kindled by two pairs of cold lips coming together on those slopes.

Of course the relationship between my wife and me had also changed. She had freed herself from the confines of death to enter my dreams. But what could explain the murderous look in her eyes, as though she were collecting some debt or avenging some injustice? I had a feeling that now she had come back she would not let me go, she would continue to invade my dreams, maybe even my waking life.

Finally, there was my relationship with Misoka. Even as I ran home from the mountain with tears rolling down my cheeks, I realized that it would not be the same. No matter how hard I tried to hide things from Misoka she would know that something had happened between Celia and me. I only hoped that she would not pry too hard into this private corner of my life. I did not want whatever it was that drew me to her to be undermined by the discomfort and unease such a confrontation might make me feel.

The next day I did not wake up until one in the afternoon but even after such a long rest my mind was still in a disoriented state. I turned on the computer, hoping I might see an email from Celia that explained what she thought about the previous night or at least informed me that she had made it home safely. Seeing no reply I found that I was not too disappointed. I stared at the screen for a while. In the end I decided not to write telling her how I felt.

The next morning when I walked into the pavilion I saw neither Celia nor Misoka. I looked out the window and to my relief Misoka was not at her usual spot by the lake. I didn't do my usual warm-up on the smaller ice rink and instead went straight to Beaver Lake. When I was halfway around the lake I noticed Misoka by a section of the lakeside far from the pavilion. It was slightly unnerving seeing her there, a position that seemed deliberately chosen so as to be invisible from both the pavilion and the ice rink. It was as if she were trying to avoid me. But then I noticed that the wheelchair was moving. She seemed to be looking for something. I called out her name but she barely responded and I wondered if there were any way for her to know what had happened between Celia and me. Whatever the reason for her indifference, I thought it best not to go over to her. At the same time I did not want to avoid her in case it led her to suspect that something had changed. For a while I neither approached nor departed, skating slowly and maintaining my distance before calling over to ask what she was looking for.

Misoka did not respond and continued to drive her wheelchair around the edge of the lake, occasionally coming closer to its edge and leaning over to peer at its frozen surface.

I suddenly understood what she was doing. "Do you want to come onto the ice?" I asked.

The dark skin of Misoka's cheeks flushed red and she nodded.

I told her that the snow on this side of the lake was not firm enough. If she wanted to come onto the ice with her wheelchair she should go to the other side where there was a ramp that service vehicles used to access the frozen lake. She immediately turned around and started heading that way and I skated across the lake to wait for her at the ramp.

When Misoka got onto the ice, a look of amazement appeared on her face. She looked all around her and said, "This is a completely different feeling to looking from the side."

I thought of the multiple times she had seen Celia and me skating on the lake and it dawned on me that such a sight was bound to make her want to experience it for herself. I felt a strong pang of guilt. "Do you want me to push you?" I asked. "It'll be just like skating together."

Misoka turned her head and looked at me knowingly. She nodded.

There was something unfamiliar yet beautiful about pushing Misoka on the ice that morning, and it only intensified the guilt I was feeling. Misoka was also clearly moved by the experience. At one point she turned around to look at me and I saw the gratitude in her eyes.

As we skated around the lake together I leaned down slightly so I could get nearer to the top of her head, to her scent. I remembered the first day I saw her. What would I have thought if I had known that at some time in the near future I would be as close to her as I was now? It truly was an unusual winter, a remarkable winter! Misoka's identity was still unrevealed to me, a riddle to which I did not know the answer, but despite this I could feel how at that moment I needed her and she needed me. I looked down at the top of her head. Like her eyes when she had turned around to look at me, I saw in it something playfully suggestive, an invitation to a kind of intimacy as pure as this winter on Mount Royal. I leaned down farther until I felt the ends of her hair fluttering in the wind brush against my face. That was when I heard her say quietly, as if speaking to herself, "They also skated together once."

I quickly straightened up. "Who?" I asked.

Misoka turned to look at me again. This time, I could see in her eyes that her thoughts were elsewhere. "Sorry," she said. "That was a long time ago."

I sighed with relief. If it was long ago then she could not have been talking about Celia and me. "Is it something you remembered or something you imagined?"

"I'm not sure," she said. "I've been getting my memory and imagination confused a lot recently."

After we had done a complete loop, I pushed Misoka to the middle of the lake and pointed her in the direction of the sun. Then I walked around and stood in front of her.

Misoka closed her eyes and stretched her arms in the air as if enjoying the moment. Then she opened her eyes and looked at me. But rather than tell me how she had found her first skating experience, she asked me a question. "Have you ever been to Miyun Reservoir?" she said.

"You even know Miyun Reservoir!" I said. I still could not work out why she was so interested in Beijing.

I thought I saw a hint of sorrow appear on her face as she said, "Of course I know," before asking me the question again.

Another "of course," I thought to myself. Another "of course" I would never be able to truly understand. I shuffled back and forth on the ice before telling her that I had been to the reservoir around thirty years ago. She asked me what time of year I had been and I told her summer. I remembered her interest in the winter of 1974 and asked if she would have preferred it if I had told her I had been in winter. She ignored my question and asked me how I had gotten there. I told her I had cycled with two classmates. Her eyes widened and it was clear that this time my answer better suited her tastes. She asked me how long it took to cycle there. I said that it must have taken at least five hours. She did not want to hear "it must" or "at least." She wanted to know exactly. I had no idea why she was so hung up on these details and could not remember the exact time, but I told her it had taken six hours, adding that we had left in the afternoon and by the time we had arrived it was already dark. She asked what the reservoir was like and I told her it was far bigger than any of us had imagined. She then asked where we had slept and I replied that we had slept in a wooded area by the water. I added that at midnight we had gone for a swim. This apparently trivial detail had a strong impact on Misoka.

"What?" she said. "You actually swam in Miyun Reservoir?"

"Yes," I replied. "At midnight."

"You're saying your body has touched the water in Miyun Reservoir?"

I had swum there. Of course my body had touched the water. I did not feel as if this warranted explanation. "Of course," I replied.

Misoka stared at me with wide eyes as if something she had always been waiting for had finally appeared before her. I suddenly felt shy. I could guess the request she was about to make.

"Do you mind if I touch your hand?" she asked.

I took the glove off my right hand and bashfully extended it toward her, looking around in all directions. The last thing I wanted was for Celia to appear at that moment.

Misoka stared avidly at my hand. Then she took off her glove and brushed the fingers of her right hand against my skin. "What does the water feel like there?" she asked as if directing the question to my hand.

I had no idea how to answer.

She lifted her head to look at me. "Is the water cold?" she asked.

"It was the middle of the night. It was a little cold."

"What about the time leading up to Qingming festival? Would it be colder at night then?"

"Before Qingming festival? It would be freezing."

I had barely finished speaking when Misoka lifted her red scarf to her face and started to cry.

"What's the matter?" I asked. "Did I say something wrong?"

She didn't reply but continued sobbing into her scarf. I knelt down on the ice and leaned closer to her face.

"What's the matter?" I asked, trying to speak in as soothing a voice as possible.

The sound of her weeping reverberated through the deadly quiet of Mount Royal. Where had this sudden grief come from? I leaned even closer to her. "What is it?" I asked, getting slightly agitated. "What's the matter?"

Misoka buried her face deeper into her scarf and wept even louder. I placed my hand on her shoulder. I did not know what to do to calm her down. Then she said something I could not understand.

"Why do you have to be like that?" she asked. "Why?"

Me? Like what? I had no idea what Misoka was talking about but her reaction frightened me. "What did I do?" I asked. "Tell me. Please tell me."

Misoka lifted her head and looked at me through tearful eyes. For a moment it looked as if she wanted to say something, but she must have thought better of it because she pressed a button on her wheelchair and it started moving away. I was still kneeling on the ice as I watched her wheelchair move slowly up the ramp and head toward the car park. What had happened? What was the matter? What had I done wrong? Was it something I had done wrong just now or was it something I'd done wrong thirty years before?

I got to my feet and began to move around the ice but it quickly became clear that I was not in the frame of mind to enjoy it. I couldn't stop thinking about Misoka. An unsettling thought had occurred to me. Perhaps the person who had made her burst into tears was not me, the man kneeling beside her wheelchair, but someone somewhere else entirely. Or perhaps that person was with us on the ice somehow, but not in the way that Misoka and I were. Who could he be? What did he have to do with Miyun Reservoir? I was starting to think that all the questions Misoka had about Beijing were not the result of an overactive imagination but of real memories, not her own memories perhaps, but memories she had to access via her imagination. But why?

The whole morning I was restless. I was not only worried about Misoka but also impatient to know what was going on with Celia. I checked my computer again when I got home. She still hadn't written. Disheartened, I left my desk and sat on the sofa. I picked up the copy of *Wuthering Heights* I had found in a pile of old books left by my floor's communal garbage chute and thought of the contrasting opinions my wife and Celia had about reading. Celia thought that reading was a sign of someone's worth, that a life without reading was not worth living. My wife, on the other hand, thought my interest in reading was a sign of my irresponsible attitude. A week before she died, she had even reminded me that I ought to take things more seriously and not spend so much time reading "useless" books. I wearily began flicking through the pages of the book until I reached a passage that caught my attention. It was about how the air in the hills was so "full of life" that "whoever respired it, though dying, might revive." This romantic phrase seemed as if it could have been describing Mount Royal and how its air had brought me back to life that winter. Excited, I continued to read, but the more I read the less it affected me and the more tired I became. Before long I had lain down and fallen asleep.

My wife appeared again. Like before she was dressed in a white shawl and accompanied by the same melody as she approached, repeating the same phrase, "I won't let you go. I won't let you go. I won't let you go."

I was not startled awake at this moment. "Is it because of them?" I asked, almost whispering as if I were afraid the two women to whom I was referring might hear.

"What does it have to do with them?" she said, responding immediately. "I'm already dead."

The directness of her response frightened me. "Then what's the reason?" I asked, trembling.

She continued to glare at me furiously as she said, "I want to know the truth, the truth, the truth ..." extending her skeletal hand toward my face.

I sat up with a start. I now knew why my wife had come back to me. However, I was unsure what to do about it. I went to the kitchen, opened the fridge door, looked inside, and then closed it again. I walked a few times back and forth in the kitchen before picking up the television remote control and then putting it back. I went to the desk in my room and turned on the computer but before it had booted up properly I turned it off again. What could I do?

That's when I heard a light knocking on the door. My first thought was of my wife and a shiver ran up my back. The knocking continued. I waited until it was finished before walking quietly to the door and peering through the peephole. It was my talkative Taiwanese neighbour. I opened the door and, seeing how flustered she was, I suggested she come inside. She ignored my offer. After looking left and right, she asked me if I had ever seen a ghost. I managed to conceal my shock at the uncanny pertinence of her inquiry and asked her where such a strange question had come from. She looked around her again and told me that she had just seen one of the tenants who had died the week before, the one who was younger than I was, standing outside the launderette. She said if he was really there it would cause trouble for the management of the building because three weeks before he had had a huge argument with them about paying his rent. She wanted me to accompany her downstairs to see. I tried to tell her I was busy but she insisted and I eventually found myself with her outside the launderette. There was no one there, but of course she maintained that the recently deceased tenant had been there just a moment before. I made no further comment about it, but in the lift on the way back to our floor I asked my neighbour what was the best way of dealing with a restless ghost. She told me that ghosts only came "over here" to collect a debt, which happened when they were in need of money for "over there." Dealing with it was simple. One simply had to burn them some joss paper, symbolic money that when burned transformed into currency that could be used by ghosts in the land of the dead, and do it as quickly as possible.

What if, I asked, the debt was not a question of money but of blood? What if the ghost was collecting its emotional dues? She laughed and said I was too immature. Couldn't everything be fixed with money these days? I just had to burn some joss paper and everything would be fine. What if, I went on, the ghost had explicitly said it didn't want money but something else? She replied that you should give whatever it was the ghost wanted. These days you could burn paper versions of anything ghosts might want to use in the afterlife: BMW sports cars, Boeing jets, villas by the sea ... Whatever the ghost needed you could send.

"What if it's not a material thing that the ghost wants?" I asked.

"What do you mean?" my neighbour replied.

"Like truth," I said. "What if what the ghost wants is truth?"

She laughed. "Then make one up! Write it on a piece of paper and burn it! You think ghosts know the difference between what's true and what's not?"

My wife would not let me go, but the reason for this had nothing to do with Celia and Misoka, which was a relief of sorts. I knew the truth that she wanted. It was not something I could just make up like my Taiwanese neighbour suggested. I would have to offer her the truth, the real truth. That was the only thing that could bring her peace, the only way I could bring myself peace.

I decided how to deal with the problem of my wife, and for the rest of the day I was much more relaxed. I still checked my email every hour or so to see if I had received anything from Celia, but I soon got used to the sight of my empty inbox. I was certain that our evening on Mount Royal had been just as much a miracle to Celia as it had been to me, even if she had always seen it coming, even if she had anticipated what would happen between us from the first day we saw one other. Like me she probably needed time to appreciate and process what had happened, to become accustomed to the new stage of our relationship. Misoka's reaction on the ice was also replaying constantly in my mind, but I was beginning to consider it from a more objective perspective. I had come to realize there was both a logical and an emotional connection between her interest in the ruins of the Old Summer Palace and Miyun Reservoir, just as there was between the absent third person she had addressed on the lake and the tears she had shed into her scarf. I was sure that one day Misoka would tell me the story that linked these things together. It was inevitable, a fact of our relationship set in stone from the moment we met.

That night in bed I flicked through the French copy of Victor Hugo's biography I had borrowed from the library the day Misoka had first mentioned her interest in the Old Summer Palace. As I read I was struck by certain numbers that marked moments in his life. "One day, two bandits entered the Old Summer Palace. One plundered, the other burned." Hugo had written his fierce critique of the West's assault on the East on November 25, 1861, some three months before his sixtieth birthday. At an age at which in the modern world people prepared for their retirement, this great poet was still as impassioned and incisive as ever. Did such vigour have anything to do with love? At the time he had penned his attack on the French and the British, the love between Hugo and Juliette Drouet that would span half a century had entered its thirtieth year. One of the many wonders of their relationship was that throughout their long affair they wrote to each other every day. Did his writing play a role in providing him with such an inexhaustible spirit? It was also the year that he finished *Les Misérables*, which he would publish the next year, and thirty years after he had finished writing his first book, *The Hunchback of Notre Dame*. I thought of what Hermit Wang had called the "bigger picture." It seemed that by considering all of these numbers together, one could get a better understanding of Hugo's outrage at the sacking of the Old Summer Palace. His righteous fury came from a position of someone who combined universal values with a genuine humanism.

An enjoyable read and a serene state of mind meant that I slept well that night, and I woke up the next day feeling fully recovered from the emotional storm of the previous few days. On the way up the mountain I found myself singing an old Soviet song from my youth. I was looking forward to seeing Celia. I was looking forward to seeing Misoka. I was not even worried about them both appearing in the pavilion at the same time.

I was disappointed that neither of them was in the pavilion. In fact it was more than disappointment. I was beginning to worry about Celia. More than two days had passed and I had heard no word from her. But I forgot these concerns when I looked out and saw Misoka by the lake, not sitting in her wheelchair but standing beside it! She was facing the sun with her arms extended straight out in front of her. She slowly moved them apart until they were stretched out in both directions, and then she lifted them gradually until they came together above her head, then repeated the sequence. Carrying out these motions against the backdrop of Beaver Lake she looked the picture of health. I approached the window, thrilled to think that her condition might have taken a turn for the better, or that perhaps it was not as severe as I had previously thought. Perhaps it might not be long before she did not need the wheel-chair at all. Maybe then I could take her to the Old Summer Palace and Miyun Reservoir. I cheerfully imagined the various possible futures lying in store for Misoka as I changed into my skates. My plan was to go first to the ice rink to warm up so as not to disturb her as she did her exercises. But out the window I saw that she was no longer standing by her wheelchair, nor was she *in* the wheelchair! I rushed outside and saw her sitting in the snow with her left hand on the wheelchair's armrest. At first I thought this might be another one of her exercises, then I realized what had really happened. Misoka had fallen.

I ran to her as quickly as I could in my skates on the hard-ened ice and saw that her face was pale and covered in sweat. I kneeled down and offered my arm.

"What happened?" I said.

She looked more frail than I had ever seen her as she reached into her coat pocket and passed me a piece of paper. "Call this number," she said. "Tell her to get the driver to come as quickly as possible."

I took the piece of paper and read the number on it. Misoka nodded at me.

"Don't tell her who you are," she said, "and don't tell her what happened."

I hesitated for a moment, not knowing if I should help Misoka into her wheelchair first. Misoka seemed to know what I was thinking.

"Call her now," she said. "I'll be fine here."

I stood up and stumbled back toward the pavilion where there were two public phones. I chose the one outside my usual entrance because from there I had a clear line of sight to Misoka while I made the call. The person on the other end answered in rapid and fluent French. She asked who I was, I murmured, "A friend." Then she asked what had happened, to which I only said what Misoka asked me to say about contacting the driver. She hung up the phone without any comments. I rushed into the pavilion, changed back into my shoes, and ran out to see Misoka.

She was sitting in the same position as before, big beads of sweat rolling down the sides of her face. I bent down and put my hands under her armpits to lift her back into the wheelchair. But her body was completely limp and I found it difficult to bear her weight. It was totally different from how I had imagined it when I dreamt of lifting her onto the bed. I shifted into a better position, which enabled me to lift her and place her back in her wheelchair. As I did so, her lips brushed against my ear.

"Sometimes I lose control over my body," she said. "It will pass in a moment."

I passed her a tissue and waited for her to wipe the sweat from her face. Then I walked beside her as we made our way back to the car park.

"The car will be here any moment," she said. I could tell from her voice that she was beginning to regain her strength.

I gave her back the piece of paper with the phone number on it and asked if she would mind if I gave her my number. I had been meaning to ask her from the first time we discussed the Old Summer Palace but I had never found the right moment. She thought about it before passing the piece of paper back to me. I wrote my home phone number and my email address.

"If you ever need anything, please let me know," I said. As I expected, she did not offer me her own contact details.

Sure enough the car arrived very quickly. After Misoka had been helped into the car, the driver asked in strongly accented French whether I was getting in too. "Of course," Misoka answered for me before I had a chance to respond.

That was the last thing I'd expected and I had no idea how to react. I timidly got into the car next to Misoka, in a space that was even smaller than the room I had shared with her in my dream. Misoka tried to adjust the position of her wheelchair to leave me more space.

"We just came from the great expanse of Mount Royal," I said quietly. "Now we're in a taxi and there's no room even to stretch your legs."

Misoka looked at me and smiled. At that moment I felt closer to her than ever and a joyful sensation flowed through my body.

"How are you feeling?" I asked.

"Much better," she replied, without breaking eye contact.

"Did it just come over you all at once?"

"It happens about once a year. I've gotten used to it."

"Is it related to your mood?"

Misoka knew I was referring to what had happened the previous day and obviously did not want to talk about it. Instead she pointed to my second pair of skates. "You have a daughter," she said.

"How did you know?"

"*She* told me."

I wasn't particularly pleased to be reminded of Misoka's relationship with Celia. I didn't respond.

"She said the reason you keep coming to Mount Royal is to find your daughter."

I let out a humourless laugh. I was hoping she would change the subject.

"I knew of someone in the opposite situation."

"What do you mean?"

"I once knew a daughter who spent her life looking for her father."

The conversation had sapped all the joy I had felt after entering the car. I was sure that the daughter Misoka was talking about was herself, and I could hear the pain in her words. I decided it was time to finish this game of hide-and-seek. I wanted to let her know how much I already knew about her.

"And this girl looks for him not only in her memories but also her imagination," I said.

Misoka must have felt the meaning behind my words but she did not act as if I had said anything out of the ordinary. She continued to look me in the eyes before slowly lifting her head to stare at the ceiling. Then, in a rare moment of candour, she said softly, "She often gets her memory and imagination confused."

Shortly after passing through the Jewish quarter, the taxi came to a stop in a small alley. An old woman was standing perfectly straight at the side of the road. Her features were East Asian and she spoke perfect French. She must have been the person I had spoken to on the phone, I realized. The old woman chatted amicably with the driver as he helped Misoka out of the car, but had a haughty, disapproving attitude when addressing Misoka, and when Misoka introduced her to "a friend of mine," she replied curtly that she had guessed it from the start. The atmosphere was unbearably tense, and I thought it would be best if I did not hang around. I asked the taxi driver where the nearest subway station was, and I said an awkward goodbye and left. I had not walked very far before I heard Misoka and the old woman arguing behind me. I did not know what they could be arguing about and I did not want to turn around to find out. In fact, I started walking even faster.

I spent the rest of the day checking for an email from either Celia or Misoka. Celia's silence was really starting to trouble me and I was desperate to hear some news from her. From Misoka I wanted to know who the old woman was, how she and Misoka were connected, and what it was they'd been arguing about. Unfortunately I received no emails from either of them, so before going to sleep I wrote Celia again, expressing my concern about her whereabouts. I went to bed feeling dispirited and picked up the Hugo biography. I read how Hugo had written in a love letter to Juliette Drouet that he had two birthdays: the first was the day his mother had given birth to him, and the second was the day he had met her. The first brought him "light," the second "passion." I knew that for Hugo, both of these were indispensable. Without them he could never have written *Les Misérables*, nor his fiery account of the two bandits who entered the Old Summer Palace.

That night I had a strange dream. I dreamt of a huge fire that reached into the sky. In the racket I heard voices speaking French and English, just as I often do in Montreal, but I knew this was not the site of my life as an immigrant in French-speaking Canada. It was the Old Summer Palace in flames. It was history, history in the guise of a nightmare, and the figures of bandits were darting in and out of the blaze. Then I saw my wife. She was running toward me, completely naked, from a distance. With each step she took I could make her out more clearly, and as she approached the fury in her eyes grew. She ran to the Big Fountains site and stood on the domed roof, which in the frenzy had just fallen to the ground. "I want to know the truth! I want to know the truth! I want to know the truth!" she yelled at the top of her lungs.

Once again I found myself sitting in bed covered in sweat. I had not fully adjusted to being awake but I already knew there was no more time for delay. I got out of bed, walked uneasily to my desk, and began to write the truth my wife wanted.

∞ Celia

I SAW NEITHER Celia nor Misoka for the next three days, nor did either of them contact me in that time. I did not feel there was much to worry about with Misoka. Although she had collapsed in the snow, she had told me she was feeling much better and I had even seen her home. There was, of course, the unsettling argument that had ensued between her and the old woman, but it did not concern me nearly as much as the question of what had happened to Celia. I had heard nothing of her since our passionate midnight encounter. The locker with her skates remained locked and her skis were still in the hollow of the elm tree, signs that she intended to return, so why had she not appeared? Somehow I was sure she had made it home safely that night. There must have been another reason for her absence. One possibility, which occurred to me the first time I disappointedly turned off my computer after seeing she had not sent me an email, was that I would never see her again. Perhaps that evening's romantic encounter was not really romantic, but merely her way of saying goodbye. But why would she want to do that? Yet again, it was her silence that confounded me more than anything, just like the first time we spoke and she refused to answer my question about China. This time, however, the silence was more remorseless than ever. This time I could not even see her.

The next afternoon I sent Celia two more emails. I made a point not to mention how worried I was about her, choosing instead to write as if nothing had changed. I asked her about one of Shakespeare's sonnets, number 71, which I chose pretty much at random. However, when I saw how this sonnet about death was directly related to our situation. I realized that my choice was not as random as it seemed. In each email I asked a different question. In the first I asked why Shakespeare was so magnanimous in the face of death yet so exacting toward love. In the second email I asked why Shakespeare described the world as "vile" in the fourth line (such that he seemed not too upset to be leaving it), yet in the thirteenth line described it as "wise"? Was this kind of contradiction evidence of what Celia had once said was the "savage" quality of his sonnets? I spent the day imagining how Celia might respond to these questions and continually went back to the computer to see if she had replied. That evening I wrote a fourth email, asking if she had received the previous three and whether something was wrong. I finished by telling her that I was anxious to hear from her, to know how she was doing, and saying that I wanted to see her again.

The next day as I was skating on Beaver Lake I was struck by a strange notion. Celia and Misoka were both nowhere to be seen and up until now I had always assumed their absences to be unrelated. Was it possible that their both being elsewhere meant they were together? I started to think that maybe they were in Celia's cabin at the ski resort. It was a painful thought. It had been two months since these two women had simultaneously appeared in my life and now they had simultaneously disappeared. The idea of them vanishing from my world was difficult enough to bear, let alone the idea that it was something they had done together. I did not want to think about it. I did not want to think about them in the scene of my dream, leaning back to back in Celia's cabin next to the stove, speaking of the daughter in search of a father and the father in search of a daughter. It was the last thing I wanted to think about, but I couldn't help myself. I thought about them sharing their lives' secrets, satisfying their curiosity about one another; I thought about the unspoken bond that was forming between them, the intimacy they shared. I saw the steam rising from the hot shower as they washed. I felt the blanket over their bodies as they lay in bed. I heard them at night whispering to one another, the sound of their breathing.... It was intolerable! I cursed my imagination that knew no bounds, that left no stone unturned. The only thing off limits to the world my mind had created was the lonely wolf. I so wanted her face to appear at the window half-obscured by snow, to smash it with her fist — or perhaps her paw? — to let out a solitary howl ...

I wasted no time in getting off the ice, changing into my shoes, and leaving the pavilion. I trudged down the mountain feeling the weight in my feet. With each step my anguish deepened until it had utterly inundated everything else. A terrifying phrase appeared in my mind: "The End." Maybe my most unusual of winters had come to an end. Maybe it had finished, just like that, unannounced, just as it had begun.

My mind was all over the place. I knew I had to smother my unruly imagination if I was to escape this cycle of terror and despair, if I was to return to a normal state of mind. First of all, I would not check my email when I got home. This was crucial. Then I would have to stop thinking about Celia and Misoka, and make an effort to focus my attention on something else. Perhaps I could finish reading Hugo's biography or I could finally get around to cleaning the kitchen, something I had been putting off for a while. Most important of all, I had to complete the truth I still hadn't finished writing. In the previous few days my wife had appeared in my dreams every night. I could not put it off any longer.

I had just picked up the piece of paper on which I had begun writing "the truth" when the phone rang. My first thought was of Misoka so when I picked up the phone I was a little flustered. I soon calmed down, however, when I heard the voice on the other end. It was my classmate who was trying to emigrate to Canada. I had not heard from him since he had made me speak to his wife, and I assumed that he would be calling to share the news of his coming move. But things had not turned out as planned. He told me that after their immigration application had been accepted his wife had completely broken down. Their every encounter would end with his wife shouting at him, telling him that his insistence on emigrating was proof that he did not care about her anymore. It was no longer a question of whether or not to move to Canada. His wife now wanted a divorce. My classmate had tried to resist but in the end he agreed when he saw that the situation was threatening his own psychological state. He was calling to tell me the divorce had just been finalized. I wanted to know how this would affect his emigrating. He replied that his life had been hollowed out by the breakup and he no longer had any interest in it. I said that it might not be such a bad idea to "stay put." He seemed pleased by this vindication of his decision and told me that he now thought that life was the same no matter where you lived. He would pick a pretty young girl in China to spend the rest of his life and money with. I said that maybe it was for the best.

My classmate had succeeded in tearing my mind away from the two mysterious women, now missing. I hung up and reflected on the conversation. There was something almost absurd about it, but it also struck me how timely the phone call had been. I had never ended a call with him and felt better than I had when it started. I picked up the piece of paper from the desk in front of me and started reading through what I had written. I quickly saw that this was not the truth I wanted to tell. First of all, it was too detailed, full of information I did not think my wife wanted. Second, it was not objective enough. Certain parts read like a confession, and in others I seemed to be trying to justify myself. I realized that I would have to start over, to find another way of disclosing my truth. Once again I felt that familiar lack of confidence in my skills as a writer. This time, however, I had no choice but to continue. I wrote for an hour and a half before having dinner and then, after a brief post-prandial walk, I wrote until I was almost falling asleep at the desk. In terms of content, I still had not gotten as far as my previous draft but I was much happier with the way I had written it. This was what was important, I told myself, no matter how much time it took.

As I lay in bed I thought about how all truth was either written or spoken, how different modes of expression revealed different truths. It reminded me of how Eric had told me there was no definitive judgment on the truth of history. Ever since I had begun trying to write I had been aware of a certain uncertainty, a lack of bearings, which made me feel that a huge gulf existed between what I experienced and how I wrote about it. The more I wrote the more it seemed to me that what I had written was not what had happened, or perhaps that what had happened was concealed by the words I had used to describe it. Perhaps this was similar to what Misoka meant when she said she often got her memory and imagination confused.

The next morning I was able to resist checking my emails before leaving the apartment. I had not felt so carefree for days, and on the way up the mountain I thought back to what my mother used to say about "wanting" and "getting." The more you wanted something, she would say, the less likely you were to get it. If there was any truth to this old cliché, I thought, it was all the more reason not to get hung up on Celia and Misoka. Not only would it improve my frame of mind, it might even make it more likely that I see them again.

The adage was proven right just as I was about to finish skating. Misoka had appeared by the side of the lake, and I eagerly skated over to her. As I got closer I saw that not only was she not excited to see me but she looked completely forlorn. A sense of foreboding came over me.

"Where have you been?" I asked.

Misoka must have noticed that I had used the French second-person plural "vous" and she looked at me nervously.

"Where have you been?" I repeated.

She did not immediately respond. She turned her eyes away from me and looked into the depths of the woods. "She won't be coming back," she said quietly, as if she were talking to herself.

She was clearly talking about Celia, but I did not know what she meant. "How do you know?" I asked.

"From the look in her eyes and the sound in her voice."

I still did not understand. I had noticed nothing unusual in Celia that midnight on Mount Royal. "What do you mean?" I asked.

"I know that look and that voice too well," Misoka said. "They were not hers. They were the look and voice of the dead."

"In what way?" I asked.

Misoka turned and looked at me again, hesitating slightly as to whether she ought to go on. "My mother ... that was the look and the voice of my mother ... at the very end."

I shivered. "I'm sorry," I said guiltily.

Misoka continued to look at me as she spoke. "I really want to help her. But —" she paused "— it's already too late."

I was annoyed that Misoka had not answered my question about where she had been over the past few days, but that's not what was on my mind as I made my way home. I was scared about what was going on with Celia. I didn't believe Misoka, or at least I didn't want to believe her. Things could not be as serious as she made out, and in any case I felt there must have been something we could do to help. When I got home I wrote Celia three emails again, one after the other. In the first email I asked how she was doing and shared with her two Jewish jokes about old men. In the second, I asked if she was free next week to see a widely acclaimed German film. In the third and final email I told her that I hoped that once we had finished with the sonnets she would read *Hamlet* with me. Inspired by the sonnets, I wrote, I had read it through once already and had many questions I wanted her help with. For example, was it possible that Hamlet was gay? Did she think that Ophelia could be related in any way to Shakespeare's Dark Lady?

In the two days that followed I did not receive a reply. I saw Misoka both days and each time I asked her if she had any news from Celia. Misoka, on the other hand, never asked me the same question; she had clearly concluded that I would not have heard anything. Misoka was a shadow of her former self. The notebook lay on her lap as always but she could no longer be seen feverishly writing. She also seemed to have lost all enthusiasm for our conversations. Outside of Celia we had nothing to talk about.

"Perhaps she's no longer with us."

This is what Misoka said when we parted ways that day and it filled me with dread. If it was true there would be no way for us to find out. We knew none of Celia's other acquaintances. We didn't even know where she lived. Apart from an email address we had no way of contacting her. I refused to entertain such a desperate notion.

"Impossible," I said. "Utterly impossible."

There was a certain distrust in Misoka's eyes as she looked at me then, as though there had never been any sincerity between us.

That night when I turned on my computer I was stunned to find an email from Celia waiting for me. It had arrived only moments earlier and was empty except for an attachment. My heart raced as I opened it and saw the long letter Celia had written:

I don't know if you remember, the first time we spoke you asked me if I had been to China, an ordinary question for most people perhaps, a simple question with only two possible answers. But I didn't answer. I remember how confused you looked at the time. I can tell you now, I didn't answer because I did not know how. If I had said no, it would have been in conflict with what I knew to be true. If I had said yes, it would have been in conflict with how I felt. Perhaps what I should have said is "If only I hadn't." That's maybe how I would have answered if I were speaking with someone I knew well. The next time it was me who asked you a question. On the ice rink I asked where you were from in China. You could probably tell how afraid I was at the time. How you answered could affect everything, the very substance and significance of this remarkable winter. I am not well. You probably guessed long ago. But I doubt you could imagine how severe my condition is. I have to scrupulously monitor everything that happens around me. What most people would consider the most insignificant details — a gesture, a colour — can push me over the edge. I don't know how many times I have suffered such a collapse over the years. I cannot drop my guard. It is a matter of self-defence.

I told you before, this has been the most remarkable winter of my life. However, it has also been the most painful, both psychologically and physically. I know the reason for this is you and her, how the three of us came to meet this winter, how our meeting rendered ineffectual the spiritual defences I have been erecting all these years and brought me face to face with the abyss of my memory and imagination. Did this happen by chance or was it determined from the start? The old question that used to haunt me has returned and I am still unable to answer it. She once described us as three "insignificant grains of sand" brought together by "the winds of this globalized age." I like this expression, though it does little to clear my confusion. The age implies determination; our insignificance implies chance. Either way, I am sure that were it not for the curious encounter between the three of us, I would never have written what I am about to write here.

Yes, I have been to China. It was the last time I travelled abroad. That night on Mount Royal I spoke to you of my darkest memories, those at the very core of my being. I am their prisoner. They are my death sentence. I already told you about my memory of my father. Now I am going to share with you the second of my darkest memories, my trip to China, from which I never truly returned.

I think I told you that I have never had a proper job. That's because I met the man who would become my husband (the man I now call my ex-husband) while I was a Ph.D. student. He had just graduated from medical school and was working at the Royal Victoria Hospital in Montreal. He had a good stable job, was very good-looking, and committed to a loving relationship — the ideal husband. We got married the day after I completed my thesis defence. He did not want me to work. He preferred that I stay at home, and I was happy to oblige. I spent twenty years as a housewife, though perhaps not the standard picture of a housewife in many people's eyes, because there were no children in the house I looked after. My husband was obsessed with Jean-Paul Sartre and like his idol he did not want to have kids. He said that children would get in the way of our love. He told me that he himself was a child and needed my undivided attention. I did not want children either but for different reasons. My own childhood formed the backdrop to the darkest of my memories and I did not believe I had what was required to bring a child happiness. Our decision not to have children did in fact make us freer to appreciate one other. For twenty years we enjoyed a tranquil and fulfilling marriage.

My husband did not like change. He kept the same job for twenty years and we stayed in the same house. His resistance to change was no doubt the main reason he didn't want to work in China, but it was also true that he had no real interest in the country. So when he heard that the hospital was planning to send him to China for two and a half months to lead a teaching course there, he spent the better half of a week moping around looking depressed. During this time he did, in fact, resemble a child, and like a mother trying to allay a child's fear of school I spent my time trying to get him interested in China. Every other day I went to Chinatown and brought back food from different areas of China to try; I bought a map of China and stuck it up in our living room so he could see for himself where each of these cuisines came from; I borrowed a bunch of films about China from the library so we could watch them together. I even used his idol as a means of winning him over — I told him how Sartre had gone to China in the fifties and witnessed the National Day celebrations at Tiananmen Square, how toward the end of his life Sartre had praised China's Cultural Revolution, applauding its role as a means for the masses to challenge authority.... In retrospect it's a cruel irony that I was the one encouraging him to embrace China.

We arrived in Shanghai toward the end of summer, which we had heard was the best time of year to visit. The hotel we were staying in was designed in a European style and was about *five kilometres from the hospital where my husband would be teaching. Our every need was attended to. A car was arranged to pick my husband up from the hotel each day and he had his own room at the hospital where he could work and rest at any time between sessions. On the first two days, my husband asked me to go with him to the hospital. On the third day I accompanied him without his prompting. On the way, however, I realized that I was no longer needed. He had completely adapted to his new environment and was getting on well with the assistant he had been assigned and whom he described as "very capable." That evening, as I foresaw, he told me that I did not need to accompany him to the hospital anymore. He even suggested I buy a bicycle so I could enjoy the city while he was at work. He promised that one weekend we could visit some of the sights near Shanghai, like the canal towns of Zhouzhuang and Wuzhen.*

Before long I had fallen in love with Shanghai. I kept making new discoveries, discoveries I knew my husband would like, and I kept a list of places to take him to see on the weekends. But after two such trips my husband began to lose interest in these outings. He said there were too many people and cars, and on top of that the air was terrible. He preferred to stay at the hotel and rest. However, at the hotel he was unable to relax. He seemed a completely different person, unable to sit still, his mind always wandering. I found it a little strange but didn't think too much of it at the time. Soon things got stranger still. He started to come home late. When we were together he barely talked to me and when he did he could not maintain eye contact. There were two nights he even refused to sleep in the bed. He told me he found it more comfortable on the sofa. That Saturday when he woke up he went straight to the hospital. He said he had students' homework to grade.

The following Saturday he told me again that he would have to go to the hospital. I asked him when he'd be back and he said it would be the same as last week, when he had not returned until 9:00 p.m. I didn't say anything, but around noon an uneasy feeling began to take hold of me. I decided to go to the hospital to see the man who was becoming a stranger to me. I wanted to ask what had happened in these preceding weeks to cause such a dramamtic change in him. The security guard who was always sitting with an English-language textbook called Family Album U.S.A. greeted me at the entrance. Using the phrase he had just learned, he asked me, "What are you doing here?" I told him I was here to see my husband. He told me that my husband was not there because it was a Saturday. I said that my husband had come the previous Saturday too. He shook his head. He was there all day on Saturday. If my husband had come he would have seen him.

That's when I realized that a word that is so important in Shakespeare's plays had become part of my reality: "betrayal." I decided not to say anything, which is to say I decided to deceive my husband, not to let him know that I knew he was deceiving me. I wanted to know how long he could endure his duplicity, our duplicity.

I never asked him about his promise to take me to the sights near Shanghai and he didn't speak of it again either. I also made no mention of our plans to use the week-long national holiday to travel to Beijing and Xi'an. With only three days to go before the holiday he finally brought it up, but only to suggest that I make the trip alone. He would arrange the flights and hotels. All I had to do was pack a suitcase and go see the sights. He simply had too much work to do, he told me, and would not be able to leave the city. Of course this was another lie. It was for his own benefit that he offered to organize the trip for me, to make himself feel less guilty or to clear the space for himself in Shanghai to pursue his other "interests." I politely declined his "thoughtful" offer. After all, every day was a holiday for me. There was no need to go out of our way to organize a special trip.

We spent our final month in China in a state of mutual deception. He came up with all manner of excuses not to spend time with me and I pretended to believe them, putting on a show of a loving wife's reluctant acceptance of her husband's busy work schedule. I found it difficult to maintain the facade and there were multiple times I was almost overcome by the urge to look him in the eyes and ask, "Who is she?" On two occasions I was on the brink of booking a flight home on my own. However, each time I lost my resolve. Perhaps I was taking it too seriously, I told myself. I pictured our life on our return to Montreal, our shared little world of twenty years, when everything would get back to normal.

So in the end we went back to Montreal together, even if something separated us as we sat shoulder to shoulder on the flight back. An incident on the flight awoke me to the almost laughable contrast between the journeys to and from China. On the flight there my husband had complained non-stop to his neighbour about China, how the food was too oily, too salty, how the people were too materialistic and cared only about money and status. Yet on the flight to Canada when my husband spoke to the person next to him of his trip, he had nothing but praise for the country he had previously scorned, even saying he found the noise and crowds charming. It was unsettling to find that for each of the two flights, there was a different man sitting next to me, each with completely contrary *appraisals of China. I knew the former man so well; the latter was a stranger to me.*

My husband did not return to normal when we got back to Montreal. If anything, he only seemed more uncomfortable in his own skin, more irritable and restless. My illusions of a return to our shared little world were shattered. I should never have played into his deception. Just as I was thinking about how best to drop the facade and come clean to my husband, a moment of negligence on his part caused his facade to fall away. He had always been a very attentive person but recently he had been having more and more moments of negligence, like the time he left his debit card on the counter at the bank, or the time he forgot to turn off the stove before leaving the house. I had already made the decision to confront him that evening when I saw his digital camera. He normally took it with him everywhere but that morning I saw it on his desk as I was doing the household chores. I picked it up and turned it on. I was hoping to see pictures of us on the Bund on our first night in Shanghai. That's when I saw the picture; it made me sick to my stomach. I was not at all surprised to see who it was with my husband. I had had an uneasy feeling from the very first moment my husband mentioned his assistant and how "capable" she was, a feeling that remained with me until our last day in China when she was the only colleague who didn't come see us off at the airport. What shocked me was the photo they had taken together. My husband was the kind of man who would blush when speaking with a stranger. How could he take such a disgusting photo?

I stared for about two minutes before turning it off. I had no interest in knowing the truth, certainly not that kind of truth. I put the camera back on the desk and returned to the living room just as the front door opened and my husband walked in. He was in a panic, turning his head this way and that, evidently looking for the object he ought not to have forgotten.

"It's on your desk," I said calmly.

His face turned white. He did not go to fetch his camera but sat down at the dining-room table, his head drooping like a rag doll's. He stayed that way some time before raising his head and looking at me pathetically.

"Yes," he said. "I don't love you anymore."

"Do you love her?"

He could tell that this was a trap, that I would use it to attack what he had once described as his commitment to love, so he hesitated before answering. "Of course," he said reluctantly.

"The way you used to love me?"

"Don't draw comparisons."

I wanted to keep my cool, but I couldn't. All the rage that had been building inside me for over two months exploded. "So was it because you stopped loving me that you fell in love with her or was it because you fell in love with her that you stopped loving me?" I yelled.

He just looked at me and said nothing.

I immediately regretted my outburst. Why was I getting worked up about such a boring question? It was undignified. You might find it hard to believe: what came into my head at that moment was Shakespeare's sonnets. I thought I knew all there was to know about them, but until that moment I hadn't truly felt why love had filled Shakespeare with such despair. I no longer had any interest in getting drawn into a discussion about such a boring, meaningless question with the man who had been my lover for twenty years. Love seemed to me no more than a flowery and vapid word people stuck on their basest

instincts. Its ingredients always included betrayal and decep-
tion. The death of my father had forever darkened my world
and now my despair in the face of love had cast it in an even
deeper shadow.

That was how our twenty-year-long marriage ended. From
a loyal housewife I was transformed into a single woman with
nothing but contempt for the fraud of domestic life. My life of
leisure left me with neither the desire nor the ability to take on
a nine-to-five job. Fortunately the events that came to form my
two darkest memories have left me with enough not to have to
worry about money. I work as a freelancer, which means I can
take on little jobs when I feel like it. The greatest asset I inher-
ited from my father was his talent for art, and over the last
few years what I have enjoyed doing more than anything else
is drawing and illustrating. However, neither "single woman"
nor "freelancer" is sufficient to describe how I feel. What the
end of my marriage brought me more than anything else is
suffering. I am not well. I am a "sufferer." This, more than any
other identity, best describes me today. I spend my time scru-
pulously monitoring everything that happens around me. It is
exhausting. I do not know how much longer I can keep it up.

Shortly afterward my husband moved to China and we
lost contact. I was not even remotely curious about how he
was getting on. It was important for my own health to stifle
my memories and restrain my imagination. However, last fall
I bumped into his mother at Place des Arts and she recognized
me immediately. Out of nowhere she started complaining
about her son, as if I had anything to do with him anymore,
as if I were still her daughter-in-law. She said she had no idea
what it was about China that he loved so much but he had
gone completely native. Naturally he had married the woman

he loved; what I did not expect to hear was that they had had three children. When we were together this man had refused to have children because of our love. Now he has three kids and I'm sure that this time it was also love that informed his decision. I turned away and left in the middle of his mother's diatribe. I had no time for her idle racket. I have no time for these idiots' stories.

My vision grew blurry and I cupped my face in my hands. Should I reply? Should I reply right away? What should I say? The many scenes of Celia and me that winter flashed through my mind, the countless occasions when her behaviour had left me completely perplexed: from the first day when she acted as if she hadn't even noticed my presence, to our passionate encounter at midnight on Mount Royal — and then the silence that had followed, a silence that now seemed a premonition of death.... No, I refused to accept Misoka's assessment. At least this email was proof that Misoka was not right. Celia was still with us, still enduring the melancholy of all she had lost. I lifted my face from my hands and saw that it was almost eleven, the same time I had last met her on the mountain. Had Celia chosen this time on purpose? Was this email in which she shared with me the second of her "darkest of memories" in fact another tacit invitation? As soon as the thought occurred to me I stood up, put on my coat, and walked out of the building into the bitterest wind of that winter.

Celia was not standing by Beaver Lake as I had hoped. I walked to the lakeside anyway and stood at the spot where we had last met, the merciless wind whipping fragments of ice into my face. That's when I heard someone calling my name. I couldn't tell if it was Celia's voice, but it was definitely coming from the direction of her favourite old elm tree. I ran over as fast as I could. There was no one there. I reached into Celia's natural locker in the hollow of the tree and felt a curdling sensation in my stomach. It was empty.

When I got home, I fought my fatigue and gloom to read Celia's email again for a second and then a third time. The line that stuck with me was "It is exhausting. I don't know how much longer I can keep it up." Did this mean that Misoka was right? I felt myself beginning to panic. I had to do something for Celia. There had to be something I could do. I decided to reply. It was very short and I did not talk about her "darkest of memories." I simply asked when she was next coming to Mount Royal, adding that Misoka and I both missed her.

I checked my email the next morning before leaving the apartment. I was not surprised to see that Celia had not responded. When I reached the pavilion, I made a point to take a look at the locker she kept her skates in and found that it was empty, which I had also anticipated. Then I checked the old elm tree again; the results were the same as the previous night. I felt completely hollowed out as I walked over to Misoka, who was sitting by the lake.

"She's still alive," I told her, as if settling a score.

Misoka looked at me skeptically.

"Last night she sent me an email," I said.

"And that's proof she's alive now?" Misoka said, emphasizing the "now" as if to provoke me.

Misoka's intransigence was infuriating. I had no inclination to share with her my discoveries about the locker and the elm tree.

"I can imagine what she wrote in the email," Misoka went on.

I did not believe her but her claim still made me nervous.

"She will have told you about the blow she suffered," Misoka said. "The lethal blow."

"How did you —" I stammered. "How could you imagine something like that?"

"Because I know what that email was."

"What?"

"A suicide note. It was her suicide note."

The bluntness of her words was like a blow to the chest and I walked away feeling utterly miserable. I decided I would not talk to Misoka about Celia again. I could not stand her lack of hope, how stubborn she was. But it was too late; she had already infected me with her hopelessness. I could not get into the mood for skating. I wanted to go home and check my email, even though I had lost any conviction I might have had that there would be a message from Celia waiting for me.

I avoided Misoka for the next three days. I did not want to let her know that Celia hadn't written again. I also did not want to hear any more of her opinions about Celia. This situation would probably have continued indefinitely were it not for my nightmare. In it, I was back at the Old Summer Palace. It was once again in flames, but this time Celia was there. She walked toward my wife, who was yelling by the Big Fountains, looked her in the eye, and said, "Why do you want to know the truth? The truth only brings memories, fatal memories." My wife stared indifferently for a moment, before returning to her usual refrain: "I want the truth! I want the truth! I want the truth ..."

Seeing my wife's scorn for her counsel Celia turned and walked away. I greedily watched the outline of her body as it disappeared into the flames. In contrast, on the first day I had seen her it was into the snowscape of Mount Royal that she disappeared. From ice to fire, from reality to dream ... Celia, is this the story of our encounter?

I lay in bed, reluctant to open my eyes. I could feel my ear against the pillow, wet with tears. A part of me was starting to believe Misoka.

∞ Misoka

THE MORNING AFTER my nightmare I jogged up the path that snaked up the mountain, keeping a steady pace past the pavilion and to Beaver Lake where Misoka was sitting in her wheelchair. I wanted to tell her about my dream, to hear what she had to say about it. To my astonishment, she started speaking before I could catch my breath.

"I dreamed of her last night," she said.

The latest of this winter's uncanny coincidences did not fail to unnerve me.

"It's the first time I've dreamt of her," Misoka went on.

"Where was she?" I asked, wondering just how similar our dreams were.

"The Old Summer Palace."

I stifled a gasp. "Who was she with?" I asked.

"She was on her own," Misoka said. "Sitting on the rock by the Big Fountains, just like you used to do."

I felt strangely relieved to discover our dreams were not exactly the same. But we had both dreamt of Celia, and we had both dreamt of her by the Big Fountains of the Old Summer Palace. The extent of the similarity was still bizarre. I considered it for a moment and decided I would not tell Misoka about my dream. "That's strange," I told her. "She has never been to the Old Summer Palace."

"How do you know?" Misoka asked.

"She told me in her suicide note."

There was a knowing look in Misoka's eye. She clearly thought I had come to accept her suicide note theory.

"She said she never made it to Beijing," I said. "If she had, maybe this unusual winter would never have happened."

With that, I started walking away.

"Why are you avoiding me?" Misoka asked.

I stopped and turned around to face her, not knowing, however, how to respond.

"Is it because of her? Because of what I said about her?" Misoka asked. "That's just what I think. I know you're upset. I am too. I am really upset."

"Let's not talk about her anymore," I said. A silence followed. "You were right. We are just three insignificant grains of sand, destined in the end to be blown apart by the winds …"

"Was that in the suicide note too?" Misoka interrupted me, clearly disquieted to hear her words repeated back to her.

"Yes," I nodded. "I had a premonition that this winter was coming to a premature end in the few days you disappeared together."

A flash of sorrow appeared on Misoka's face. "I'll be moving away soon," she said. She told me she would be returning to her home on the South Shore. The apartment near here had been rented so that she would be able to go up Mount Royal every morning, which was part of her treatment. However, the people she lived with no longer approved of her coming to the mountain. "They are very sensitive," she added.

I was sure she must be talking about the old woman so I did not know why she said "they." Could the fact the old woman "no longer approved" of her visits to Mount Royal have anything to do with the argument between them on the street? I walked back toward Misoka. Again, I was tired of playing hide-and-seek. "That day you had an argument," I said.

"Yes," Misoka said. "That was when it first came up — us moving back."

"Who is she?"

Misoka did not answer.

"Who is she?" I repeated.

"They're very particular about who I meet. They say that everything they do is for my benefit."

Misoka had still not answered my question but I did not feel I could ask a third time. I looked at her, thinking this might be the last time I saw her. If I left at that moment she might disappear from my life forever, just as Celia had done, when there was still so much I wanted to understand about who she was, where she came from, what she was writing. Celia had said that it was up to Misoka to tell me and that she was sure Misoka would do so in her own time, in her own way. I had always been skeptical, now I was even less sure that I would ever hear Misoka's story. We were running out of time. If I left now I might be leaving behind my last chance.

Little did I know that this was the moment Misoka had been waiting for. She sat motionless, staring at me as if considering her options. I looked back at her and from the change in her eyes I saw that she had decided.

"The first day we met, you asked me about the story I was writing," Misoka began. "It's not because I didn't trust you that I didn't tell you. It's more that I didn't trust myself. I was struggling with two questions at the time: why I was writing and whom I was writing for. I've always had a rather extreme view about writing. Every piece must exist for one reason and one reason alone. Similarly it must be written for one reader and one reader alone. I now know the answer to both of these questions, so I can tell you about the story." She paused before going on. "I am writing a classical love story and the narrator is a Japanese-Chinese woman. She is based on a classmate I had at the Paris Academy of Fine Arts, my best friend. There are many gaps in the story of her past. She was born and grew up in Paris. She has not been to either of her homelands and can speak neither Japanese nor Chinese. She has never seen her father and he has never seen her. Her family consists of three women of three generations: her grandmother, her mother, and her. Her grandmother and mother were both formidable women who kept a watchful eye over all aspects of her life. Her mother could speak fluent Chinese but never did. She didn't even like to bring up anything related to China and was wary of her daughter developing an interest in the country." Misoka stopped for a moment. Perhaps she'd noticed the irritated look on my face. She sighed and went on. "In our last year of university, my friend fell in love with a student from mainland China. When her mother found out she was furious. Not only did she force the daughter to drop out of school, but she wouldn't let her out of the house for more than a month. I was the only person who was allowed to see her in that time, and I would go to their house every other day. On my third visit my friend could not stop complaining about her mother and was even thinking about running away from home. The fourth time I went to see her, however, her attitude had completely changed. She told me that since finding out the truth of her mother's past she had not only forgiven her but was filled with a newfound admiration for her. From that day on, every time I went to visit, we spoke about what had happened to her mother, the people with whom she had met and from whom she had parted ways. It is a story entangled with history and on many occasions I was brought to tears. The classical love story I am writing is based on the life of that friend's mother."

I was unable to hide my frustration that Misoka was still playing games with me. I knew enough now. "I know what happened to this friend of yours," I said.

For a moment, a vulnerable look appeared in Misoka's eyes, but she quickly regained her composure and sat waiting for me to go on.

"There was an accident," I said. "She damaged her spinal column and now she's in a wheelchair."

Misoka did not move for a few seconds. Then she rotated her wheelchair and began to leave. She did not get very far before stopping. "You're wrong," she said, turning her head to look at me. "She's dead. She jumped into the Seine. Just like Paul Celan."

I had no idea if I was really wrong or if she was making up stories again. I stood motionless, not knowing what to say.

At that moment, Misoka said something that surprised me: "And just like her father." Then she abruptly turned her wheelchair around and left.

This last comment seemed to hang in the air for some time. The memory of her strange reaction to our conversation about Miyun Reservoir came back to me and suddenly everything seemed to become clear. A part of Misoka's past had revealed itself to me, or at least so I believed. Unfortunately it was a revelation that brought me nothing but sorrow.

The sorrow remained with me all morning. I regretted having let my frustration get the better of me and interrupting Misoka when she was simply telling me about what she was writing. On the other hand, I was sure that what she had said before she left was evidence that she was keen to keep talking. My suspicions were confirmed when, just as I was making lunch, I got a phone call from her. It was the only time Misoka had used the phone number I had given her the day she collapsed in the snow. She was on her own at Windsor Station, she said, and asked if I would like to meet her there. Windsor Station is an old train station that is no longer in use, but the interior is well preserved and it is open to visitors. With only four benches remaining in its expansive waiting room, it must be one of the quietest public spaces in the city. I had walked past the old station only twice during my time in Montreal and each time I looked in it had been utterly empty.

"What are you doing there by yourself?" I asked.

"Come and find out," Misoka replied.

I left my half-made lunch on the counter and headed straight out, but it still took me thirty minutes to get there. Misoka, the only person in the waiting room, was sitting on one of the long benches. She had placed a tablecloth over her wheelchair beside her, and on it were various neatly arranged snacks and some disposable cutlery.

"I'm preparing a little celebration," she said proudly as she motioned me to sit on the bench.

I tentatively sat down. "What are you celebrating?"

"The birth of a myth."

"What myth?"

She leaned over and retrieved a notebook from the pouch under the seat of her wheelchair.

"You've finished?" I asked.

She ran her fingers over the surface of the notebook. "Late last night," she said.

"Congratulations," I said, realizing how extraordinary her previous night must have been. On the same night that she finished her "myth" she had dreamed of Celia. It was also probably when she had made her decision about how she would say goodbye to me, how she would reveal to me the story of her life — an evening of tying up the loose ends of this winter.

"I need to thank you," she said. "Without you I wouldn't have been able to write it. We created this myth together."

"You should thank Mount Royal," I said, "and this unusual winter."

"Yes," she said. "This winter is a myth of its own. Ever since it began, I have had a strange feeling about how it would unfold, who I would meet, and how it would end."

That was when I noticed how red and swollen her eyes were. "What happened?" I asked.

She sighed and said, "Oh that's from this morning, when we parted ways, some things that shouldn't have been said."

Clearly our conversation earlier had touched on painful aspects of her past, and I did not want the same topics to mar the afternoon celebration. I told her to put the notebook on the tablecloth and after pouring two drinks we raised our glasses to the birth of the myth.

The rest of our afternoon was a delight, and the conversation between us flowed in a way it had not done before. Misoka told me that she had chosen to celebrate in Windsor Station because this was where the myth had begun. The old train station played a prominent role in her classical love story: it was a sort of "Garden of Eden" for the male and female protagonists, and also the starting point for the narrator's imagination and memory. She then said she had made the salads and sandwiches for the celebratory meal herself. "I love cooking," she said shyly. "Were it not for my accident I would have made an excellent housewife." She also told me that she had grown up surrounded by women who monitored everything she did very closely; this was the "unique" time she had ever eaten alone with a man ... and so the conversation continued. It was a joy to be with Misoka as she chatted so freely and happily.

After the celebration we went to the subway station together. I accompanied her to her platform, where she reached into the pouch under the seat of her wheelchair and pulled out an envelope. "I photocopied some bits I thought you might find interesting," she said. "It's only the first draft of course, so I'll definitely be changing it in places." She hesitated for a moment before holding out the envelope to me. "Would you like to have a look?" she asked tentatively. "When you have time of course."

I enthusiastically took the envelope from her. "Of course," I said. "I've been dying to read what you've written." The scene of her refusing my first inquiries into her writing reappeared in my mind. It had taken the whole winter but I felt as if Misoka was finally opening up to me.

"My story's for you," she said. "You are the reader I wrote it for."

I remembered what she said about writing that morning. I was touched to know that the "one reader and one reader alone" of her book was me.

This was when Misoka tore off a piece of the newspaper I had picked up at the entrance to the subway station and wrote the kanji characters of her name and its romanized spelling. Following me, she pronounced her own name in Mandarin before pointing to the character for "Mi" and saying, "That's the same 'Mi' as the one in Miyun Reservoir." This was the last thing she said to me before turning away to get on the train that had just arrived at the platform.

I stood and watched until the lights of her train had disappeared into the black of the tunnel. My own train was quick to arrive on the opposite platform and when I got in there was barely anyone in the carriage. After taking a seat I tore open the envelope, removed the manuscript within, and turned over the cover page to reveal the photocopies of Misoka's story.

On the morning of my twenty-sixth birthday my mother came into my room and told me she had a special present to give me. Sitting on the edge of my bed, she handed me a red scarf and an old photograph. She pointed to the man in swimming trunks in the photo and said, "This is your father."

It was the first time I had seen my father. He was completely different from the father who often appeared in my dreams. The man in the photograph was far warmer, closer. As soon as I saw him I knew he was my father.

"You two couldn't be more different," my mother joked, "you so dark and ugly," and in the joking tone of her voice

I could hear the sincere love she had for both me and my father.

My father and I share a birthday. I was a premature baby, born two weeks early. My mother used to say that I had chosen my birthday on purpose but it was only with the arrival of my twenty-sixth birthday that I saw the sick irony of my ill-fated choice. I had never been able to share a birthday with him. When I was born he was already dead.

The only birthday my parents were able to celebrate together was my father's twenty-sixth, and the red scarf was my mother's gift to him. On one end she had embroidered his name, on the other hers. It was only later that she realized her unforgivable mistake. She should not have put their names on opposite ends; she should have brought them together, tightly knit, inextricably and illegibly occupying the same space ... like their souls in love. She told me that the evening when my father drowned in Miyun Reservoir, the red scarf had been hanging off the handlebar of his bicycle, as if waiting for him to swim back to shore.

I held my mother tightly as my tears wet her shoulder. I remembered the answer my mother had given me three years earlier when I asked her why she had never complained of loneliness, an answer that I did not understand at the time. She had said that since she was twenty-four years old, she had never been lonely. Now I realized that her loneliness had been taken away with her life's first and last love. The tragedy had left her with a stubborn conception about love: that it happens once and once only, just like death.

Below is my parents' love story, the story, if you like, of how I came to be.

More people were getting on the train, which was also beginning to become less steady on the track, and I decided I would need a quieter environment if I was to give Misoka's story my proper attention. I returned the sheets of paper to the envelope, leaned back against the seat, and stared vacantly at the subway map on the wall beside the doors. Over the past few days I had come to sketch a rough outline of Misoka's life from the clues she had left me, and I was keen to find out the extent to which this outline resembled the story she'd written.

Judging by the speed with which I had read the previous passage, I estimated it would take me six or seven hours to read everything Misoka had given me. I was intent on finishing it in one sitting, and I bought a burger from McDonald's on the way home from the subway station so as not to have to waste time making dinner. As soon as I got home I started reading and did not stop until I had finished at eleven. Misoka's neat handwriting was very easy to read, but because she had only selected certain extracts to give me, I found that I was reading what contemporary critics would call a "fragmentary text," which kept jumping back and forth in terms of mood and content. Furthermore, every half page or so would present me with a new word that I had to look up in a dictionary in order to understand the passage, which slowed me down a great deal. However, despite all this, reading Misoka's story was a thoroughly enjoyable experience. Many details confirmed what I had previously suspected about Misoka and I relished the series of small affirmations I received from her work.

I read through the manuscript again over the next couple of days. In the few years since I left Montreal I have continued to read it once through every year, and I have come to know it and understand it better each time. What appears below is based on what I have gleaned from the text. It is, of course, not a literal translation, perhaps not even a translation at all, but a sketch of the truth I have read from the fragments left to me by Misoka. It could be said, perhaps, that it is our shared creation.

The year is 1974, the place China's capital, the people involved a Chinese man and a Japanese woman.

Their love began in Chinese language class. It was a beginning that ought not to have taken place at all given the histories that stretched before them: the history of two families, the history of two countries. The China-Japan war had left indelible scars on both of their families. Her father had lost his left arm to a cannonball in the first Battle of Changsha, and his father was a hero of the Battle of Pingxingguan, whose abdomen and thigh still bore the wounds of five gunshots. They knew full well all that had taken place between the two nations more than three decades before and its impact on each of their families, but neither of them thought that these histories would return to form an insurmountable obstacle to their love.

She had a rebellious nature. With the normalization of relations between Japan and China, she defied her family's wishes to join the first wave of students who travelled to China to study. He was her third-year advanced reading lecturer and she was fascinated by him the first day he walked into her class. With his genuine smile and easygoing air he seemed different from the other Chinese teachers. The wind was roaring outside, and the first thing he did upon entering the room was throw open the window and announce to the class, "We shall set off with the wildest of winds." Both his opening gesture and the sound of his voice kindled inside her a longing for romance.

From that moment on she did not see him as a teacher, but as the object of her passion.

She was not the only student to fall prey to his charms and he quickly became the topic of many post-class conversations. The students discussed what he had taught and how he had taught it, the manner and speed of his walk, his life outside of school. They had managed to discover that he came from a highly respected and cultured family. From an early age he had gained a great deal of experience and read a great many books. They were delighted to find out that he was an athlete too, an excellent swimmer, and he also had a beautiful voice. He had received professional training and had been the lead singer for the Beijing Children's Palace Choir. One student had heard him singing Schubert's "Serenade" in the corridor of the teaching building and she said that the way he sang "Darling" in the Chinese lyrics was enough to arouse amorous notions in even the most dispassionate of women. Naturally, the subject that most intrigued them was why he was able to arouse these notions in others but seemed impervious to such temptations himself. When they asked other teachers why he did not have a girlfriend, the answers they received were strikingly similar: he was too "proud." The students could not make sense of this explanation because to them he seemed like the humblest of all the teaching staff. That was just how he appeared on the surface, the other teachers would say. Deep down he was a very proud man. But it was precisely his inner pride that attracted his Japanese student. One day, she told herself, she would become the object of this pride.

She also loved his sense of humour. Other teachers taught class with expressionless faces, as if every moment had to be sorely endured, and said no more than was necessary to impart

information to their students. He, on the other hand, was re-
laxed and offbeat. His lectures were peppered with off-the-cuff
ironic remarks and jokes. His humour struck at the essence of
things and revealed flashes of truth, providing shortcuts in her
learning of the language. He began and ended each class with
a joke. He said he learned all his jokes about "stupid husbands
and their clever wives" from his grandmother. That generation
of Chinese women had no power in society and had to satisfy
themselves with telling jokes.

He had a lot of respect for his grandmother, who he said
was beautiful, intelligent, headstrong, and generous — a
tough and astute woman. It was precisely these qualities that
he sought in a woman. "Alas, there are no women like that
anymore," he once sighed. She could hear the sorrow in his
voice as he said this, a sorrow in the face of the era in which
they lived, in the face of their history. She knew this sorrow
came from a place deep inside him, just like his honesty, just
like his pride, just like his humour.... She had never seen a
sorrow like it in any other man. Like everything else about
him, she was drawn to his sorrow.

She would never forget what happened on that special
afternoon in late autumn. It was the last lesson of the day and
all her classmates had already left but she was crouched over
her desk, apparently lost in her studies. In reality, however, all
of her attention was directed at him, looking to see if he no-
ticed her. He leisurely closed the window and headed toward
the door but, just as she had hoped, he didn't walk out. He
turned his head and asked her why she had not left. She replied
that she still hadn't finished her homework. He said that it was
about to rain, that she should not stay for much longer. She
replied that it was fine, that she liked the rain, before worrying

that maybe she had said too much. Would he see the similarity with his own penchant for the wind? She felt the blood rush to her face and the sweat forming on the back of her hands. She longed for him to take the next step, which he did, to the front of her desk where he asked her if she needed any help. She said she didn't and immediately regretted it. But strangely enough he paid no attention and sat on the chair of the desk in front of her with his legs out to one side. She lowered her eyes to her work. She felt as nervous as if she were standing completely naked in front of him. She had been waiting for this moment. She had dreamt of it four times. She did not want to let it pass without grasping the opportunity it contained. She had to let him know how she felt, that she had felt this way since the first class, how every day since then these feelings had only grown stronger. The unbearable silence at that moment was inter-rupted by a loud clap of thunder, and she lifted her head to look longingly into his eyes.

"Sir, why don't you have a girlfriend?" she asked. Her stom-ach was in knots.

He seemed completely unfazed.

"What kind of question is that for a student to ask a teach-er?" he said. The seriousness in his voice caused her to lower her head timidly again, which kept her from seeing the smile that had crept across his face. "I suppose students like to talk about their teachers," he added, as if in forgiveness of her trans-gression. Encouraged, she lifted her head once more.

"Especially the teachers who captivate them," she said boldly.

He stood up slowly and asked her if she had an umbrella. Without waiting for an answer he offered to accompany her to her dormitory.

They walked side by side out of the teaching building. She had never shared an umbrella with someone of the opposite sex before, let alone someone of the opposite sex in a different country, let alone someone of the opposite sex in a different country who so captivated her. The pouring rain separated them from place and time. Their little umbrella became their sky and the space beneath it their new world, a world that was so wholesome, so harmonious, so true.... She felt a contentment she had never felt outside of dreams. It was as if she had always been here, alongside the man with whom she now shared the world under the umbrella; it was as if the walk would never end.

They said nothing the whole journey back to her dormitory. They both walked rigidly, as if terrified their bodies might touch, yet this did not prevent the occasional brushing of shoulders, arms, and even knees. Each moment of contact caused a shock more intense than the lightning above their heads to tear through her heart, to tear through her body. She wanted to burst out from under the umbrella and dance in the storm until she was wet, soaked, dripping with rain, in an act of self-cleansing, a baptism of love.

By the time they had arrived, everything was dripping with rain and flowing across the ground was a stream of water that barred their way to the stairway that led to her dormitory. He stretched out his hand and she grabbed it, perfectly naturally it seemed to her, as if it were the thousandth time she had held his arm for support, as if they were something other than teacher and student. They jumped over the river of rainwater together, walked up the stairs, and arrived at the entrance to her dormitory. He was not bothered by the fact that there were students all around them. He looked down at the damp trousers that clung to her legs and a worried expression appeared on his face. "Go in and get changed quickly," he said, pointing to her trousers. "You'll catch a cold." She had never heard such caring words from the male members of her own family. She was moved to the brink of tears. She did not want to go in "quickly." She wanted to stay and watch him leave. She did not want him to leave at all.

In their next class, from the moment he arrived to the moment he left, she was too nervous to raise her head. The previous night she had tossed and turned in bed picturing their next encounter, and it was precisely how she had imagined it. She had also foreseen that at the beginning of class when he returned their homework, he would pause ever so slightly before placing her exercise book on her desk. When, with her eyes still fixed on her desk, she saw out of the corner of her eye that he did indeed hesitate before returning her book, she decided not to check her grades right away like she normally did. She waited until the end of class when everyone had left and then slowly lifted the cover. She immediately closed it and looked all around her before jumping to her feet and charging out of the classroom. She did not want to be seen by anyone. She ran to the toilets, went into a cubicle, and locked the door before opening the notebook to reveal the strip of paper placed between the pages. On it he had written an answer to the question she had asked the previous day. "Because, until now, no one has ever made me feel that way." She understood right away and as she read the words "until now," her eyes welled up with tears. She felt a fulfillment she had never felt before.

That strip of paper was the first letter he wrote to her. In the next class, he left her a second, again tucked into the pages of her exercise book. In it, he wrote that he had noticed the look *of astonishment and adoration in her eyes in the first class, a look, he said, that gave him a powerful sense of loneliness. She decided to write a letter in response, in which she said that from that moment she had been his captive. That winter, he wrote her a total of eighty-seven letters, approximately one every day, and she wrote him forty-one in return. To begin with she found it took a lot of effort, but with time she came to enjoy the process of writing letters in Chinese. As the winter progressed, her letters became longer and her writing better. Even her Chinese language writing teacher said her progress was "hard to believe."*

The place he chose for their first date was the Old Summer Palace, a place she had never been or even thought to go to before. It was a Saturday afternoon and they arranged to meet beneath the willow trees not far from the north entrance to the university campus. He told her he was going to take her to a place that she was sure to find enchanting. As she approached the meeting place, he caught up with her on his bike and she jumped onto the back. After passing through three villages they entered an area of vegetable fields, and his evident familiarity with the winding paths filled her with a powerful curiosity about their destination. He took her to the ruins of the Big Fountains in the Old Summer Palace. She jumped off the back of the bike. He was still straddling the bicycle with both feet on the ground as she looked all around her and sighed deeply.

"How did you know I'd find it so enchanting?"

"Because I have been enchanted by you," he replied.

She turned her face toward him, the first time she had brought her face so close to his. He placed his bicycle on the ground, took her by the hand, and led her to a piece of stone that must have been part of a domed roof. He ran his other hand over its surface.

"All ruins are a magnet," he said. "One end points to the past, the other to the future." He paused a moment before going on. "It is a wise observer who can see the future from the ruins of the past."

She heard in this statement his passion for ruins and his concern about the future. She was proud that she alone was here to enjoy his beautiful words.

There was also his beautiful voice. From that day on every time they entered the ruins she sat between his arms on the crossbar of the bicycle while he sang lyrical ballads that were banned at that time in China. He had managed to get hold of hand-copied versions of the songs that circulated in the black market. He collected a great deal of this samizdat material, not only songs but also literary works that were deemed to be "toxic." He sang one song after the other and she got lost in the touching melodies as the breath that carried them brushed against her cheek. In the gaps between phrases he would often lean forward and kiss her, while she often could not resist turning around to kiss him as he sang. Her favourite piece was Schubert's "Serenade," and he would frequently sing it many times in succession, "Lover, I await thee in the tranquil grove …" Sometimes she would place her hand over his mouth, concerned that his singing might destroy the tranquility of their surroundings, but he would always pull free and sing even louder: "Worry not, my darling, no one will disturb us. Worry not …"

He had a peculiar power of vision. He was able to see both the past and the future, which is to say that he could see the bigger picture in life. It was another quality of his that fascinated her. One day he asked her if she knew what was special about September 25. She of course knew that it was the day that Prime Minister Kakuei Tanaka travelled to China to finalize the normalization of relations between China and Japan. But this was not the whole answer: it was also the day of the Great Victory (or, for Japan, the Great Defeat) of Pingxingguan. He said that even his father had not noticed this fact. He was convinced that this had happened not by chance but by design, but whose? If it was China, it was a display of their shrewdness; if it was Japan, a display of their sincerity. However, things were more complicated still because the previous year the commander who had led the Chinese army in the battle of Pingxingguan had suffered as great a fall from grace as could be imagined, a great hero of the people accused of treason. Who would want to connect the victory of this national traitor to the latest diplomatic achievement of the country he had betrayed?

He also talked to her of China's future. He told her that in ten years' time, China would no longer be the China of the Cultural Revolution. In fact, it might even have become its opposite, a nation obsessed with opulence and wealth. Such a logic was summed up by the Chinese idiom "Things reverse when they meet their extremes." He had based his conclusion about China's coming transformation on two premises: "All humans eventually die," and "The Great Leader is also human." Many Chinese people believed in the myth of immortality and found it difficult to accept the second of these premises, but he was not one of the believers. It had not been long since President Nixon had visited China and the reports of the great meeting had only strengthened his conviction. From the images broadcast, he estimated the Great Leader had no more than five years left to live. He was certain that within five years great changes would come to China, changes that would without doubt be beneficial to society and the people, but the long-term repercussions of which would be hard to predict. He did not want to live in a China obsessed with opulence and wealth. All he wanted was a simple and quiet life. A simple and quiet life was a life truly lived.

She wanted to know what had furnished him with such a visionary gift. He was so different from all her other Chinese teachers, so different to all the Chinese people she had met. He told her that his own teachers were philosophy and death. He had read the works of the Greek philosophers from a young age and was obsessed with their metaphysics and methodical reasoning. His earliest encounters with death came via his father's experiences in the wars of the Chinese against the Japanese, then the Communists against the Nationalists, and finally the Chinese with the North Koreans against the United Nations. Two of his father's closest friends had fallen on the battlefield, one of them right in front of his father. Later it was his own experience of death that came to deepen his reflections on the relationship between the necessary and incidental in life. At the age of nine he was swimming in Miyun Reservoir with three friends from his compound when he suddenly got a cramp a great distance from the shore. His companions were terrified and had no idea what to do. Had it not been for the two farmers who just happened to be passing at that moment, that day would surely have been his last.

Aside from the Old Summer Palace, there was another hidden place they liked to go: a small abandoned railway station. He pointed out that this railway station, the Big Fountains in the ruins, and their classroom formed an equilateral triangle. He told her that it was the madman on their university campus who first took him to the station. The madman was famous for being able to recite all of Chairman Mao's poetry by heart, although nobody knew his past: Where was he from? What had turned him into a madman? He told her that one day, the madman had asked him a mysterious question.

"Do you want to know the truth?"

He fixed the madman with a cool gaze and asked him, "What truth?"

The madman responded without hesitation, "The truest of truths."

"What is the truest of truths?" he asked, genuinely curious.

"Come with me," the madman responded, gesturing for him to follow.

He followed the madman all the way to the abandoned railway station. The madman stood in the middle of the twenty-or-so-square-metre waiting room.

"Here it is!" the madman said.

"What do you mean here it is?"

"The truth!" the madman said impatiently. "The truth is right here."

The madman then hobbled through the waiting room and to the edge of the platform, before leaping in an exaggerated motion onto the tracks. He followed the madman to the edge of the platform and looked down. The madman gestured to him to jump down but he remained still. The madman did not insist. Pointing downward to the tracks beneath his feet, he said: "The truth is right here." Then he went on to recite Chairman Mao's poem about lost lovers: "I lost my dear Poplar, you lost your Willow; Now Poplar and Willow float up into the Heavens ..." as he shuffled away along the sleepers buried in weeds.

A vague grief had descended upon him as he stood alone on the platform watching the madman walk away along the tracks. He returned to the dusty waiting room and sat down on one of the chairs that lined the wall. Something about this place, isolated from the city of people around it, appealed to him. He had no idea what it had to do with truth, but he knew it would become his refuge from the world outside. He liked to go there at dusk with his illegal hand-copied books or simply sit on the edge of the platform swinging his legs back and forth like a child.

She also liked the quiet of the abandoned railway station and its subtly melancholy quality. Like him, she had fallen in love with the station as soon as she had seen it. When he told her the story of how he discovered it, she responded without really thinking that judging by the poem the madman had recited when leaving, the truth he was talking about was a truth about love. Suddenly his eyes lit up as if everything had become clear and he embraced her tightly.

From that moment on his refuge became their Garden of Eden where they imagined their future together. She told him that her mother was a francophile and that she had been brought up surrounded by French culture. She liked the French way of life and said that in the future they should move to France. More than a place to contemplate their future, however, the station was a place for them to savour their passion for one another, their present. One evening they were snuggling up in a corner of the waiting room when a bolt of lightning abruptly illuminated them, just as it had done the day they were alone in the classroom. She said she was cold. He undid the buttons on his coat and she took off her own before nestling into his open coat. She rested her *head under his chin, as innocently as a child. But she was still a little cold she said, and he did not know how to help her warm up. She took off her jumper and unbuttoned her shirt, and he pressed his face against the softness of her breast, as innocently as a child.*

The Chinese lyrics of Schubert's "Serenade" turned out to be correct: no one disturbed them, either in the ruins of the Old Summer Palace or at the abandoned railway station. What lay in store for their hundred-day romance was less a disturbance than an ambush, which came from both sides. Both fathers believed their relationship brought disgrace upon their families. A unified cause made allies of these long-time enemies. His father used his influence to try to force the school leaders to prevent the continuation of their relationship. In the principal's office, when he was reminded that relations between Japan and China had been normalized, he simply bellowed, "That is a national matter. This is a family matter!" The next thing he said was heard by everyone in the vicinity. "I don't care where my daughter-in-law comes from as long as she's not Japanese!" Her father, on the other hand, used diplomatic channels to bring pressure to bear upon the school leaders. He told his daughter that if she continued to see this son-of-a-bakayaro, she could consider their father-daughter relationship over. The two fathers did not realize that it was already too late. Inside him was a determination that would choose death over submission. Inside her was a new life they both awaited with devoted anticipation, their child.

Ever since finding out that she loved swimming, he had told her numerous times that one day in summer he would take her to Miyun Reservoir. In the end, however, he went on his own, in the middle of a bitterly cold night at the beginning of spring.

Before getting into the water he kissed the scarf she had given him for his birthday, while she stood perfectly still beneath the plum tree of her home in Tokyo, thinking about the abandoned railway station, that bolt of lightning ...

∞ I

WHILE MISOKA'S MANUSCRIPT clarified many things for
me, it also posed a whole new set of questions. For example,
why had she not written more about the circumstances that
caused the lovers to separate? I was particularly keen to know
how everything had affected the young exchange student, the
narrator's mother, who was forced to leave China and return
to Japan. The only other information to be gleaned from the
manuscript was that she went on to defy her family's wishes for
a second time by moving to Paris, where she gave birth to the
child that was the "fruit of their love." Nineteen years later, the

narrator's now widowed grandmother called to make up with her estranged child, and then travelled to France to live with her daughter and granddaughter, three generations of women under one roof.

This was not the only gap in the story. At no point did the manuscript describe what its narrator looked like, and the ultimate fate of her mother was only touched upon briefly at the very end. To this day when I read the last photocopied page of her manuscript, I do not know if Misoka intentionally left out the information that so intrigues me from her novel or simply from the parts she chose to give me. In the final days of that most unusual of winters, I continued to hope that I might see Misoka and share with her my thoughts and enthusiasm about her work. I wanted to let her know how much I wanted to read the full, unabridged version, and especially how much I enjoyed the way it ended:

> On the morning of my twenty-sixth birthday my mother came into my room and told me she had a special present to give me. Sitting on the edge of my bed, she handed me a red scarf and an old photograph. She pointed to the man in swimming trunks in the photo and said, "This is your father."
>
> It was the first time I had seen my father. He was completely different to the father who often appeared in my dreams. The man in the photograph was far warmer, closer. As soon as I saw him I knew he was my father.
>
> With these gifts she told me the story of how I came to be. More than once I was unable to hold back my tears, but my mother never lost her composure, recounting the events of her winter in China, the season when the seeds of my life were sowed, in that same measured tone of voice. It was only

after she had finished and had stood up to leave that her self-possession began to crack. She said that she did not have the courage to return to Beijing but she would like it if one day I had the chance to see it myself. She would be surprised if anything remained of the abandoned railway station, but I would definitely be able to visit Miyun Reservoir and the Old Summer Palace. She hoped I would be able to run my fingers over the remains of the Big Fountains, through the water of Miyun Reservoir ...

Over the next year my mother's illness worsened. It began to affect the sound of her voice and the look in her eyes. I began to dread speaking with her. I was afraid of causing her harm and also of the harm she might cause me. What frightened me most was how she would often spend whole nights unable to sleep, alone in her chair on the balcony, looking resolutely out into the limitless black.

She now lies in a cemetery on the north side of Mount Royal, and every time I visit her grave I take a trip to Beaver Lake, which is not far away from where she is buried. One day as I was sitting on one of the benches that overlook the lake, a strange idea came to me — that one winter, my father, mother, and I, three insignificant grains of sand, would be brought together on the slopes of Mount Royal, and in that remarkable winter I would write about my parents and the story of their love.

By the time I read Misoka's manuscript I had already finished writing the truth my wife needed, and I could not help but read Misoka's ending in the light of my own situation. It seemed to me that the mother's deterioration was a result of her finally telling her daughter the truth. Just like Celia had said, for the psychologically fragile the truth can have lethal consequences.

In her final days I had struggled with the question of whether to share the truth with my wife, the truth she had begun to ask from me. At times I was certain it was the right thing to do, that it would put my own mind at ease and give her the comfort she needed. But each time I saw her lying in bed, her body withering to its bones, the spirit fading from her face, I would lose my nerve. What could the truth mean to someone who had such a tenuous hold on her own life? This state of indecision was almost brought to an end three days before she died. She was looking better that day and I discerned a light in her eyes that I thought had been long extinguished.

"There's something that I've always been meaning to ask," she said faintly. "What made you suddenly agree to emigrate?"

I shuddered. "Didn't you say it was for the child?" I said.

"That's what *I* said. I want to know what made you change your mind."

I hesitated for a moment, but in the end did not tell her what she wanted to know, the truth I would write much later, in the winter after she died:

After the incident with our paper's series of exposés on education in Guangdong province, I lost my passion for work. I knew that I could not change society and I was unwilling to let society change me. I became an outsider. In the office I lost my former drive to excel and only concerned myself with completing my assignments, just as outside the office I stopped having new interests or long-term goals. In this sense, there was some truth to my wife's complaint that I was irresponsible. This "irresponsibility" was part of the reason I thought it strange that my wife suddenly became so intent on emigrating. It all happened after a get-together she had with former classmates during which, I later discovered, she had had conversations with two friends that had left a deep impression on her. The first friend worked in the provincial education department and revealed to her the "inside story" of schooling in China, whereas the second, who lived in Canada, spoke glowingly of Canada's "far more humane" education system. The question of emigration became a source of bitter disagreement between us and in our more heated arguments she even threatened divorce, saying she would take our daughter to live abroad without me. I signed the divorce papers twice but each time she tore them up in a fit of emotion before she was able to submit them.

It was a Thursday evening when everything changed. I stayed late at work that day to tidy up a report written by one of the interns about the chaotic state of an audiovisual equipment market in Guangzhou. As I was getting ready to leave I noticed that, aside from the light that was still on in the office of our new supervisor, there was no sign of life on the whole floor. It had been some time since I had worked so late and there was something surreal about walking through the dark and quiet of the deserted office space. When I reached the elevator, I heard what sounded like sobbing but it didn't really register with me at first. The report on the chaotic Guangzhou market was still in my mind, and I was also thinking about where I would go to buy my daughter's favourite brand of bread. However, as I walked into the elevator, I suddenly felt that something wasn't right. Who would be sobbing in the office at this hour? Later I would often reflect on how, had this thought not occurred to me, everything would have turned out differently. I don't know where it came from, whether it was a matter of fate or of chance, but for some reason as I stood in the elevator something came over me, a peculiar sensation the repercussions of which would eventually include my consenting to emigrate. Just as the doors were closing, I pressed the button to open them again and stepped out into the corridor. I stood there for a moment and sure enough I could still make out the sound of someone crying. I began to make my way toward where the sound was coming from, making an effort as I walked to measure my stride so it would appear as natural as possible. It was a bizarre situation. I was an outsider who cared little for work, yet here I was after hours gripped by a sudden concern about what was going on in the office. I did not know what had come over me. Was it curiosity, empathy, or a sense of responsibility? As I approached the door to my supervisor's office it became clear that the sobbing was coming from there, the only room on the whole floor with the lights on, but I did not stop. There were CCTV cameras everywhere, and I imagined the security guard downstairs watching my every movement on the surveillance monitors so I continued to walk without breaking my stride until I had reached the editorial office. I entered the room, sat at my desk, and thought about what I should do. It was a simple predicament, I quickly realized, and I had three options: knock on the door to my supervisor's office, get the security guard to knock on the door, or ignore it and go home. In ordinary circumstances the third of these options would have been the most appealing to an outsider like me (and the first option the least) but for some reason I picked up the report I had just been working on and walked slowly to my supervisor's office door. Even if the security guard had been watching me at that moment, I thought to myself, he would not have seen anything he thought out of the ordinary. I paused for a moment outside the door, and when I was sure that I could still hear somebody sobbing I knocked softly. The sound stopped. Then I heard a drawer being closed and the sound of footsteps. The door opened to reveal the smiling face of my supervisor.

"You're still here?" she said.

I handed her the report and said, "I don't know if this is what you were hoping for." I glanced briefly around the room and saw that there was no one else there. Was it my supervisor who had been crying just now? She looked up from the report I had given her with the same rigid smile on her face.

"Leave it with me," she said. "I'll get back to you tomorrow."

I didn't know what else I could say. I smiled awkwardly and said thanks before turning around and walking away. My eyes were trained on the corridor that led to the elevator but my mind was still in the room behind me as I heard the door close. Then I heard it open again, then a period of silence, and finally the voice of my supervisor. She was calling after me. I stopped and turned around.

"Come here a moment," she said.

She asked me if I was in a hurry, and I replied that I had nothing to do except buy my daughter's favourite brand of bread.

"We can chat for a bit then," she said, as she stepped aside to give me room to walk into her office. She closed the door and told me to make myself comfortable, so I sat on the sofa nearest the door and farthest away from her seat behind the desk. I hoped increasing the distance between us might calm my nerves, but to my dismay she turned the chair on the other side of her desk around and sat right in front of me. I have never liked talking face to face with my superiors at work, and the whole situation made me tense. She, on the other hand, seemed completely at ease as she began to tell me that she knew how difficult it was being a parent, especially of girls. A daughter always caused her parents much more distress than a son did.

Her own daughter was studying in the U.K., and the older she got the more worried she was about her. I did not feel confident enough to chat as an equal with my supervisor, parent to parent, so I simply replied that my daughter was still young and we had not reached that stage yet. My supervisor went on to ask me who cooked in our family. I replied that I enjoyed cooking but my wife did not like the food I made. A solemn look appeared on her face as she said, "All families have these problems."

We chatted for almost forty minutes and in that time we did not speak once about anything related to work. Neither did she say anything that shed light on the sobbing that had emanated from her office moments earlier and naturally I was too nervous to bring it up. She did not give the impression of someone who had been crying; she seemed utterly relaxed the whole time I was in her office. In the end she was the one who brought the conversation to a close, standing up and reminding me that I had to buy bread for my daughter. "It's best not to keep a child waiting," she said. "Your children are the most important thing."

The next day in the canteen at lunch, my supervisor walked past my table and asked if she could sit in the empty chair opposite me. I felt my face immediately turn red. Ever since leaving her office I had been thinking about our peculiar encounter. I had never sat so close to a superior and spoken at such length, especially about such personal topics. In fact this was precisely what had been on my mind when she interrupted my train of thought with her question and, before I could reply, sat down. She asked if I had been able to buy the bread yesterday, and whether my daughter was upset that I had returned home too late. She even asked if my daughter looked like me. As I answered her questions I was as nervous as I had been the evening before, nervous about what I should say, about how she would react, and about what my colleagues would think about us sitting together. I realized that what worried me most was not simply the fact that she was my supervisor, but that she was also a woman; a woman who was my supervisor who had chatted with me at length last night about things completely unrelated to work. I did not ask a single question and I said no more than was absolutely necessary. Our conversation revolved around children, and she continued to chat in the same placid tone of the evening before. She told me how her daughter used to behave when she was my daughter's age, and then what she thought of the mother-daughter relationship and the best education for a child. It was only when she stood up to leave that she brought up anything to do with work. She said she had read my report, and she asked me to come to her office that afternoon to talk about it.

After lunch I found it difficult to concentrate on work. All I could think about was my work boss (my supervisor) and my life boss (my wife), and I found myself comparing them. At first, I considered their attitudes toward parenting and education, and discovered I preferred my supervisor's approach. Her way of looking at and dealing with these issues seemed both more sensible and more sensitive than my wife's. The longer I considered these two women, the more the scope of my comparison grew until I found myself weighing up their educational backgrounds, their thinking styles, even what they wore and how they looked. My supervisor was more easygoing in terms of her convictions, whereas my wife was fastidious in her views. When it came to clothes, however, it was my wife who paid no mind to what she was wearing, as long as it was comfortable, whereas my supervisor took great care to dress well. Although she was older than my wife, my supervisor's skin and general physique were in better condition, and there was a youthful femininity to her movements and the way that she walked. The more I compared them and the more things I compared them on, the more the prospect of visiting my supervisor unsettled me, and it only got worse as I continued to think about the two encounters that had already taken place. Ten minutes before the end of the workday I finally went to her office and knocked tentatively on the door. I heard a voice say, "Come in," and I opened the door to find my supervisor absorbed in her work. She looked up from the documents on her desk to see me standing in the doorway unsure of whether or not I should enter. She smiled and said, "Do you mind waiting a moment while I get this sorted?"

I took a step back out of the office, closed the door, and returned to my desk. My colleagues were beginning to pack up their things so I pretended to be getting on with some work. When everyone had gone I retrieved a copy of Harvest *literary magazine that I kept in my desk drawer. When I looked up from the magazine I noticed how much time had passed. It was already around the same time I had left the office the previous day. I walked to the door, looked out, and saw that the light in my supervisor's office was still on. I took a deep breath and, making an effort to appear relaxed, walked slowly to her office. I knocked softly on the door and she opened it. "I've been waiting for you," she said. She closed the door behind me as I walked in and then locked it.*

I sat in the same place on the far side of the sofa as the previous evening and looked at the chair I assumed she would place in front of me like she had done the night before. She did not touch the chair, however, and I felt a flutter in my chest as she took a seat on the sofa next to me, only an arm's length away.

My body and larynx tensed up, even more than they had the day before. I had no idea what to say and so I waited. I hoped she would bring up my report so I could hear what she had to say and leave as quickly as possible. Unfortunately, this is not what she had in mind.

"Do you have a picture of your daughter?" she asked.

I thought it a strange request but was grateful that the silence had finally been broken. I retrieved the photo of my daughter that I kept in my wallet. After studying the photo for some time she turned to look directly at me. I smiled awkwardly, wondering what she would say next.

"I think I can picture what her mother looks like," she said.

I was about to say that my daughter did not look much like her mother but decided it would be better not to complicate things. Little did I know my supervisor was about to complicate things a great deal.

"Do you love her?" she asked.

I stifled a gasp. Her words seemed to pierce me like a knife. "Who?" I said, unable to prevent my voice from breaking slightly.

She flicked her eyes toward the photo again. "Her mother of course," she said.

No one had ever asked me this question before, let alone a woman, let alone a woman I did not even "know" twenty-four hours ago. I told myself that I did not have to answer truthfully. "Sure," I said as I took the photograph back from her.

"Oh, that's such a male answer," she said. "What the hell does 'sure' mean?!"

I could not believe it. This wasn't the way a female supervisor usually spoke with her male subordinates!

"Do you know how difficult it is for women?" She brought a hand to her face and began to cry.

I had no idea what to say. My mind was all over the place as I thought about what I had heard the previous night from the elevator.

"You men are all the same," she added through her sobs.

There was a pack of tissues on her desk. It was the only thing I could think of to help so I walked to the desk, pulled out three tissues, and handed them to her.

I would later regret this decision. If I had not tried to comfort my supervisor, perhaps her emotional outburst would have simply been a one-off, an exceptional incident that would not go on to affect my entire life. Rather than taking the tissues she grabbed my hand and feverishly pulled it toward her face. She planted her lips on the back of my hand as her crying intensified.

Never before had I felt another's tears roll down my hand, nor had my hand been kissed so passionately before. It was the first time I had seen someone reduced to such an emotionally raw state, and the dreamlike scene had a powerful impact on me. It kindled a strong sense of empathy and responsibility that made me forget that the woman in front of me was my supervisor, someone I barely knew twenty-four hours earlier. I leaned my face closer to her dishevelled hair. She was now a woman whose suffering it was my responsibility to help lessen, a woman who needed my support.

She must have felt my breath as I leaned closer to the back of her head because she suddenly stopped sobbing. She lifted her head and looked at me through teary eyes.

"Men don't know how lonely women are," she said before lowering her head and placing it back on my hand. "You don't know how lonely I am."

I noticed how she had changed "men" and "women" for "you" and "I." She had moved from a comment about people in general to one that brought the two of us in particular together, and the link that connected us was loneliness. A pang of sympathy caused me to realize even more keenly my duty of care toward her.

"I know," I said. "I know."

She lifted her head and looked me in the eyes as she grabbed my hand with both of hers and placed it on her chest. This was not what I expected. I was too afraid to look at her, so I closed my eyes and turned toward the door as I tried to pull my hand away. She misunderstood my concern.

"Don't worry, I locked the door," she said. She placed her hands on either side of my face and pulled me back to look at her. "No one will disturb us," she added softly, as if cajoling a child.

I opened my eyes and saw that she had undone the buttons on her blouse. Before I had a chance to react she had taken off her bra, grabbed my hand, and placed it on her breast. I was both shocked and excited, and I could not help but notice that the breast in my hand must have been twice the size of my wife's. This almost unconscious comparison filled me with a strong sense of guilt, both about the half-naked woman before me and the woman who was at that moment waiting for me at home. I felt paralyzed. I could not bear to look my supervisor in the eyes, nor did I dare to look at the bare breast in my hand. I closed my eyes and clenched my teeth, as if subject to some terrible torment. That's when I felt my supervisor undoing my fly. I immediately pushed her away.

"No, please don't," I said. "We shouldn't be doing this."

My protestations did not dissuade her. If anything they only seemed to spur her on. She knelt on the ground, undid my trousers, and brought her face toward my crotch. On a physical level I seemed immune to her provocations, which only aggravated my conflicted mental state. On top of the nerves, excitement, and guilt I had been feeling, I was now struck by a painful sense of shame. I was acutely aware of every movement of her mouth and tongue, but there was no reaction whatsoever from my body.

"Don't you like it?" She lifted her head and looked at me disappointedly.

I could not look at her. I did not know what to say.

"You're nervous," she said as she did up my fly and pressed her hand softly against my crotch.

She got to her feet and tidied up her clothes before sitting on the sofa next to me. I took a deep breath and leaned forward, placing my head on my knees. She put her hand on the back of my head. "It's fine. You're nervous, that's all," she said. "It'll be all right next time."

She began to tell me about her marriage. She said that for three years there had been no relationship to speak of between her and the man she had married, even though they continued to live in the same house. She had known for some time that he had a mistress, but at first she had thought it was just one of those moral lapses so typical of men. She was sure it would pass and that things would return to normal. However, it became clear that their marriage could never be what it once was when she discovered he wanted to marry his mistress. He had been asking her for a divorce ever since their daughter had left to study in the U.K., but she was against it. Her husband did not understand her attachment to their marriage, which was, after all, a marriage in name only, and could not see what difference a divorce would make to her. He had presented her with divorce papers four times now, with what he considered very favourable conditions for her, but each time she'd refused to sign, tearing the documents to pieces and throwing them in the toilet without even looking at them. Eventually he had decided to change his approach, and it was yesterday, the day I had first heard her crying in her office, that she had received a package by registered mail from her husband. It contained a fifth set of divorce papers and an accompanying letter on which were written only two sentences. The first explained that the package included a draft of the final divorce papers he would send her. The second sentence stated simply that if she still refused to sign, he would see her in court. When she got to this part of the story she began to cry again.

"What should I do?" Her question seemed half-posed to me and half-posed to herself.

I knew this was not a question I could answer directly, but I still felt I ought to comfort her. I put my hand on her back and was trying to think of what I ought to say when she stopped crying.

"But today is a happy day," she said. "I shouldn't let this boring stuff get between us."

As she said these words she looked deep into my eyes. She leaned forward and placed her lips on mine — slowly, as if performing some kind of sacred ritual. It was a sensual moment, more sensual than anything that had taken place between my wife and me, and I did not pull away. I was excited, my whole body was excited, and when our lips gradually parted I saw the same hungry look in her eyes.

"From now on don't think of me as your boss, and don't worry about the age difference between us," she said. "From now on I am simply a little woman who needs your compassion."

By the time I got home my wife and daughter had already finished their dinner and cleaned up. I worried they might be able to smell an unfamiliar scent on me, so I went to the bathroom to brush my teeth and wash my face before going to the kitchen to eat some leftovers. My wife told me to heat up the food first so that I would not get indigestion. I said it was fine, that my stomach was not usually affected by that sort of thing.

"If you can't even be responsible for your own body, how are you supposed to look after this family?" my wife said.

Normally, I would not have responded to this all-too-familiar criticism, but something about everything I had just experienced had rendered me unusually sensitive. "What do you mean by that?!" I said, raising my voice. My wife was evidently not prepared for my answering back, and she simply looked at me confused with her mouth slightly open. "Why do you always speak to me like that?!" I went on. "Why can't you behave like a little woman when you're speaking to me?"

"You've had a bad day," she said, the softness of her voice barely concealing her contempt.

"Actually, it's been a great day," I said, lowering my voice to mimic her spite.

My wife clearly had no idea what to make of my reaction. After standing stunned for a moment she left to tell our daughter to get ready for bed.

After I had finished cleaning up the kitchen I went to the bathroom to wash before bed. In the shower I looked down and saw my body in a way I had never seen it before. It was the first time I had ever noticed my body, the first time in my life. Less than thirty hours before, it had been just another forgotten relic that had outlived its usefulness. Now it was the site of a newly born passion. It had been noticed, needed.... Pride burst out of my chest. I looked up to the nozzle and enjoyed the wonderful heat of its spray as it ran down my face and over my body. But then I felt a sharp pain in my head and a fearful solitude came over me, just as it had done a couple of hours earlier when I had left my supervisor's office. "What should I do?" I heard her question echo in my mind; this time, however, the desperation was mine. I went straight to bed after my shower, but by half past eleven I was still wide awake. I was thinking about how helpless my situation had been since I met my wife, and how stifling and dispiriting this helplessness was. I remembered the talented but unfortunate woman, and the girl I was "meant to meet" in the Old Summer Palace. My wife had never been able to fill me with wonder as they had or to affect me as they had with their purity. She had aroused in me nothing that resembled the emotional turmoil I had experienced only hours before.

My wife had only come to bed at eleven but she'd fallen asleep immediately. As I listened to the rhythmic sound of her breathing I felt a painful contraction in my chest. Tears started to run down my cheeks and into the pillow. I could not locate the source of this hurt. Was it guilt? Remorse? Shame? Or despair? I turned toward my wife, and something about her figure in the dark triggered a strange sensation in my body. I looked at her chest as it rose and fell under the sheets, and the physical sensation that had come over me began to grow stronger. I stretched out my hand. I wanted to put it under her shirt and hold her breast — no, my breast. It belonged to me. No one had ever held it before except me. We had lived together for many years; this was the first time I had ever felt such a forceful sense of belonging, of possession. It was short-lived, however, because the real master intervened. "Stop that," my wife said, the annoyance audible in her voice as she pulled my hand roughly from her shirt and pushed it away. She turned swiftly away from me and went back to sleep.

For the next two months I was pulled between two extremes. On the one hand my wife's unflappable indifference was diffi- cult to bear, while on the other my supervisor's unbridled ap- petite had me constantly on edge. I was split between two pre- dicaments that meant I dreaded both going to work and going home. I never did get used to my supervisor calling me to her office to "discuss work," even if what she had said turned out to be correct: it was "all right" since the second time. But the physical pleasure was not enough to dispel my mental anguish. Each time I left her office after one of our "discussions" I felt as if a great weight had been lifted from my shoulders. She, on the other hand, was always reluctant to let me leave and said that she found it difficult to think of me going home to spend time with another woman. I told her I felt the same way so she decided not to let "boring stuff" (which meant anything to do with her husband) interfere with our encounters. This did not solve the problem, however. There was something disconcerting- ly conspicuous about her very silence on these matters. I did not know what it was she really wanted from me. Why did she refuse to let go of her marriage if it was, as her husband had said, a marriage in name only? I found it difficult to accept the fact that each time we parted ways she was going home to another man.

This was perhaps the main reason I refused to go to her house. During our two-month affair she invited me three times, twice on the weekend and once during work hours. She told me there would be nobody home and said I was "bound to be more relaxed" there. However, the thought of sitting on the same sofa he sat on, using the same bathroom he used, even seeing the same windows and walls that housed him, this man who had once satisfied the woman I was having an affair with, filled me with revulsion. I made no excuses to explain why I could not go and simply said that there was no way I would be more relaxed. But she seemed intent on having me go to her house, and it was obvious that my unwavering refusal disappoint- ed her. It was only when she invited me for a third time that it finally dawned on me that my role in our relationship was not simply to satisfy her bodily cravings. I was also there to address a shadowy psychological need: she was using me to get back at her husband, as a strange way of reinforcing her refusal to divorce him, and something about me being in her house had a symbolic function that would help her deal with the hurt she had suffered. With this realization I only became more adamant in my decision. "Find someone else to go with you," I said angrily. From that moment on I began to think that my situation, divided between two extremes of passion, was even more boring than the "boring stuff" my supervisor endeavoured to keep from me.

All this meant I was neither particularly surprised nor that upset when my supervisor happily told me one day that her husband had changed his mind. It was not what she said, but where and when she said it, that left a sickening taste in my mouth. We were in her office; she had just finished breathlessly saying, "That was great," and was pulling up her trousers when she smiled at me and said, "My husband finally changed his mind." I looked at her in stony silence. "It doesn't bother you, does it?" she said as she pulled me up from the sofa. "I'm so happy he finally saw sense," she said. "It's just …" She paused. "We won't be able to do this anymore." She held onto me tightly. I stood rigidly in her arms, my hands motionless by my side, waiting impatiently for her to let me go.

That night when my wife turned off the bedside lamp I turned over, put my hand on her left breast, and nestled my face into her shoulder. It had been some time since I had acted so intimately with her.

"Let's do it," I said.

It took a while for my wife to realize what I was saying. "Do what?"

"Emigrate," I said.

I could tell my wife had turned her head toward me.

I did not move, my head still stuck to her shoulder. "You were right," I said.

"When?"

"When you said that it's what we must do for our child."

∞ The End of the End

THE ICE RINK on Mount Royal officially closed in the second week of March, and on the very last day I arrived before sunrise. The pavilion had yet to open so I changed into my skates on one of the benches outside. I thought back to the Korean student who was the first to bring me up the mountain that winter. She should have left Canada and been back in Korea by now. I did not know if she had ever returned to Mount Royal or whether she had even thought about it during her time here. If she had any idea what a remarkable winter our apparently chance encounter would lead to I was sure she would regard it with the same wonder as I did.

The temperature had risen the previous evening and the workers who tended to the ice rink hadn't yet arrived, which meant the surface was uneven and it was difficult to pick up any speed. After around twenty minutes I grew tired of skating. I took a seat on the bench where I had just changed my skates and looked out vacantly over Beaver Lake, covered in snow. Perhaps it was a result of the wistful mood that was coming over me as winter drew to a close, but there was something exhilarating that morning about the radiance of the sun as it inched over the horizon. I had had no news from Celia since her "suicide note," and what remained of Misoka was no more than a pile of photocopied fragments of a novel. This most unusual of winters was coming to an end … I was struck by the uncanny sensation that I was fading away. I thought back to the first question Hermit Wang had asked me: What was I doing here? Over the course of this winter the answer had been getting more and more complex, the number of causes for my circumstances steadily increasing. Appearing on the mountain for the last time that winter, it seemed that I was *here* because of Misoka, because of Celia, because of Mount Royal and its glittering white snow, because of Beaver Lake and its frozen thick surface. But as winter slowly departed it would take all of these reasons for being here with it. I felt myself fading away with the season and a new idea was appearing in its place: it was time to leave. There was no reason for me to stay. The sound of a woodpecker interrupted my thoughts, its empty *tap-tap-tap* breaking the silence of the woods, hollowing me out even further. Yes, it was time to leave.

On the way home I stopped by my wife's grave and burned the pages on which I had written the truth she needed. I had come to the conclusion that she would not care about all the details of what had happened or exactly how I had felt at each stage of the process, so in my final version I had simply recorded the key events and all the things I had done for which I was genuinely sorry. My list of regrets was exhaustive, from my consistently "irresponsible" attitude to the day I raised my voice to her in the kitchen after my first transgression with my supervisor. I even expressed remorse for the worst argument of our time in Montreal, which had started when she decided she wanted to buy the house we would later live in for nine years. She had been determined to buy it ever since she came across the advertisement by chance one day, but I completely disagreed. Aside from being uninterested in owning property in general, I did not think much of the location of the house, which I said was too far from both my daughter's school and the convenience store. In my letter I conceded that I did not have her head for business or her eye for the economy. I explained that although I had sold the house after she died, it was out of respect and admiration for her and had nothing to do with my original opposition to her decision.

I waited until nothing remained of my truth except ash, but as I walked away I remembered my epiphany at the top of the mountain. I returned to my wife's grave and told her that I had begun to consider leaving Montreal.

My Taiwanese neighbour's method turned out to be as effective as she claimed it would be. That evening my wife did not appear in my dreams, which meant that I had given her what she wanted and she had accepted my apology. More importantly she had forgiven me, she had consented to "let me go," and to this day, after so many years, my wife has not reappeared. The following day when I woke up in bed I opened my eyes feeling completely reinvigorated. It was time to draw my fifteen years of life as an immigrant to an end.

I decided to go back to China. I knew I had grown unaccustomed to its air and its ways, its joys and its strife. In the fifteen years I had been away, my native land had become foreign to me. Or was I the one who had been transformed, who had become a foreigner? The last time I was back, my friends and relatives all said I was different. I no longer understood what they were talking about when they smiled and joked or grumbled and moaned, and I felt separated from their memories of jubilation and hardship. I had no desire to share with them my own views of China as an outsider, an emigrant returning home, nor had I spoken about my life abroad. In general I kept to myself. It was clear, they all said, that Canada had changed me.

The fact was we were all different. In this globalized, information age everyone was changing and no one could understand anyone else; we could not see the change in ourselves so we assumed that it was everyone else who was changing. The absurdity of our condition struck me but it did not shake my resolve. I had made my decision. I would return to my native land, no matter how unrecognizable it was.

The first thing I had to do was tell my daughter. I had no intention of letting her know how sudden my decision was or how it had sprung from that empty *tap-tap-tap* I had heard coming from the woods of Mount Royal, so in the email I explained that it was the result of a winter's long consideration. Of course what I meant by "a winter" was all the events that had led, albeit indirectly, to my decision. I closed the email saying I hoped she could find time to see me as quickly as possible so we could put things in order before my departure.

It took almost a month to get everything ready for leaving, during which time I eagerly waited for my daughter to get in touch. Although my disappointment grew with each day that she did not get back to me, I was mentally prepared for such an outcome. I knew there was a possibility that she would not respond at all. I also wrote to Celia twice. I was now pretty much convinced by Misoka's theory but I still held out hope for a miracle. With everything that had happened that winter I no longer believed anything was impossible. In my last weeks in Montreal I even saw Misoka once through the windows of a subway car as she adjusted her wheelchair on the platform. It was clear she had just arrived at the station and we must have been on the same train. But why could we not have also been in the same carriage? Was it meant to be or had it just happened to turn out that way? I feverishly knocked on the glass but she didn't hear. As the train pulled away from the platform I was hit once again with the realization that winter was truly over.

I only bought my ticket home a week in advance. I agonized for two hours before deciding to adopt the "senior-junior principle" and send a final grovelling email to my daughter, in which I told her I hoped that we could see each other before I left. I filled it with sentimental phrases like "I don't know when the next chance will be," and attached my flight information in the hope that she would see for herself how little time there was left.

I learned the "senior-junior principle" from my Taiwanese neighbour. The first time I had complained to her about my "oblivious" daughter she had responded by shaking her head and telling me that it was exactly the same with her family.

Since moving out to a place only fifteen minutes' walk from the apartment, her son's record for the amount of time spent without visiting was one year, three months, and eight days. She went on to tell me that over many years' observation she had developed two principles for dealing with children: the "arm-leg principle" and the "senior-junior principle." A parent could never force children to do anything because "the leg is stronger than the arm," she said, "and they are the legs." Furthermore, one had to abandon one's sense of seniority and learn to act as though they were the child's junior, which meant putting up with all manner of humiliation — no matter how painful — and patiently, humbly, shamelessly waiting for them to come around. She concluded that the child would always return to the parents' side in the end, and reconciliation would eventually be achieved.

I never did receive a reply from my daughter but two days before my flight, just as I was thinking that all hope was lost, she phoned me. It was the first time she had called since moving out of our home and out of my life. I hadn't heard any news from her all winter (perhaps one of that winter's darker miracles) so when I heard her familiar voice I found it difficult to contain my excitement.

She seemed completely relaxed, utterly natural, as if it were just an everyday conversation between us, as if an entire winter did not separate this phone call from the last time we spoke. She asked me where I was spending my last night in Montreal and I told her that my Taiwanese neighbour was letting me sleep in her living room. "Why not stay here?" she asked, before telling me her address for the first time. She even said she would leave work an hour early to see me. It was hard to believe. Was it possible my fortunes could be reversed so completely in a moment? The reconciliation my Taiwanese neighbour had promised had arrived.

This was the final miracle of that most unusual of winters. On the evening before my last night as an immigrant I walked, for the first time, into my daughter's home. It was her very first home as an independent adult, a home that was hers and hers only, but I could not help but think that in some way it also belonged to that winter. I was over the moon, but I did not want to make my daughter uncomfortable so I stifled the tears that I knew would be hard to hold back once they had started to flow. She showed me around the apartment and then sat with me at her dining table and told me about the neighbourhood. Everything in the apartment was arranged much more neatly than I would have expected, and I wondered if she had tidied especially for me. The image of her preparing the apartment for my visit filled me with joy. Was it possible she truly cared what I thought? I had always assumed she had long stopped caring.

Afterward she took me to an Italian restaurant three blocks from her apartment. She was still not as talkative as she had been when she was younger, but I was grateful to finally have the chance to have a normal conversation with her. We had not spoken like this since she started high school. She answered my questions, shared her opinions, and even asked me questions of her own. As we ate, she told me she approved of my decision to return to China.

"You won't be so lonely there," she said.

I sighed. "Who would have thought this is how the winter would end."

My daughter seemed to take this as a criticism directed at her. "I really have been very busy," she said guiltily.

"I'm not blaming you." I paused. "In fact I should be thanking you."

My daughter looked at me quizzically.

"For some time now I've not had a life of my own," I explained.

"You deserve a life of your own," she said, and I felt the solicitude in her words.

"Do you remember when we used to go skating on Mount Royal?" I asked.

"That was a long time ago."

"This winter I went skating there pretty much every day," I said.

The surprise was visible in my daughter's face.

I smiled and said, "Yes, I've not been so lonely this winter."

"That's the way it should be."

"And each time I took your skates with me."

"Really? Why?"

"I wanted to get that old feeling back."

My daughter paused for a moment. "Did you?" she asked.

I looked her in the eyes, thankful for the chance to be sitting with her, and thought about telling her that this was the old feeling I had been looking for. But I did not want to make her feel uncomfortable so I simply said, "This winter has never failed to amaze me."

My daughter did not pursue the topic any further and instead asked about her grandparents. In the first email I had sent her I had mentioned that my parents' health had taken a turn for the worse, and that one of the reasons I was going back was to look after them.

After we had finished eating my daughter took me to the park behind her home. As we walked I told her about our family's financial situation. We had managed to save up quite a lot of money after thirteen difficult years running the convenience store. Plus we had made a reasonable amount from the properties we had bought. I took the opportunity to praise her mother's financial foresight. She had been right to insist on buying both the convenience store and our house. Then I told my daughter that I lived very simply and so she was sure to receive a sizable inheritance. This news left little impact on her. She said there was no need for me to be so tight with my money, especially if it was with a view to leaving her a larger inheritance.

"Did you not say that if you had the time and the money you would like to travel the world?" she said.

"You remember I used to say that?" It was something I had begun to talk about after Hermit Wang left, but I was touched to hear that my daughter had taken note of it.

"I really want you to be able to live the life you want," she said.

It had been a long time since I had felt such empathy from my daughter and I looked into the pristine night's sky and sighed. What had I done to deserve this blessing?

"You're going to miss Montreal's clear skies," my daughter said.

"I'm going to miss Montreal's miracles," I replied.

This was clearly not what my daughter had expected. She looked at me and seemed for the first time to perceive the change that had taken place in me.

As we came to the park entrance I reminded my daughter to go to her mother's grave once in a while when she had time. As I said this, a peculiar thought came to me. I stopped walking and turned to her. "You must know that there wasn't much feeling between your mom and me," I said, "but when I die I'd like to be buried next to her."

My daughter pulled on the corner of my coat to indicate that we should keep walking. "That's still a long way away," she said. "I always thought you should think about finding someone else to spend the rest of your life with."

The next day my daughter said she would come with me to the airport. I made a show of refusing but of course was secretly overjoyed when she insisted. For some time in the taxi we sat in silence as I wondered what she was thinking. I thought back on the first evening we arrived in Montreal fifteen years earlier but my reverie was interrupted by my daughter. She said that from now on I could email her if I had anything I wanted to talk to her about. I understood of course what she meant. She was telling me that from now on she would reply to my emails. The magical reconciliation had truly taken place and I felt the full strength of my love for my daughter. I told her that I had put the cheque she had refused to accept the night before under her pillow. She scolded me good-naturedly for my deception, telling me she was not in need of money. I said it would make me feel better, that I wanted her to keep it for emergencies.

When we arrived at the airport I suggested she get back in the taxi, but she refused. She accompanied me as I collected my boarding pass and even stayed with me until I got to security. I began to feel self-conscious, because I did not know how to say goodbye. I didn't want to regret this moment, but I also was worried about embarrassing my daughter. Before I could make a decision my daughter reached out and gave me a hug. She had not hugged me since her mother's funeral, and after our relationship had soured I had come to think that that might have been the last time I would ever hold her in my arms. I would never have imagined that she would be the one to put her arms around me, rest her head on my shoulder, and, in the voice I had been yearning to hear all winter, wish me a safe trip. The emotion building inside me finally became too much to bear and the question I had been holding back for more than twelve hours burst out of me.

"Do you like it here?" I asked, my voice cracking slightly.

My daughter didn't seem to think there was anything out of the ordinary about my question. "I do," she said.

This was the answer I was waiting for, the answer I needed to hear. My eyes began to well up. "Do you remember the first time I asked you that question," I said, "when we stepped out of this airport fifteen years ago?"

My daughter nodded.

"I remember you took a deep breath of the icy air, turned to me with a dreamy look in your eyes, and said exactly the same thing: 'I do.'"

She nodded again.

"After that I asked you again, do you remember? Every time we were alone together I asked you. When we went up Mount Royal to go skating I would ask you," I said. "Your answer never changed. In my whole life, this is the thing for which I am most grateful."

My daughter hugged me again and reminded me I had a flight to catch.

The tears began running down my face. "You know it's the one thing in the last fifteen years of my life that hasn't changed."

With that I left the city I had lived in for fifteen years, seen off by my daughter and the one constant that kept me going in that time.

On the plane I remembered what Hermit Wang had once told me was the mysterious thing about being an immigrant: "Once an immigrant, always an immigrant. For someone who has emigrated, returning home is simply a second emigration. You can never go home! You will forever and everywhere be a stranger!" He was right of course. The last two times I had been in China were proof enough. In the last fifteen years I had only experienced my native land through some medium: the news, what people said, the internet. I had not felt for myself its moments of elation and suffering. Similarly, as far as the people back home were concerned, I was no more than a distant "insignificant grain of sand." They had no way to know the pleasure and pain I had felt while I was abroad, and they had no need to know. If anything the winter I had just experienced would only have estranged me from them further. I reminded myself that I would have to be prepared for the difficulties this "second emigration" would bring.

One thousand nine hundred and fifty-two days have now passed since I left Montreal. During this unremarkable time, images and memories of Mount Royal have often returned to me. These reveries have done little to bring me closer to that winter and if anything only seem to draw me further away. In the end the dream is always rudely cut short and I find myself back in a reality that makes it hard to believe the events of that winter: the mysterious appearance of two enigmatic women, their equally mysterious disappearance ... It seems the world in which I now live could not have less to do with Celia and Misoka.

I have spent most of my time since my second emigration looking after my parents. They became my world. For the first three years this mostly involved being at home, but on the third

day of the Chinese new year in the fourth year, my father started coughing up blood and had to go to the hospital. It did not
take long for the doctors to diagnose him with lung cancer.
One week after my father was admitted, my mother suffered
a stroke and was sent to the same hospital. My father was on
the eighth floor and my mother on the third, which my father
knew about but my mother didn't. From the day my mother
was admitted to hospital they did not see each other.

Even though my brother had arranged for a helper to look
after each of them, my parents still required a lot from me. I
decided to split my day between the two of them. I got to my
father's room at nine in the morning and left at noon, then
went on to look after my mother from one until five. It was like
having a nine-to-five job, except of course without weekends
off. Life was beginning to resemble my time working in the
convenience store.

After the stroke, my mother quickly lost awareness of her
surroundings. Before long, she could not even recognize the
son "who did everything right," let alone me, the one "who did
nothing right." She began to call me "Dad," perhaps because
deep down inside that was the only person she could imagine
tending to her every day. Her mood began to get worse. Apart
from "Dad," of whom she seemed slightly afraid, she treated
everyone else, including the doctor, with contempt and was
very uncooperative when it came to her treatment.

My father and I, on the other hand, got much closer. We
spoke much more than we ever had before and he even asked
me about my time in Montreal. I found his attitude toward
my mother slightly disconcerting. He never asked to see her
but each morning when I arrived in his room he would ask
me how she was doing. "Is she still alive?" he would often ask.

The vulgar turn of phrase made me wonder if his condition had not also affected his mind in some way. One day I lost my patience.

"Would you prefer it if she was alive or dead?" I asked.

He appeared slightly confused. "I'm just afraid," he said.

"Afraid of what?"

"Afraid of her dying before me," he said, and then before I could think of a comforting response he added, "and afraid of her dying after me."

At first I didn't know what to say to this contradictory answer but then I saw a chance to get back at him for his years of scorn. "That's a puzzle mathematics cannot solve," I said, laughing coldly.

My father picked up on my petty act of revenge and sighed before saying, "Mathematics could never solve anything."

The regret in his disconsolate response made me drop my hostile stance and I put my hand on his. "She's still alive," I said softly, "but barely. She doesn't recognize anybody anymore."

He coughed before saying, "I've always thought our marriage was a mistake."

I had never heard my father say a bad word about his marriage before. "Why?" I asked.

"She's a very intelligent woman," he replied. "She should not have had to spend her life in a small town with a nobody like me." He paused for a moment before going on. "She deserved a completely different life."

That was the first and last time I heard my father talk this way about his marriage. It was also the only time I had ever heard anybody find fault with their marriage on behalf of their partner. After that my father stopped asking me about my mother's condition.

Around half a year ago my father asked me about my plans for the future. I said I didn't know. He replied that it wouldn't do to be alone, that I ought to find someone "suitable" with whom I could share my life.

"Easier said than done," I said.

"Of course. You don't need me to tell you that. You've seen for yourself the repercussions of getting it wrong."

I laughed coldly and told him it was impolite to make fun of the dead.

He looked at me sternly and said, "Yes. I'll be there soon myself." He motioned me to lean closer. "Actually, I think there's someone."

"Who?" I asked apprehensively.

He pointed to the door and I stared at it but did not understand. Then he mimed injecting himself with a needle and it dawned on me. He must have meant the head nurse he liked so much. "I hear she's recently divorced," he said with a grin, as if a divorce was something worth celebrating.

I would be lying if I said my father's suggestion did not strike a chord with me. I was also fond of the head nurse he was talking about. I liked the way she looked and the way she spoke, but perhaps most of all I liked the fact that she read. I had noticed she often walked around with a "useless book" in her hand. It had never occurred to me that something might happen between us, but when my father pointed it out I realized that she was someone I would consider "suitable." My father said he could tell she was interested in me. She often asked about me and had even wanted to know what book I had recently been reading. My father went on to criticize me for being an "insensitive dope." Three weeks earlier the head nurse had recommended a novel called *The Empty Nest*, but I had not given her recommendation much thought. I had yet to get my hands on a copy. "If I'm not mistaken," my father said, "there is something in that book she wants to communicate to you."

I had not forgotten the head nurse's recommendation and even remembered that she had said it was a novel that my father and I could read together. The problem was that I had long before lost interest in Chinese contemporary fiction. But that day at noon I went straight to the bookstore and bought a copy. I read it all afternoon at my mother's side and when I got home I didn't stop reading it until I had finished it, late into the night. I didn't discover a secret message in its pages as my father had predicted, but I enjoyed it a great deal. Not only was it written in clear, concise prose and carefully structured, but it had genuine emotional heft and conceptual depth. As I read I kept thinking back to the period of my life in which I had lived in an empty nest, during the winter in which I lost contact with my daughter, when I too felt as if life were cheating me. Were it not for Celia and Misoka, perhaps I would have come to the same end as the one implied in the novel — cutting my own life short in the cold of a night when everything had become too much to bear.

The next day I waited until there was no one else in the head nurse's office before going in and sitting at her desk. I thanked her for her recommendation, adding that I had finished reading the novel the previous day and had liked it a lot. I told her that my father had once almost fallen victim to a telephone scam so many of the novel's details rang true. It was the first time I had properly spoken with the head nurse and the first time speaking to her at all since finding out that she might be "interested" in me. As we spoke I was pleased to discover nothing contradicted my initial positive impression of her. In fact as the conversation went on I only liked her more.

From that day on, the head nurse and I spoke more and more frequently. It was not long before our conversation expanded beyond the confines of literature to cover every detail of our lives. I was gratified to discover that we had similar ways of looking at all of life's problems, and one day I even ventured to talk to her about Celia and Misoka. To my delight and astonishment she had a profound insight into the words and actions of these curious women and immediately understood what had drawn me to them. She offered perceptive speculations about their lives, which in turn aroused fresh speculations of my own. She even expressed a desire, "if there's an opportunity one day," to visit Beaver Lake. As our conversations flowed more freely and touched upon deeper topics, I couldn't help but imagine our life together.

My mother passed away on the last weekend of August. My brother and I decided it would be best to keep this information from our father, who was only just holding onto life himself. But three days after her funeral as I was leaving his room, my father called out to me.

"From now on can you come and look after me in the afternoons as well?"

I froze. "I — I have to go downstairs to —"

"She's gone," my father interrupted me. "What do you have to go downstairs for?"

I didn't know how he knew and I did not want to know. I returned to his bedside and sat down.

The doctor said that depending on how my father reacted to the chemotherapy, he either had a few months to live, or a few weeks. This death sentence meant little to my father, whose mood only got better as time went on. That was because he could see the relationship forming between the head nurse and me and knew we had already begun to plan our future together. He saw it as a sign of reconciliation between father and son. He smiled and told me that it had taken a while but I had finally done something that made him happy. He saw it as a personal achievement, and one day he even said, "All this cancer business wasn't for nothing."

The head nurse and I attended my father's funeral together. As his ashes were placed beside my mother's and the grave sealed, I remembered what I had said to my daughter the night before I left Montreal. When I died where would I be buried? Who would I be buried with? I glanced at the head nurse beside me and she tenderly squeezed my hand. At that moment my daughter's words rang in my head: "That's still a long way away."

Yes, maybe this is where the story of that most unusual of Montreal winters should end.